DEAD NORTH

BOOKS BY SUE HENRY

DEAD NORTH

AN ALASKA MYSTERY

SUE HENRY

WILLIAM MORROW • 75 YEARS OF PUBLISHING
An Imprint of HarperCollins*Publishers*

HarperCollins books may be purchased for educational, business, or
sales promotional use. For information please write: Special Markets
Department, HarperCollins Publishers Inc., 10 East 53rd Street,
New York, NY 10022.

FIRST EDITION

Designed by Kate Nichols
Map illustration by Eric Henry, Art Forge Unlimited

Printed on acid-free paper

Library of Congress Cataloging-in-Publication Data
Henry, Sue, 1940–
        Dead north : an Alaska mystery / by Sue Henry.—1st ed.
            p.   cm.
        ISBN 0-380-97881-4
        1. Women mushers—Fiction.   2. Alaska—Fiction.   I. Title.
    PS3558.E534 D38   2001
    813'.54—dc21   00-048077

01   02   03   04   05   RRD   10   9   8   7   6   5   4   3   2   1

This one's for my friend
and sometime travel companion
Barbara Hedges
with love and thanks
for always being there

That black bear in the field of sunflowers
wouldn't have been half so funny without you

It is also dedicated in
loving memory to my dear
friend Alice Abbott

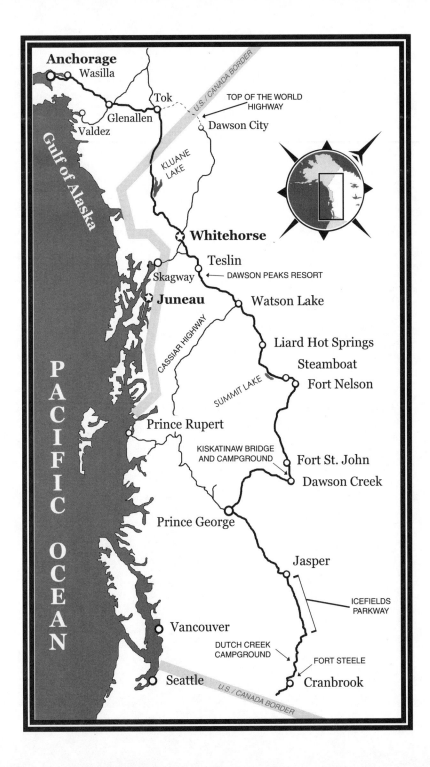

C H A P T E R

The old man woke still tired from a restless sleep in the back bedroom of his small house on the outskirts of Cody, Wyoming, and grumbled to himself as he rolled over, seeking comfort in a new position. His legs were aching again and there was a charley horse in his right foot. He slid down far enough in the bed to brace it against the footboard and push hard against the cramped muscles of the arch, stretching them until the spasm finally eased, then for a while longer, just to make sure it wouldn't immediately return.

Wide awake now, he pushed himself to a sitting position so he could swing his feet painfully out of the bed, stood up, and tottered toward the bathroom. Couldn't sleep through the night anymore without his bladder waking him at least twice. A couple of times lately he had even dreamed that he got up and made it to the toilet, only to come suddenly awake in the middle of the action and find himself lying shamefully in a wet spot like some goddammed kid. The doctor said there was nothing really wrong, that it was just age and a body that couldn't be entirely depended on anymore—but it worried him anyway.

Young medical whippersnapper—maybe he'd missed something. *Whippersnapper?* Where the hell had that come from? He'd never said *whippersnapper* in his life. Even beginning to *sound* old, he chided himself.

As he stood poised for action, one hand braced on the door frame, he realized that, through the slightly open bathroom window, he was faintly hearing voices from the house next door—angry voices, one male, one female. They were at it again. If they had to fight, why did they always have to do it in the middle of the night? But he knew why.

That bastard McMurdock came off his shift with the Cody Police Department at midnight. At least one night a week he would come home, have a snort or two, and provoke his wife into an argument that rapidly turned physical—pounding out frustrations and aggression on her that would have had him up on charges had he done it on the job. Sometimes lately the hostility wound up involving her young son, Patrick, who hated his stepfather and, now that he was older and bigger, sometimes came to her defense.

Finished with his business, the old man flushed the toilet and, impatient for the rush of water in the tank to stop so he could listen, flipped off the bathroom light and went to the window. Working to raise it as far as it would go, he peered out into thirty feet of dark yard between the two houses, worried about the woman, but more about the boy. The upstairs bedroom light was on next door and he could almost, but not quite, make out the sense of McMurdock's belligerent shouting. The tank water quit running and he heard McMurdock's wife wail in pain and her body thump against a wall.

A dim light came on in Patrick's basement room and the old man hoped the youngster would stay put and out of harm's way. His interference would only make things worse, as usual. Though he might divert some of his stepfather's brutality from his mother, he was not large or strong enough to stop him, to do what the old man longed to do—though he knew he was no more up to the job of giving McMurdock a taste of his own savagery than the boy.

He would call the police—if the dammed police would do anything. But from sad experience he knew they wouldn't arrest one of their own—he'd already tried that twice to no avail. All it had earned him was a threat across the back fence from McMurdock and embarrassed pleading from young Patrick not to call his stepfather's *friends* again.

He was a good kid, really. Showed up unasked on a regular basis to mow the old man's lawn when he mowed his own, sometimes helped out with things too heavy for the old man to lift or too high for him to reach anymore, or ran a few errands. Then they would sit in the kitchen over a glass of juice or soda, talking—though never about what went on in the night next door. Patrick tried to act as if everything was perfectly normal, but his casual smile often didn't erase the hurt and confusion in his eyes, as he shied away from anything approaching the secret he was clearly ashamed of and bent on keeping to himself.

The old man knew that Patrick had been in trouble once for helping to spray-paint four-letter words on a police car parked outside a restaurant where the two officers who drove it were taking a dinner break. That particular mischief made some sense when you thought about it—acting out, he'd heard it called—a kind of getting back. A black eye and bruises from McMurdock were the result, and the old man had fervently wished that there were something he could . . .

Another cry from next door interrupted his thoughts, accompanied by the sharp splintering of glass, then the shriek was abruptly cut off. Something heavy fell, then there was silence. The elongated shadow of a person passed over the shade that covered the window. There were no further sounds from the upstairs room.

The old man waited, listening in the dark, but the episode appeared to be over. Tomorrow, and for several days, she would not leave the house, hiding out inside. If he, or anyone, knocked, there would be no answer. Then any lingering cuts and bruises would be the result of a *fall—an accident*—her own *clumsiness*. And young Patrick would make himself scarce, probably with those two friends of his, hoping not to cause further trouble.

When there was nothing more to be heard or seen, the old man closed the window to its normal narrow crack and padded back to bed, lay down, and tried to go back to sleep, fighting disgust and impotent fury. Most of his anger was, of course, directed at McMurdock, though there was some disdain reserved for Patrick's mother—for putting herself in this situation and staying there, risking her son as well as herself. Why the hell didn't she leave—just take Patrick and go? Even if the house belonged to her, it could be worked out later and wasn't worth staying for. It made no sense to him at all. For three years, off and on, he had been made glaringly aware of the violence that haunted the family next door, and it was growing worse, not better—a bomb ready to go off and cripple or kill someone, if something didn't change.

Well, perhaps it would soon—he comforted himself with the thought that Patrick was about to graduate from high school. He had heard McMurdock yelling contemptuously that after that benchmark Patrick would be on his own—that he was through supporting a *lazy* kid—that Patrick would have to get out, find a place of his own, and a job.

The old man sighed and shifted again in his bed. Getting up had not helped the ache in his legs, but the cramp in his foot had not returned as it sometimes did, driving him crazy with its persistent intensity. Consciously, he made himself relax and turned his mind to other things. He began to lay out the garden he was about to plant. Two rows of carrots this year—good for the eyes, and his weren't as sharp as they'd once been. Maybe he'd try some of those cherry tomatoes instead of just the regular kind. He'd already loosened the soil in his bean patch, turned it over, ready to plant runner beans, which would climb up strings on the side of his storage shed. Visualizing a summer's worth of fresh lettuce, spinach, radishes, and cucumbers, he fell into a light, uneasy sleep.

He did not see the light in the upstairs bedroom go off, or the one in Patrick's basement room stay on for some time afterward. When it finally went off, he did not hear the back door open and close quietly—didn't see the dark figure slip into his backyard, where it remained beside his shed for a few minutes hidden in the shadows, then went on between the two houses to the street. Though booted, the feet made little sound on the sidewalk as they hurried away, and the huddled figure of young Patrick disappeared into the night beyond the streetlight at the corner.

The old man was unaware that the upstairs bedroom light came on again some time later. But a siren coming up the street woke him as the gray light of early morning made it just possible to see the shape of the house next door, the driveway full of police cars, an ambulance, and the coroner's wagon, and many people going hurriedly in and out. From the window he saw McMurdock assisted into the ambulance and whisked away. And much later in the morning, he watched a covered body carried out the front door and learned over the back fence, to his relief, that it was not Patrick but his mother they had taken to the morgue.

Patrick, it seemed, had disappeared—had taken a few things, including the money from his stepfather's wallet, along with his own small savings, and run off. Patrick, according to Officer McMurdock, had battered and killed his mother with a baseball bat he'd carried up from the basement and tried to kill his stepfather, knocking him cold and sending him to the hospital for a day. It was everyone's gossip in a town the size of Cody—how you could just never tell about kids and what they might do these days—how even with a policeman for a stepfather . . .

The old man thought differently. He didn't believe a word of it, but no one asked him, so he kept his mouth shut. If they found Patrick, there would be time for talking. If not, who could he talk to anyway and, especially, what could he prove? Nothing. All he could do was wait and see, but he sincerely hoped Patrick would be all right, wherever he was, and that they wouldn't find him.

He liked that boy.

The next afternoon, when the old man was neatly stretching string from nail to nail on the side of his shed to support the beans he had just planted, a detective came around the side of the house into the backyard. He was so nonregulation that at first the old man thought he was probably a salesman of some kind.

Daniel Loomis was a quiet man in his late thirties, slender and fit, with broad shoulders. He had a manner of slow speaking that almost, but not quite, hid the quickness of intellect and wry humor that shone in the half-lidded eyes that peered out under the brim of a baseball cap, above a slightly hooked nose and scrubby mustache. He wore a black windbreaker and moved almost silently across the small patch of grass near the back door to the path between the old man's two raised garden plots, where his feet finally made a sound on the pebbles, attracting the old man's attention. He did not respond, but continued to fasten the string to the nails and waited.

"Mr. Dalton?"

One last knot in the string before he turned to watch the stranger cover the last few feet of the path.

"You selling something I don't want?"

"Detective Loomis, CPD. Got a minute?"

Slicing the string at the knot, he folded his knife, blade worn thin with years of use, slipped it into his pants pocket, and carefully wound the dangling string back onto its spool.

" 'Spose you better come on in."

They settled at the kitchen table with the last of the breakfast decaf—Loomis's black, the old man's with sugar and low-fat milk. He stirred it slowly for a time after the sugar had dissolved, watching the spoon follow the shape of the cup. "This about what happened next door?"

"Thought you might have heard or seen something we should know about."

"Why would you think that?" But he knew the defensive tone that crept in had given him away.

The detective waited until Dalton raised his head to meet the question in his eyes. It was easier to see, now that he had removed the cap and laid it on the edge of the table.

"Never wanted anything from me before."

"Nobody died before, Mr. Dalton." The tone was soft, with a note of regret that suddenly infuriated the old man.

"Nobody *should* have died last night. You had plenty of warning. I called before—not that it did any damn *good*."

A silence hung for a few seconds over the table. With a habit of the solitary, the old man sucked the liquid from the spoon and laid it on the Formica beside the cup and saucer. His shoulders slumped and he suddenly looked even older than his years.

"When did you call, sir?"

"Last year—summer. Then again sometime in October."

"There's no record of your calls on file."

"Doesn't mean I didn't make 'em," he retorted, scowling.

"No—it doesn't." A frown wrinkled the detective's brow. "What exactly did you report?"

"That he was *beating* on her, of course," the old man snapped, the anger and resentment boiling again. "I may be half-blind, but I'm not deaf."

"So you did hear things from next door. How about last night?"

"Same thing. Her yelling when he hit her."

"The son, Patrick, you mean?" A mild question.

Dalton jerked to rigidity in his chair and almost quivered in indignation. "*Never!* That boy would *never* have hurt his mother. He was her only defense, and he suffered for it, too."

It all came pouring out then in a jumble—the sounds in the night of McMurdock battering his wife and stepson, the boy's attempts to protect his mother, reports ignored, calls responded to late, if at all, the old man's frustration at being unable to do anything but watch and listen.

"You cops killed that woman—McMurdock's *buddies*." He spit the word out like something rotten he had accidentally tasted. "Not Patrick. Sure as I sit here, you killed her by letting it go on happening and pretending it wasn't." One fist of arthritic fingers at the end of a scrawny arm pounded the table top until the coffee made waves in the cup and spilled over into his saucer. Then the thumping grew weaker until he finally left his hand lying limp for a second or two before raising it to swipe at the helpless, angry tears below the thick lenses of his glasses. "You bastards are worse than McMurdock."

It was very still in the kitchen, until Loomis drew a deep breath and leaned forward with an air of apology and an odd hint of collusion.

"Sir, do you have any idea where Patrick McMurdock might have gone?"

The old man stared at him in disbelief. "Like I'd tell *you*, if I did? And it's Cutler—he kept his real father's name."

"Look, Mr. Dalton . . ." He held up a hand to stop another flood of words that were obviously about to start. "No—give me a turn, okay? I'm fairly new in this department—came in from Denver a little over a year ago. I've been assigned specifically to this case and—just between you and me—the chief has an idea that . . . ah . . . well, that we should be looking into it more closely, let's say. McMurdock says that the kid knocked him out with a baseball bat, then killed his mother. Maybe that doesn't quite fit with what we found at the scene, or a couple of rumors I've heard—okay? Maybe we'd better wait to hear the other side of the story—right? But to do that, I've got to find Patrick—Cutler. So if you've got any ideas, I need to hear them."

"I'm supposed to believe that?"

"I certainly hope you'll give it a chance. Otherwise he may not have one."

It took a while, but there was something different about Loomis, something sincere about him that gave the old man a glimmer of hope for the boy. When the detective left, he knew everything Dalton knew about the two friends Patrick hung around with in Cody and the best friend—Dave somebody—whose family had moved to someplace he couldn't remember in Alaska.

A day later McMurdock came home from the hospital. Late

that evening, when he tossed a bag in his Chevy Suburban, drove away, and didn't return, the old man was watching. But when he tried to call Loomis, there was no answer to his message, and a second call told him only that the detective was out of town—sorry.

He went back to his gardening, wondering if he had been conned into making a bad mistake. It worried him in the night, hindered his sleep that was always uneasy anyway. But there were no more sounds of any kind from the house next door. Empty and silent, it sat dark, uninhabited, and he finally stopped bothering to peer through the crack in the bathroom window each time he made a trip to the toilet or walked the floor to ease the ache in his legs.

But he wished he knew where Patrick had gone—wished he was young again and could have been of some good to any of them—even himself.

C H A P T E R

Sometime during a night in early May, Jessie Arnold was jerked awake from sound sleep by the sudden roar of rain hitting the fiberglass roof over her head. She rolled over, disoriented by the unfamiliar sound and unaccustomed to the firmness of the bed on which she lay. A flare of lightning lit the world outside and, in narrow bands that fell like a camera flash through the slats of a venetian blind, a green blanket she did not immediately recognize. A reverberating crash of thunder so loud it hurt the ears was quickly followed by another lightning bolt.

Sitting up, she heard her Alaskan husky, Tank, shift position on the floor beside her, and recognized the interior of the Winnebago motor home she had driven from Coeur d'Alene, Idaho, to the Dutch Creek RV Park a little over a hundred miles north of the border between northern Idaho and British Columbia.

Throwing back the green blanket, Jessie jumped up to crank the bathroom vent closed and, through the opening, saw a jagged bolt of lightning split the sky as the cover came down and shut out the raindrops that were splashing in from above. Quickly she padded barefoot to a second vent in the front part of the motor home and closed it as well.

Brushing dampness from her short, honey blond hair, she headed back toward her bed. His dark silhouette told her that Tank was awake and alert to the cacophony outside, for he was sitting up and his ears twitched at the next reverberating growl of thunder. Thunderstorms seldom occurred where Jessie lived in Alaska, but as a child she had learned to love their power and excitement almost as much as Fourth of July fireworks and was not unhappy to find herself in the midst of one now. Tank, evidently, was not so sure about it.

"Hey, guy, it's just a lot of noise," she told him, laying a soothing hand on his head.

He licked her wrist but remained attentive, reassured but not completely satisfied that all was well.

Through the slats of the blind beside her bed, she peered out into the tumultuous dark, delighted with the sound and light show passing overhead, and was instantly rewarded with an almost blinding flash that lit up the campground surroundings as bright as daylight—trees, grass, two other nearby motor homes, a picnic table and fire pit, a figure hurrying with a coat over its head from the direction of the washroom. Reaching, she raised the blind, cranked the window—which swung out from the bottom—as wide as it would go, and settled down cross-legged on the bed to enjoy the pyrotechnics and the cool fresh air that washed over her with a hint of ozone, damp earth, and vegetation.

Slowly, over the next half hour, the storm passed to the east and the staccato of the rain lessened to a faint soft patter. Water dripping from the tree under which she had parked tapped intermittently on the roof. Leaving the vents closed and the window partially open, satisfied with her middle-of-the-night experience, Jessie lay back down, snuggled into her warm bed. She closed her eyes and, drifting back to sleep, considered the unexpected series of events that had brought her from Knik Road in the Matanuska Valley of Alaska to this unaccustomed place, bed, and thunderstorm.

* * *

Three days before, with the help of her friends Hank Peterson and Oscar Lee, she had finished clearing away the charred remains of what had been her log cabin until a few weeks earlier, when an arsonist had burned it to blackened rubble, destroying almost everything she owned. Though the ground was soaked with rain, it was not yet thawed deeply enough for Hank to dig space for a basement, but most of the snow was gone, except for a few filthy remnants of what had been the deepest drifts, and cleanup had been possible. So, Jessie and Oscar had employed her chain saw to cut up the larger pieces of the little that was left of the burned logs, while Hank used his Bobcat to shove them into a pile for burning and to load anything that could not be burned into a truck to be hauled to the dump.

Work completed, the three had stood surveying the results of their efforts, clothing grimy with the soot and charcoal the fire had created.

"That should do it for now," Hank said, leaning on the tire of his Bobcat and pulling off his dirty gloves to dig for a crumpled, half-empty package of cigarettes in his jacket pocket.

Raising an arm, Jessie wiped the sweat from her forehead with her sleeve, leaving another dark streak on her already grubby face. "How long till we can start?" she asked, pleased with the results of their labor but impatiently wishing they could begin to rebuild immediately. "I've got to give Vic some idea when they can start raising logs."

Since the fire, she had been living in a large canvas tent, hauled in and set up by a generous neighbor, but sorely missed the cozy log cabin she had helped to build and hated the destruction site. It was a relief now to have the remains of it cleared away and know she would not be constantly reminded of the fire every time she went outside to work with the sled dogs in her sizable kennel. With a contractor, she had been busily planning the construction of a new cabin to be financed with insurance money from the old, but spring had come late to Alaska this year. For most of April it had seemed the snow would never completely disappear nor the sleet and rain stop falling, and breakup had clung for weeks with a tenacious grip.

"Depends on the weather. If it gets warm and dries out—another three weeks or so. If it goes on raining and I dig the hole too soon, there'll be nothing but mud and the sides'll cave in." He shook his head at the idea. "Besides, it'd be too wet to pour concrete."

"So we wait and hope for warm and dry." Oscar looked up at him, frowning thoughtfully as he kicked at a puddle of standing water.

"Yeah," Hank agreed. "It'll be at least a month—maybe more—before we have a basement poured and the forms off. Sometime the first couple of weeks in June, I guess."

Jessie scowled and sighed, discouraged and frustrated.

As they stood contemplating with resignation the uncertainties of construction during this late spring, a pickup turned off Knik Road, rocked its way through the muddy potholes of the driveway, and stopped beside them. Vic Prentice, the contractor in charge of Jessie's building project, a barrel-chested man wearing a red plaid jacket and a baseball cap, climbed out of the truck and lifted a hand in greeting as he came to join them, splashing heedlessly through the puddles in his black rubber breakup boots.

"Hey, nice job, guys. Looks like you're about ready to dig a basement—ah—if it ever dries out." Vic's voice, soft and slow, hinted of a past spent in some sunny southern state and belied his rugged appearance, but Jessie knew from experience that he could raise it to a bellow if necessary.

For a few minutes they discussed the timing of the planned basement construction, but Vic obviously had something else on his mind and soon got to it in his easygoing manner.

"I've—ah—run into a snag, Jessie. We got us some time before we put this place up, so I figured you'd—ah—maybe take on a job for *me*. I'll knock a chunk off the bill if you will."

"What kind of a job, Vic?" It wasn't in character for him to ask for help.

"We-ell"—he scrubbed at the top of his head self-consciously with the baseball cap and pulled it back over his bald spot—"I had this motor home, you see, that I been hauling around for fifteen years to sites like this one here to use for a project office. But last fall it really fell apart—roof leaking pretty bad, engine won't run—couldn't even take it hunting. So I ordered a new thirty-one-foot Winnebago from where they make 'em in Iowa—ah—costs less than buying it here, ya know. I was going to fly down and drive it back—but I've got a project in Eagle River that I can't take off from right now or it won't get done in time to start your place. Anyhow, I got to thinking maybe you'd go instead—bring it back up the highway for me . . ."

"From *Iowa*?" Jessie asked, frowning as she considered the long stretches of unpleasantly crowded midwestern highways that such a drive would involve and how much she disliked that kind of traffic.

"No—no, not Iowa. The company's agreed to have somebody drive it to Idaho, so you'd pick it up in Coeur d'Alene. It's the part through Canada and Alaska that'll cost me big bucks to hire a professional driver for—and I don't want to depend on some tourist that I never met who doesn't know the road. I *know* you know trucks. Waddaya think?"

Prentice grinned, settled back on his heels, and folded his arms, awaiting Jessie's reaction to what he clearly saw as the perfect answer to the problem and was pleased with himself for thinking up.

Jessie, amused at his purposeful satisfaction, had to smile as she considered the idea and how typical it was of Vic Prentice to intertwine the *give* of one project with the *take* of another in finding a solution.

Part of her reason for choosing him as her contractor for such a big job was that he approached both his work and life as a series of challenges—problems to be solved in the most efficient and cost-effective manner. If anything would ensure that enough of the cabin would be completed to allow her to move into it in the fall—and spend the winter finishing the inside—it was this characteristic approach of Vic's. The necessities would be his top priority. He would work hard to be sure that the log walls would be up, roof on, doors and windows installed, plumbing and electrical done, and furnace functioning in the basement by the time snow fell. The cosmetics and conveniences—paint, trim, shelves, cupboards, and all the odds and ends—could wait to be done in a more leisurely fashion, and she planned to do most of them herself.

Because of the short northern building season and the high cost of materials and construction, half of Alaska was built this way. Rural people often lived in unfinished houses—some that were never completed because their owners became so used to raw plywood walls and floors that they never got around to it.

With growing enthusiasm Jessie considered the motor home transportation job Vic had just presented to her. It would give her a project to focus on during the weeks before they could start building walls—something that needed to be done. It would also help finance some of the things that the old cabin had lacked— the concrete for a basement, for instance. She didn't need to ask how much of a chunk he would knock off her bill, knowing it would be more than fair.

The idea of this particular trip was also appealing for other, more personal reasons. She had driven the Alaska Highway three times in the past, once in the fall, once in the spring, and once in the dead of winter—but never alone. Though she had not traveled its length in a motor home, the fall trip had involved a camper on a pickup, and she had enjoyed being able to stop and stay in places along the way without searching out a rented room each evening in some lodge or motel and eating nothing but restaurant food. Camping overnight by a river or lake or some other scenic spot had been much more to her liking. The enormous and ever-changing wilderness through which the highway ran had been captivating, and she had been fascinated by the way each season had defined the varied and mostly uninhabited land along its route. A motor home would be even better than the camper, with a kitchen and bathroom handy and a roof over her head in all kinds of weather. It would at least be fun to try, and doing it alone would give her more opportunity than ever to concentrate on the country through which she would be passing.

Thirty-one feet was a medium-sized rig, not that different from the school bus she had once driven for several winters to earn the money to set up her kennel and sled dog racing business. The idea of maneuvering a motor home did not particularly concern her, especially as many sections of the highway had been widened and paved in the last ten or fifteen years. Except for one or two spots still under construction, it was now for the most part smooth and easy driving all the way from the Lower Forty-Eight to Alaska. This was a job she could comfortably do and a trip she would enjoy making, especially if she didn't have to rush through it.

"When do you want it here, Vic?" she asked, giving away her capitulation with her smile and the eagerness in her voice. "If we've got a month before we can start on the logs, I'd rather not push it—take a couple of easy weeks."

"Take three, if you want. It'll be parked here at your place all summer anyway."

"Two would be fine. If it dries out soon, I don't want to miss the basement pour. But I'd like to stop at a place or two I've gone right by on other trips. Could I take Tank along for company?"

"That lead dog of yours? No problem. Tinker'll spend most of the summer in it with me."

The dog Vic referred to and doted on was a lilliputian Yorkshire terrier, who often kept him company on the job. The decided contrast in their sizes and appearance had always amused those who knew him, but Tinker, true to his breed, exhibited astonishing audacity and bravado in challenging far larger adversaries, animal or human, with courage well outweighing his size.

"So you'll do it—right?" Vic returned to the question at hand, as tenacious as his pet.

Jessie grinned and nodded her agreement. "Why not? Billy Steward can take care of my mutts—puppies and all. It's too soggy for training runs. When do you want me to go?"

"They called from Idaho yesterday," Prentice told her with a satisfied expression. "It's there."

* * *

Two days later Jessie and Tank had flown to Seattle, then into Coeur d'Alene, and taxied to the local dealer where the Winnebago was waiting as promised. There she had used part of the afternoon to assure herself that the motor home's automotive and coach systems were functioning correctly and that she knew how to use them all—thanks to a two-hour session with a patient and knowledgeable mechanic and the dealer's best instruction. Before leaving she had paid a visit to their RV shop and purchased chemicals for the holding tanks, toilet paper that would dissolve and flush out without clogging, a hose for the potable water system, and a heavy-duty extension cord. She also picked up extra filters, belts, and fuses for all the systems, and containers of oil, brake, and transmission fluids, all recommended by Vic Prentice. "If you have 'em, you'll probably never need 'em."

The rest of the day was spent in a nearby shopping mall checking off a long list of other things she and Prentice had agreed would be necessary for the trip or should be added for later use. "Might as well get this stuff down there, where it's less expensive," he had said when they finished brainstorming. "This is all stuff I want in the rig for moose hunting this fall, and you'll want most of it on the way up."

So Jessie had filled shopping carts with pillows, sheets, blankets, and towels; a few pots and pans and other cooking equipment; a broom, dishwashing detergent, and window cleaner; and a few items of her own, including several paperback mysteries, a road atlas, a copy of *The Milepost*—the travel authority for anyone heading north—a large flashlight and batteries, and—remembering that she had wondered about the elevations of the road on past trips—an altimeter for the dashboard. At a nearby super-market she stocked up on basic cooking supplies and food for herself and Tank, thankful that the Winnebago's refrigerator and small freezer would allow her to carry dairy products and meat. Wheeling a shopping cart through the aisles of the unfamiliar store, she enjoyed picking out meals for herself with travel in mind, noticing things she might have overlooked at home as well as old favorites.

By late afternoon, loaded up with essentials, she had found a nearby RV park in which to spend the night, fed and watered Tank, cooked her first meal on the brand-new gas stove, and spent the evening stowing her purchases in the compact storage the motor home provided. The toiletries, clothes, and camera that she had brought along in a large duffel soon resided in con-venient cupboards and closets. She then practiced hooking up the rig to the campground's electrical, water, and sewage systems and was satisfied that all was in order and she was ready to travel.

Before going to bed she settled down with a cup of pepper-mint tea and once again reviewed the operator's manual for the motor home, making a checklist of things she must remember to do before leaving the campground. Parking and hooking up a motor home was different in several respects from driving it, and she wanted to be sure she wouldn't forget some important detail. Of course she must disconnect the water, sewage, and electric lines and check the status of the holding tanks—water, sewage, and propane—from the gauges in the galley. The refrigerator must be switched from the AC power provided by the hookup in the campground to the DC power with which the automotive system would keep it cold as they drove. She must also be sure that the kitchen stove, water heater, and furnace were all shut off and the propane that fueled them turned off at the tank. When she was finally satisfied that she had it all straight and would forget nothing the next day, she spread out her new road atlas on the dinette table to plan the next day's route to the Canadian border and beyond.

Having explored and familiarized himself with the motor home from one end to the other, Tank lay down at her feet and contentedly snoozed as she examined the map. Jessie was glad she had brought him along. He was well trained and behaved, would be the best of company for such a long trip, and would keep her from driving too long between regular stops that would be exercise breaks for them both. She could hardly wait to get on the road the next day, anticipating a smooth and relaxing drive, with no suspicion that it might not turn out to be the idyllic vacation she envisioned.

CHAPTER 3

At just after eight the next morning, breakfast over, everything loose put neatly away so it wouldn't fall or rattle, gas, water, and propane tanks all properly filled, with Tank on a small multicolored rug spread over the passenger seat and already applying nose prints to the window glass, Jessie headed north into the forty-five-mile-wide lake country of the Idaho panhandle. She found the big motor home remarkably easy to handle and was delighted by a first-class sound system. She found herself singing joyfully along, rediscovering how much she liked traveling, feeling like a kid at the beginning of a summer vacation, with all its possibilities and satisfactions still in the offing.

The day was warm and sunny with white fluffy clouds floating in a clear blue sky, a complete contrast to the rainy, muddy conditions Jessie had left behind in her yard on Knik Road. Cranking the window down, she took several deep breaths, appreciating the scent of green growing things. Remembering that spring had not yet reached the Alaska, she felt not the least bit guilty to be escaping the last of the northern winter.

The rugged Selkirk, Purcell, and Cabinet Mountains rose close to 5,000 feet above the valley through which she traveled and were densely covered in forests of Douglas fir, western red cedar, and hemlock—trees she did not see in Alaska and welcomed like old friends. Long ago, retreating glaciers had carved and left sharp peaks and below them huge moraines that dammed the water of melting ice to create large lakes.

Soon Jessie caught a first glimpse of Lake Pend Oreille and as the highway swung a little west and up to run for miles through ranching country on the high plateau above it, she was rewarded with a spectacular view of the large eastern arm of its inverted U. Sixty-five miles long and fifteen miles wide, it looked much larger than it had seemed on the map. Well over 1,000 feet, it was one of the deepest in the United States, and the sparkle of the morning sun on its blue water gave her reason enough to pull into a rest stop and climb with Tank to the top of a small rise for an unimpeded look across it. The tiny triangle of a sailboat made slow headway far below as she stood watching, but she decided it was probably moving at good speed for those aboard, and for just a minute she wished she could join them.

Tank sniffed at the new grass and found a dry stick that he dropped at Jessie's feet, looking up expectantly. She tossed it away, and for five minutes he surrendered his usual dignity to chase and carry it back for her to fling again.

"Okay—enough," she finally told him. "Come on, we gotta go." Then they were both running down the rise and through the tall fir trees toward the house on wheels they had left in the parking lot.

Inside, seduced by the warmth of the spring weather, she took time to dig out a pair of denim shorts and a T-shirt with Arnold

Kennels printed in tall green letters across the front, quickly changing out of the jeans and sweatshirt she had been wearing and into the lighter clothing. The sunny weather promised to continue, and she intended to enjoy it, perhaps even add a little color to her pale northern complexion. Tank sat watching, head cocked to one side, waiting for her to complete the transformation, ready to resume his place in the passenger seat when she was dressed.

"Hey, buddy," she told him with a grin, yanking the shirt over her head, "we Alaskans don't tan, we thaw, remember?"

The highway soon came down to a long causeway that crossed Lake Pend Oreille's much narrower western arm. Jessie drove across it and lessened her speed as she entered Sand Point, an engaging community of quiet tree-lined streets and a downtown area filling a few blocks with shops and restaurants that reminded her slightly of pictures she had seen of small European villages. She admired its charm but felt disinclined to stop, knowing she had gone only forty-four miles, not even half the distance from Coeur d'Alene to the Canadian border. The places she hoped to explore were farther up the road, and she was determined to save her extra time for them and try not to succumb to every interesting place she passed on the way. Besides, wilderness held her interest more than quaint urban shopping areas, and an enormous wilderness lay ahead, including the spectacular Canadian Rockies.

With the lure of the town behind them, scenery flying past the passenger window had a hypnotic effect, and Tank soon grew tired of it, curling up on his rug and settling into a nap. The valley narrowed slightly and the road rose to wind along the eastern hillside, through dense forest periodically interspersed with rural houses and barns tucked away above cultivated fields that spread across the bottom land to the Kootenay River, visible at times as the road meandered north.

Meeting a truck piled high with freshly cut logs, she immediately thought about her new cabin. The logs for her house would not come from here, but farther south, near Boise, Idaho. It seemed strange to import logs for building in Alaska when it was covered with billions of trees, but Rocky Mountain logs were kiln dried, which removed more moisture, and were a more dependable building material, shrinking and settling less, assuring a tighter, warmer structure.

The cabin she and Vic Prentice had designed, with the advice and assistance of the company that would provide the logs, would rise in the footprint of the old one. But besides adding a full basement, they had planned a second-story loft with two bedrooms, one for herself and one that she planned to use as an office for her kennel business and that would double as space for guests. She visualized with pleasure the balcony that would run across like a hallway between them and allow an open view down into the large living room that would, like the old one, fill the whole front of the house.

Directly below the loft, a kitchen would fill half the space, and the rest would be taken up by a bathroom and an ample combination pantry, storage, and utility room where a washer and dryer would reside. She had satisfied thoughts of the things she would place on the floor-to-ceiling shelves and the luxury of having room for a large worktable.

The floor plan spread itself out in Jessie's mind, so real she could almost see it, and she fell easily into the pleasing mental process of finishing and furnishing it. White. The walls and even the moldings for doors and windows would be white. This time there would be larger windows for the additional light they allowed in, especially in December, when if the sun showed up from behind the clouds at all it was only for four to five hours a day.

Enthusiastically involved in her fantasy of decorating, Jessie paid less attention to what she was passing. The communities of Naples and Bonners Ferry, smaller than Sand Point, all but flashed by, and having settled into a comfortable driving speed and rhythm, she almost missed a turnoff but caught it at the last possible minute. In a short time she arrived at the U.S.-Canadian border, where a friendly customs agent welcomed her to British Columbia with a smile and a colorful map of the provincial parks, initialed Tank's vaccination certificate, then let her go with only a few cursory questions when she learned that Jessie was an Alaskan on her way home and had no firearms or prohibited items.

Pulling away from the checkpoint into Canada, for the first time Jessie felt that she was *on* a trip, not just *going* to be, or somehow *pretending* to be. She hadn't noticed that it all felt slightly unreal until it began to feel *very* real, and crossing the border somehow completed that realization. She laughed a little to herself, aware that a large part of her present enjoyment had to do with traveling alone, and that it equated somehow to the freedom she felt driving her sled and dogs through the winter wilderness of Alaska. There, where she went and how had only to do with herself and her team. There were few distractions or intrusions, just the soft swish of runners on the trail and the wide-open snow-filled space of measureless miles around her. Here there was also much open country, though more heavily populated, but no snow or ice—nothing but the pleasant green of trees, shrubs, and returning grasses.

It had been several years since she traveled anywhere except in connection with racing sled dogs, and she realized that she had almost forgotten how much she loved to drive long distances. A map of Alaska quickly shows that there are very few roads, and except for the short 100-mile stretch that connects the state ferry system in Skagway to the Alaska Highway at Whitehorse in Yukon Territory, and the 152 miles between Haines and Haines Junction, these lie only in the eastern third of the state. Land-locked, Juneau and the rest of the southeastern panhandle have no connecting roads at all and can be reached only by plane or ferry. The rest of the state, particularly the western two-thirds, consists of endless roadless tracts of wild country that can only be accessed by air, if at all. The limited roads and highways of the eastern third run for hundreds of miles between communities. Anchorage, for instance, is a six- or seven-hour drive, 358 miles, from Fairbanks and, by the shortest route, via the Glenn Highway/Tok Cutoff, 486 miles from the Canadian border. The only driving Jessie had done on a regular basis in her truck was to Wasilla or Palmer, the towns nearest to where she lived, or to Anchorage, 50 miles to the west.

Now, rediscovering the joy of solitary driving on roads with hundreds of miles ahead of her, through country that piqued her interest, she felt smugly satisfied with her own company and the adventure to come. She could travel, within reason, at her own chosen speed, stop when and where she pleased, explore and appreciate what she liked or discovered, and there was no one to disagree with her preferences or with whom she must compromise. It seemed a treat as rare as the warm pine-scented fresh air flowing in through the driver's window. She laughed aloud, waking Tank, who did not move but gave her a quizzical look before closing his eyes again, and resolved that she would allow nothing to spoil it for her—though she could think of nothing that would. Anything that impeded or interrupted her northward progress, from a flat tire to—whatever—would simply be an interesting experience to be dealt with. She would not allow it to become a disaster. Obstacles, she decided, only became disasters if you saw them that way. She would simply toss the word out of her traveling vocabulary. Besides, what could go wrong?

The weather would undoubtedly not remain so glorious, but she was used to being outdoors in all kinds of conditions, so its changes wouldn't bother her. When dressed for it, she did not dislike rain, and loved snow for all the obvious reasons of her profession, as well as her more aesthetic appreciation of its frozen silence and the lovely softening nature of the clean white blanket it cast over a landscape. Each kind of weather had its benefits and pleasures. You just have to look for them, she reminded herself. But for now, she was not only content, but exhilarated, to soak up the sun and good roads.

*　　*　　*

At almost one-thirty in the morning, in Cody, Wyoming, two boys, one dark, one blond, sat parked in a brown-and-cream-colored pickup across the street from a dark house that they were watching. Earlier, they had seen McMurdock, carrying a duffel bag, lock the door and leave, and he had not returned. For over three hours nothing had moved, no lights had come on, it had remained as silent and empty as if no one lived there at all.

The fair-haired boy in the passenger seat slouched sideways, leaning against the door, frowning and scratching at a pimple on his chin. "It's a hell of a long ways to go when we're not sure."

His friend took a last drag on a cigarette before tossing the butt out to join several others on the asphalt below his open window.

"Well—*I* think Pat took off for Fairbanks. That's what he said he was gonna do after graduation anyway—visit Dave and see if he could find a job up there. If you don't stop picking at that thing, you're gonna make it worse."

The blond boy knotted his fingers together in his lap and sat up straighter in the seat. "But what if he didn't, Lew? He could've gone anywhere."

The boy behind the steering wheel turned to him in impatient annoyance. "Kim, *think* about it. Where else would he go? He was getting tossed out, and Alaska's all he talked about. If we're gonna find him before the police do—and help him—we gotta go looking somewhere, and that's our best bet—right?"

"Ye-eah," accompanied by an indecisive sigh. "Yeah—I guess you're right. We gotta do something, but what about McMurdock? We could run into him. He scares me. You know what he said he'd do. You know . . ."

"I know you were really dumb to let him catch up with you. But tell me again what he said—and how he said it."

"He was really mean. My arm still hurts where he grabbed me. He said that Pat must have told us where he was going and that if I didn't spill it he'd get us arrested for that spray paint on his car and—anything else he could think of." His worried tone came close to a whine. "Besides, if we don't stay and finish school, we won't graduate, Lew."

"So? I'd rather not graduate than get arrested. My dad will have less of a snit-fit. Besides, we've either gotta tell McMurdock something or go and try to find Pat. Right?"

"I—I guess so." But Kim sounded anything but persuaded and certain. He glanced out the window and bit his lip, a mixture of fear and confusion deepening his frown.

"Is there something you're not telling me? Did he tell you something else? Did *you* tell *him* anything?"

"N-no, Lew. I told you I didn't."

Lew thought the answer came a little too quickly but didn't ask again, knowing that Kim was terrified of McMurdock and that questions just made his dread worse. Anxiety could account for his reluctance. As soon as they were on the road, he would probably be fine. Still, he would like to have been there when McMurdock confronted his friend, to hear for himself exactly what had been said. He raised his arm till a beam from the street-light revealed the face of his watch. "It's one-thirty-eight. I say if that cop's not back by two—we go. Okay?"

"Okay."

As Kim Fredricksen slowly nodded his agreement, the door of the house they were parked in front of suddenly opened and a man in pajama bottoms and a T-shirt came out onto the front porch and walked barefooted across the lawn, speaking angrily before he even reached the pickup. "What do you no-good kids think you're doing? You been sitting in that truck for hours. If you don't get the hell out of here right now, I'll call the police and you can tell them what you're up to. We've had enough trouble around here."

"Yes, sir. We didn't mean to bother anybody. We're going—honest."

"And don't come back."

"No, sir." Lewis Jetter hurried to start the pickup and ease away from the curb.

"I guess that answers the question. We're outta here," he said when they were half a block away.

In their haste to be gone, they didn't notice a vehicle that pulled out of a side street behind them and cautiously followed without turning on its lights.

Driving on back streets to avoid the police, who with little to do sometimes stopped teenagers out later on a weeknight than they thought appropriate, the boys slipped through town. The road ran east and west out of Cody. If they had gone west, it would soon have taken them into Yellowstone Park and from there north to Lewiston, Montana, and Highway 90, the major east/west route across the state. But Jetter elected to go northeast on roads that eventually, near Billings, also joined Highway 90, on which they traveled west to Butte before finally heading north.

By the time it began to grow light, they had left the Rocky Mountains a hundred miles behind and were nearing Great Falls, in the center of the wide-open grain-rich part of the state that, rolling gently from horizon to horizon, gave Montana its Big Sky Country distinction.

All day they went north, one sleeping while the other drove, stopping for food a time or two. Hitchhiking, with two days head start, they calculated, their friend Patrick would probably have already reached Canada, but he might have done so by a different route altogether, so they didn't diligently look for him, choosing to cover ground instead. They had no trouble crossing the border, having brought plenty of cash and camping gear to explain the vacation in Alberta that they claimed, though the Canadians efficiently went through the pickup before letting them go on toward Lethbridge.

They camped late that night west of Calgary, thoroughly tired but eager to get back on the road early the next morning, heading for Banff, then north on the Icefields Parkway, where they intended to spend a couple of days, if necessary, in a serious search for Patrick.

Kim, as expected, had cheered up and his lack of enthusiasm had faded as soon as they were out of home territory. Even so, something still made Lew uneasy about the one-sided conversation his friend had reported having with McMurdock. It seemed uncharacteristic that the heavy-handed policeman would accept Kim's word and let him go without the information he had demanded. But under the circumstances, all they could do was hope McMurdock was not looking for his stepson in Canada.

CHAPTER 4

It had taken Patrick Cutler a long time to walk from one end of Cranbrook to the other, for the town had grown up along the highway and spread out in business after business, all wanting to be noticed by traveling motorists and easily accessed by local customers. It seemed the place would never end, but the only times he had stopped were to fill his water bottle at a gas station and to change some of his precious American money into Canadian bills and some change at a bank.

Under the golden arches of a MacDonald's, his mouth watering at the thought of a Big Mac and french fries, he had recounted the small handful of Canadian change without touching the bills in his wallet, then shoved it back in his pocket and tramped on, determined to endure his empty stomach until he stopped for the night. For the price of the Big Mac and fries he could buy a whole loaf of bread and a couple of cans of beans—two days' food. One such meal a day was all he could afford, and even that might not be possible soon, depending on how long it took to reach Fairbanks—a long, long way ahead.

When he looked at the map, he knew he had barely started, though he had made it all the way from Wyoming, through Montana, into British Columbia. It was probably—hopefully—safe now, and he could stop carefully watching every vehicle that passed him when he was hitching, always ready to run. They wouldn't know where he'd gone—how could they? So they wouldn't be looking for him in Canada—would they? The idea that they might figure it out and come after him made his stomach lurch with the terror he was attempting to leave behind, and the shrug of his shoulders was almost a shiver, as he tried not to think about it. Something else—anything else! Think about what he and Dave would do when he got to Alaska. Dave would help him figure it all out—he was smart that way. Patrick tugged at the floppy brim of his blue hat to make sure that it covered as much of his red hair as possible. Maybe he should get some dye and make it a different color that wouldn't be a dead giveaway to anyone looking for him. Black? No, brown would look more natural. He shifted the backpack into a more comfortable position, wishing it wasn't so heavy, and walked on past a small shopping center.

At least he'd made it across the border. He knew that if the guards had known how little money he had, they would have turned him back into Montana, and he *couldn't* go back—*had* to make it to Dave. Waiting for the right kind of truck to pull into the last service station on the American side had taken some time—he'd needed one with a load or cover that he could hide himself and the pack under and a driver who went into the store to pay for his gas. But it hadn't been too difficult to slip into the back of the truck between the empty five-gallon cans, crawl under the heavy folded tarp, and lie flat enough not to be seen—

to disappear into an all but empty truck bed that wouldn't be checked because it obviously carried nothing suspicious.

For that moment, Patrick had been glad he wasn't fat or any bigger—though he'd always longed to be at least six feet tall instead of five foot ten. Another couple of inches and he might have made the basketball team. He wondered what they had thought at school when he didn't show up for his last month of classes. They'd have called his stepfather, but the bastard wouldn't care, would be glad he was gone—definitely wouldn't report him missing—wouldn't dare. *He was throwing me out anyway,* he thought resentfully, or . . . His stomach lurched and he consciously didn't complete the thought. *I'm finally old enough to decide what I want to do,* he told himself. *It's just me—by myself.*

Being alone was okay—better than being in the same house with the sick shit his mother had married, but thinking about it made him ache with remembering her. He wouldn't have left if she'd still been there—been okay. But there hadn't been a choice, had there? Not after what he had seen. Sudden tears made it impossible to see the curb in front of him and he tripped over it. He missed his mother—a lot. Scrubbing at his eyes with one fist, he tried very hard not to think about that either.

Once into the truck and across the border, all he'd had to do was lie there under the tarp and ride along until it stopped and he could get out again. Luckily, the driver had gone all the way to Cranbrook, forty whole miles, but it would have been nice if he'd gone on through it instead of pulling into the first bar he came to. It was hard to hitch a ride in a town. You never knew where the driver was headed, and most were not going up the highway in the direction he wanted to go. It was easier on the outskirts, though even then they were often only going a few miles to a farm or ranch. He'd thought of making a sign, but the idea of one that read Alaska or Bust! seemed ridiculous, and besides it would make him conspicuous to anyone looking for him, so he'd given it up.

Now, finally at the edge of town, he leaned against a guardrail, waiting for some car to take the eastern turnoff. Here the road split, one part going in a thirty-three-mile loop to the west, the other nineteen miles to the east, but Patrick could see on the map that they came back together farther north. The western loop would be shorter, if he couldn't get a ride and had to hike it, but he waited, resting and hoping, with his thumb out. Several vehicles passed without slowing—a bus full of tourists, two passenger cars with local plates, a Winnebago motor home with a dog looking out the passenger window. At last two guys in a red pickup with a camper, towing a canvas-covered boat, pulled over, the passenger door opened, and one of them waved an inviting arm. Patrick grabbed his backpack and ran to climb in.

"Give you a hop to Fort Steele," the driver told him. "But it's only six or eight miles."

"Hey, that'd be great. Every bit helps."

"Where you headed?"

"Calgary."

With these men in their forties, Patrick lied without hesitation, for he had found soon after leaving home that the idea of someone his age hitching all the way to Alaska made older people uneasy. The retired couple who had given him a ride in Montana had asked a lot of personal questions, even offered to find a phone so he could "call his family." Alarmed that they would report him to the authorities as a runaway, he managed to grab another ride when they stopped at a gas station, and hoped they'd forget about him.

The incident had made him cautious. Now he told drivers that he was going to the nearest northern community, whether it was on his real route or not. Calgary was credible and staved off questions, as did the other part of the tale he had made up—that he was "going home from college for the summer." He had also decided not to use his real name. Rick, he almost always told anyone who asked, adding Carlson instead of Cutler, if necessary.

The two men in the pickup didn't ask and the short ride to Fort Steele was soon over. He rode with them into the parking lot of the historic town, assessing the assortment of vehicles scattered through it for a possible next ride. It looked promising. He also noticed that a few people were having picnics at some wooden tables. Maybe someone would offer him lunch, if he looked hungrily at their food as he walked slowly past. It had worked twice before, once in a Yellowstone campground and once in a city park in Missoula, Montana. Once the guy he had ridden with had even bought him dinner. Some folks were nice— you just had to pick them carefully. He was learning a lot about people.

Thanking the guys with the camper for the ride, he walked off without learning their names. He'd try for half an hour to get someone to feed him. Then, still hungry or not, he'd head back out to the highway and see how far north he could make it today. First, though, it couldn't hurt to try wandering past the picnic tables. He was practically starving anyway, so looking hungry would be no problem—no problem at all.

•   •   •

An hour from the border, Jessie had stopped to fill the gas tank in Cranbrook, British Columbia, where she exchanged some American dollars for Canadian, and fifteen short minutes farther up the road slowed to pull off the highway for a stop at Fort Steele, ready for her first real break of the day. Tank, who had abandoned his nap in Cranbrook, looked out the window with great interest as they passed an antique train engine, which with bell clanging, whistle screaming, and steam hissing from its boiler pulled several passenger cars away from a refurbished station near the wide sweep of the access road.

Fort Steele Heritage Town was one of the stops Jessie had had in mind when she agreed to make the trip. Tracing its origins to the Kootenay gold rush of 1864, it had caught her attention on paper when she learned that it was named for Superintendent Samuel Steele, a person Jessie remembered as having come to Dawson City during the Klondike gold rush in the Yukon to command what was then the North West Mounted Police and keep the peace.

This town, in which Steele had also been responsible for law enforcement, lay at one end of what had once been only a difficult trail from Missoula, Montana, to the small settlement of Galbraith's Ferry on the Kootenay River. First used by the Kootenay Indians, it had been developed by miners and settlers into "the roughest road" in the area and finally evolved into a modern highway with connections north. When the Canadian Pacific Railway bypassed the town near the turn of the century in favor of nearby Cranbrook, it had gradually become a ghost town. But it had now been restored to what it was in its 1890s heyday and boasted some sixty renovated and reconstructed buildings—among others, a theater, a barber shop, a hardware store, doctors' and dentists' offices, a school, two churches, hotels, a livery stable, a newspaper office, a telegraph office, a bakery, and several residences, complete with antique furnishings—all of which she was anxious to see.

Parking the Winnebago in one of the long spaces provided for motor homes in the large parking lot, Jessie decided to eat a quick lunch before heading off to explore. She gave Tank a bowl of water and quickly made herself a ham and cheese sandwich, grabbed an apple and a handful of cookies, and took them outside to a picnic table under a tree on a grassy parking lot divider.

Though the parking area was half empty so early in the year, there were about a dozen motor homes and campers, at least double that number of cars and trucks, and a couple of tour buses that had parked near the gift shop at the entrance to the tall board fence that surrounded the historic town. Jessie sat watching people come and go as she ate the first half of her sandwich.

Two boys wandered past with the self-conscious swagger of teenagers on their own, but ducked their heads and hurried off when they became aware of her attention. Across the lot at another table a family with three small children had spread out a picnic from the trunk of their car, and the mother was attempting to collect a boy of about five and convince him to sit with his sisters at the picnic table.

"*Michael*—you can't have ice cream if you don't eat your lunch."

Good idea, Jessie thought, having noticed a sign at the gift shop that advertised homemade ice cream in a variety of flavors. More dessert, she told herself with a grin. Eat up all your lunch, Jessie.

Realizing she had forgotten something to drink, she got up from the table and walked around to the coach door on the far side of the motor home, which she had left open to allow more air into the rig, closing only the screen door. She climbed back inside and rummaged in the refrigerator till her hand fell on a can of apple juice. Just the thing.

Tank, finished with his water, had been waiting patiently at the screen door, so she clipped the leash to his collar and took him back outside with her. Though she knew he was too well trained to stray, it was a public parking lot, and she intended to fasten his leash to the table for appearances but halted abruptly when she reached it to stare open-mouthed at the paper plate that had held her sandwich. Except for a crumb or two, it was empty! Not only was the second half of the sandwich missing, but the apple and the cookies had vanished as well.

A loose dog might have helped itself to the sandwich, even the cookies, in her absence, but no dog would have—could have—so quickly gulped them down and taken the apple too. A child? One of the teenage boys? Jessie quickly turned to examine the area nearby, but no questionable person was to be seen. The boys were gone, and all the family members were seated at the table—even Michael, who, unwilling to lose his ice cream treat, was now rapidly scooping potato salad from a paper plate with a plastic spoon. Who then? Someone had obviously *stolen* the rest of her lunch. The more she thought about it, the more annoyed Jessie became. Who the hell would have the nerve to take someone else's food?

The crunch of steps on gravel made her spin around frowning at an elderly couple who were walking past the Winnebago. They widened their eyes a little at her startled movement and accusing stare but did not stop moving in the direction of the Fort Steele entrance and gift shop.

"Hello," the white-haired man said and nodded. "Nice dog."

Flustered at her suspicious reaction, Jessie forced herself to relax and smile a little. "Ah—thanks."

The woman looked back once over her shoulder and murmured something to her husband that Jessie couldn't hear. He shrugged and they trudged steadily away in their matching blue windbreakers and white Adidas.

Feeling embarrassed and a little silly as she watched them go, Jessie suddenly noticed a figure moving toward the gift shop ahead of them at a faster than normal pace. From across the wide lot, she couldn't tell if the person was male or female, but it was dressed in jeans, hiking boots, and a green plaid shirt. A blue backpack with a sleeping bag tied under it bounced a bit on the person's shoulders, and a denim hat with a floppy brim covered the hair. From Jessie's point of view, the person, man or woman, looked younger than herself but larger and older than the boys that had passed earlier—how old was impossible to tell. As she watched, the figure turned slightly to glance back and she could see that the face was hidden behind a large pair of reflective sunglasses. Noticing the focus of Jessie's attention, the person immediately broke into a trot and vanished through the door to the gift shop.

But Jessie had seen enough—the round red shape in one of the robber's hands had told her that he, or she, was still in possession of the stolen apple. She hesitated, tempted to run after the departing figure and demand her lunch back, but imagining the accusation she would have to make over half a sandwich that in all probability had already been eaten, she found herself giggling. Still laughing, she sat down at the table and considered the situation. *Stop thief? You stole my lunch? Give me back my apple?*

What the heck! If whoever-it-was wanted her lunch badly enough to steal it, did she really care? Let it go. The day and her mood were too fine to waste chasing after it, or resenting a situation so insignificant. Maybe the thief was a ham and cheese addict who, finding temptation too much, had fallen off some twelve-step sandwich wagon. It had looked like a hiker—maybe a hungry one.

She considered making another sandwich, but it didn't seem worth the trouble.

"Let's go get some ice cream," she told Tank as she locked up the motor home and headed for the gift shop and the antique streets of Fort Steele.

Fort *Steele*? It now seemed a more appropriate name.

CHAPTER 5

As Jessie was exploring the historic buildings and attractions of Fort Steele, Maxie McNabb drove past it without turning in, but slowed her own motor home to watch the steam engine pull into the reconstructed station. Listening to the train's whistle tooting cheerfully to a group of tourists waiting on the elevated platform for a ride, Maxie took a look at several huge Clydesdale draft horses grazing in a neatly fenced field next to the highway.

Though she had only been on the road for five hours—since leaving Missoula, Montana—for some reason it had seemed a long and tiring day. In another hour she could reach the campground she had carefully marked on the map. It lay just south of the retirement community of Fairmount Hot Springs, and she was looking forward to taking a long hot shower and settling back in the sunshine for some late afternoon relaxation. There was also a new Kate Grilley mystery that she was eager to start, for she had always had a hankering to visit the Virgin Islands.

As she accelerated past the Fort Steele turnoff, a narrow reddish-brown head rose alertly from a padded basket that hung over the front of the passenger seat and provided a comfortable view of the passing scenery for her short-legged canine companion.

Maxie reached across to rub the ears of the toy dachshund affectionately. "Take it easy, we're not stopping," she told him in her deep husky voice.

But Stretch, curious as always, caught sight of the horses calmly cropping grass and scrambled up so his front feet were on the edge of the basket. He barked several times and followed up with a low growl.

Maxie grinned at his audacity. "You wouldn't last a round in a revolving door with those giants, you silly galah."

True to his breed, the excitable dachshund was ready to take on almost anything, though most of his overconfidence was directly proportional to the distance between himself and a perceived threat, especially if it was bigger—and almost everything was bigger. Safe inside the motor home, he watched attentively until the Clydesdales were out of sight, then, wide awake now and curious, turned to the passenger window to see what else was going by.

Nora Maxine "Maxie" Stillman Flanagan McNabb was more than glad to be heading north, though she was aware that she would soon be leaving spring behind and driving into a late breakup in Alaska. The Alaska Highway was a favorite, if long, drive, but she would be home soon enough. She liked her nomadic style of life for many reasons, but every so often it was good to take her time and spend a week or ten days driving the more than 2,000 miles home.

For the last three years she had lived and traveled in her motor home. She had spent the previous winter in the warm high desert of New Mexico, where snow might infrequently appear but never stayed long. The summer before, she had not driven back to her compact house near Homer, on Alaska's Kenai Peninsula, but had left her "gypsy wagon" with a friend in Denver and flown back for a month to check on her property during part of June and July. Now she looked forward with longing to having a whole three months, perhaps a little more, to spend enjoying the change of going to bed and waking up between walls that rested on a solid foundation. It would be good to tend to her garden, to spend lazy afternoons in her hammock on the deck watching the weather alter the colors of Kachemak Bay, to renew her relationship with her extensive library and the collection of Alaskan art that was too large and valuable to carry along on her travels. Most of all she wanted to get together with a few old friends. She had missed them more than anything else. She was famished for communal evenings with the crowd gathered congenially around her dining table to share good meals seasoned with familiar conversation and laughter.

It would have been better to have Daniel there as well, but the last five years had mellowed that specific grief from the sharp anguish of loss to a lingering nostalgia. She could go back now, and the pleasant reminders of this second husband would be welcome; time had finally made memories more significant than absence.

"We had six fine years before you nicked off, you stubborn old Aussie coot," she said to him fondly and aloud, a habit that she enjoyed and hadn't attempted to break. He was still good company.

But Daniel McNabb, Australian expatriate, from whom she had picked up the bits of Aussie *slanguage* that frequently enlivened her speech, was not the only husband Maxie cherished and had outlived. At forty-five she had scattered the ashes of Joe

Flanagan, her high school sweetheart and first husband, into the waters of the bay where he had drowned in the storm that sank his commercial fishing boat. Meeting and marrying Daniel years later had been a surprising gift when she least expected it and considered herself a confirmed widow. Once again alone at sixty-two she knew she had been lucky in both her relationships but had no inclination toward another. Her independent spirit had finally won out over her heart and desire for companionship. Daniel's careful investments had left her with no financial concerns, so she had used some of the interest to buy a thirty-four-foot Jayco motor home, found a caretaker for her house in Homer, and gone off to see the world she had missed while living in the far north for the first fifty-nine years of her life.

A no-nonsense woman with a solid sense of humor, a fine practical mind, and a zest for life, Maxie had a realistic balance in her expectations of the good and bad the world had to hand her and knew how to manage what she could not control. She no longer bothered to fool herself or others about much of anything, but took what was positive with appreciation, dealt directly and as little as possible with the negative, looked life straight in the eye, and got on with it. A plaque that hung in the kitchen of her house without wheels said it well: "Life ain't all you want, but it's all you 'ave, so 'ave it, stick a geranium in your 'at, an' be 'appy!"

As she drove up a hill and the highway began to level out, the sharp summons of her cell phone attracted her attention. Slowing slightly as she looked for a place to pull off the road, she answered it.

"Maxie."

"Hi, Mom. It's Carol. Can you talk?"

"I can in a minute or two. There's a gas station ahead. Hold on."

Parked out of the way at one side of the station with the

engine turned off, she stared at the cell phone for a moment, took a deep breath, and decided she was as ready as she could be to speak to her daughter. "All right—I'm here now."

"Are you okay? Where are you?"

Why couldn't Carol ever assume she was okay instead of the reverse? Wishful thinking?

"I'm just fine, thanks, and I'm between Cranbrook and Lake Louise in British Columbia. How are *you*, dear, and how is dear old Boston?"

"Oh, you know—the usual—too busy. I thought we agreed you weren't going to drive that appalling highway to Alaska again."

Maxie took a deep breath and held onto her patience.

"No. You attempted to get me to decide that. I never agreed."

"*Mother!* You *did!* Now I'm really concerned. Don't you even *remember?* We talked it all over at Christmas and—"

"Carol, I recall our conversation in great detail. I've not yet gone 'round the twist, whatever you may think. You gave me your opinion. But you didn't ask for mine, so I refrained from giving it. I'm going to Homer for the summer, as I planned."

There was a pause, in which Maxie could anticipate what would come next. It did.

"*Philip* won't approve of this at all. You shouldn't be driving alone in that thing. It's not sa—"

"Well, I'm sorry to hear that, but I don't arrange my life to please your husband. He may be a fine lawyer—"

"Attorney, Mother."

"Attorney then, if you wish—but your stepfather always thought he was a bit of a sook. I may be an oldie, but I'm not yet close to falling off the perch and I'm perfectly capable of deciding what suits me. Just now, heading up this beautiful highway toward home couldn't suit me more."

There was an offended silence from the phone, which Maxie waited out.

Carol's voice was frigid when she finally spoke again.

"Well. I just called to wish you a happy Mother's Day. It *is* this Sunday, you know."

Maxie had forgotten, and wished her daughter had as well—as she wished they would forget to remind her exactly how old she was on every birthday—but put a smile in her voice before she answered.

"Thank you, dear. Have a nice one yourself. How's Brandon?"

"Fine."

"Are you sending him up to visit me this summer?"

"No."

"Why not? He loves to visit—wherever I am."

"That we never know where you'll be next is part of the problem. He's playing Little League this year."

"All summer?"

"Yes."

"Oh. Well—give him a big hug and tell him I'll miss him."

Extended silence.

Maxie wavered but decided against accusing her daughter of withholding her grandson as punishment for not following unsolicited and unwanted advice. She waited, elbow in the curve of the steering wheel, forehead resting in her free hand. Why did it always have to be so . . .

"Look, I'm not trying to tell you what to do, Mother," Carol eventually said icily. "We have a right to worry about you. It's an unstable way to live—wandering around in that absurd motor home. What can people think?"

You are incessantly telling me what to do and how to do it, Maxie thought, but did not say. Did anyone but Carol and Philip really care, she wondered—not for the first time. Everyone she knew who mattered seemed to admire her having the freedom and the nerve to take off on her own—thought it sounded interesting and exciting. Everyone, that is, but Carol and her wowser of a husband, who felt they had a position and an image to maintain that were somehow threatened by a sixty-two-year-old "vagrant" mother. If they had their way, she wouldn't even return to Alaska periodically but would live tidily tucked up in some health care facility for senior citizens—near *them*—where they could keep an eye on her *instability*—with a power of attorney over her bank account.

"Thank you for the call, Carol. I'll think of you on Sunday, but I have to go now," she said brightly.

"But *Mo-other*, I think—"

But Maxie didn't want to know what Carol thought. "Bye-bye, dear. I'll talk to you when I get to Homer." Resolutely pushing a button, she hung up on the resentment in her daughter's voice and dropped the phone back into its holder.

She had always hoped Carol would be happy but suspected that her daughter didn't even realize she was not. How in the world had appearances become so important to her? As a child she had been a rumble-tumble tomboy, hated dresses, loved adventures. Now she was all volunteer efforts and civic occasions intended to help advance her husband's legal and political career. Somewhere under it must be a vestige of the bright-eyed, carefree little girl who had bound up the wings of injured birds, organized treasure hunts on the beaches of Kachemak Bay, emoted in high school dramatics, spent summers working on her father's fishing boat, and wanted to be an archaeologist when she grew up.

Stretch, who had climbed from his basket to the passenger seat, then to the floor, now stood beside her with his front paws on the edge of her seat. Her hand still lay on the phone in its holder, and all he could reach was the wrist, which he licked. Wrenched back from memories of long-ago summers and children rolling over each other like puppies down the front lawn, Maxie reached down to lift him back into his basket.

"Thanks, lovie. Shall we be rolling again?"

Firmly she emptied her mind of impossible regrets and put the motor home in gear.

Pulling back onto the highway, she passed a young man at the intersection with his thumb out, but since she never picked up hitchhikers she dismissed the figure in jeans and green plaid shirt, whose eyes were concealed by his sunglasses, his mouth by the apple he was munching.

It was time to do some nice, comforting thing for herself, and that new campground wasn't far ahead, with a shower she hoped would be hot.

CHAPTER

The sun was more than halfway down the western sky when Jessie turned the Winnebago off the highway and followed a short, winding gravel road that ended in a neatly organized campground beside a small river.

From Fort Steele the highway had continued up the long valley of the Purcell Trench, which extended far into British Columbia. It had been a pleasant drive with remarkable views of the rugged Rocky Mountains to the east, reminding Jessie that they formed the Continental Divide. From her side of their spectacular heights, every river and stream flowed west and eventually to the sea. These included the narrow beginnings of the Columbia River, which first trickled north gathering strength from a myriad of tributaries, then curved in a large loop and fled swiftly south into Washington, gradually becoming the mighty river that powered Grand Coulee Dam, watered the apple-growing country of Wenatchee and Yakima, rolled past The Dalles, and finally emptied into the ocean at Astoria, where Lewis and Clark had made camp on the Pacific.

Though she had intended to go on another twenty miles and find a place to stay in Radium Hot Springs, Jessie was a little tired from her first day of driving on unfamiliar roads. Still getting used to handling the thirty-one-foot motor home, she wanted plenty of time and light to park and get it hooked up before dark. So when she noticed a sign for Dutch Creek Resort and RV Park, she remembered her vow to stop when and where she liked and impulsively turned off the highway to take a look.

Pleased with what she found, she stopped in front of a Register Here sign and stepped out, leaving Tank to wait for her. Across a wide green lawn was an immaculate white and green office and a friendly young man who assigned her space 26 and circled it for her on a piece of paper with a map on one side, rules and information on the other.

"It's a pull-through, so you won't have to back in," he told her with a smile. "And since you don't want a sewer connection, I'll put you close to the washroom. Okay?"

She assured him that would be fine.

"In case you're interested, we have a couple of nesting pairs of osprey right now—here and here," he informed her proudly, pointing out the locations on the map. "And please—keep your dog on a leash."

The campground was about half full, and after driving slowly around a large loop that branched every thirty feet or so into individual spaces for RVs, Jessie found number 26, bordering on another, smaller loop where she could see several tents set up among the pine trees. Pulling into it, she checked the spirit levels on the dash and was glad to see that whoever had graded the parking place had done a good job; she would need to make no adjustments—front to back, side to side, the motor home was almost perfectly level. She took out the list she had made the night before, reversed the order of the things she had made sure to remember to do before leaving that morning, soon had her rig connected to electricity and water, turned on the liquid propane gas, and cranked open the ceiling vents and several windows to let the late afternoon breeze wander in along with the faint sound of running water.

Time to take Tank for a walk to the river and get a look at the ospreys—and some pictures, if she could, before it grew too dark. Retrieving her camera case from the closet, she moved the Minolta, with its usual 35- to 70-mm lens, to a light daypack, along with a second lens that would zoom from 70 to 200 mm, hoping it would let her see shy birds well enough to photograph.

A quick check of the map told her that the nearest of the two nests lay directly to the east beyond the tents, near a pool the owner had told her was available for swimming. As she walked through the area, she was glad not to have to crawl into a small tent for the night.

A boy and a girl in swim suits, with inner tubes and towels slung over the handles of their bicycles, zipped by as she passed a tent more than big enough for the young couple who were cooking dinner on the two gas burners of a Coleman stove. A small girl in a pink shirt, with matching ribbons in her hair, rocked her bicycle from side to side on its training wheels as she peddled furiously to keep up with a woman who walked ahead in the direction of the washroom with a baby on her hip. Two of the other tents were zipped tightly closed and seemed momentarily abandoned, one with a line of clothes drying nearby on a line tied between two trees. In the middle of the line a green shirt tossed limply in the light breeze, reminding Jessie of the person who had stolen her lunch, but the shirt was not plaid. She still thought the incident odd but humorous. Her vanishing lunch was long gone by now, leaving no evidence, and to go around accosting everyone she saw in green would be absurd.

Several times on the looping road that connected campsites she had to step off to one side as vehicles passed, their occupants looking for a space for the night. Most were motor homes or pickups, either with campers or pulling fifth-wheel trailers, but some were people traveling in cars who would set up tents. Once a green Suburban surprised her into an awkward leap off the road by making less noise than the heavier RVs as it came up behind her. It cruised slowly past with no one inside but the driver, who stared at her as he passed from under the brim of a western hat, and did not return her nod.

Looking for someone else, she thought, and turned away to continue the walk.

She and Tank, on his leash, were soon standing on the riverbank, where one of the bicycles had been hastily dropped on its side. She could only hear splashes and shouts, for the pool lay hidden beyond a low brush-covered ridge across the swiftly moving but shallow water.

Some distance away, also on the other side, stood a pole perhaps twenty feet high with a two-foot-square platform on the top. There the ospreys had built a large nest, and Jessie could just make out the black-and-white head of one of them, sitting on her eggs. Replacing the 35- to 70-mm lens with the stronger one, she used it to focus and zoom in on the bird and was able to make it out more clearly, body out of sight below the edge of the tangle of dry sticks that made up the nest.

At first she didn't see the male osprey. Perched in the top of a nearby tree, he was so still as to be almost invisible until, carefully searching, she spotted a slight ruffle of feathers and a flash of his white underside. Through the camera lens she could see that the gold of the sinking sun warmed the color of his feathers to a dark brown, not black, and she detected a gleam from his watchful yellow eye as he slowly turned his head in her direction.

Though they were seldom seen in Alaska, she knew that these raptors were not hawks, though they were often called "fish hawks" and lived near water—especially coastal marshes—where their finned prey swam and could be sighted from the air. Like their terrestrial cousins, the eagles she saw often at home, they hovered above the water till they located a fish, then dove and snatched it in their strong talons. Peering through her lens, she could see that the male's upper beak curved sharply over the lower, a cruel but effective scimitar for stripping flesh from its catch.

Jessie took several pictures, noticing that the bird seemed aware of her and a bit nervous, or perhaps it was the presence of Tank, who sat patiently by her side. Then, as she watched, the male osprey suddenly launched itself into the air with a sharp *kip kip ki-yeuk* and soared off above the trees. As it glided away, its powerful wings formed a distinctive M—inner wings thrust forward, outer swept back—that made it look more like a gull than a hawk or eagle, which had a wider and straighter wingspread. For a few seconds it was visible against the golden glow on the spires of the eastern Rocky Mountains as it sailed off and disappeared along with its cry. The female remained in the nest, silent and motionless.

For half an hour Jessie and Tank walked along the riverbank and through the campground, enjoying the warmth of the late afternoon and being away from the constant sound and motion of the Winnebago. Heading back toward their home-away-from-home, they were passing the space next to their own when a small brown body sprang suddenly from under a larger motor home, dragging a leash and barking loudly. He rushed toward them with all four short legs a blur of motion, slid to a halt in the road between them and space 26, and continued his noisy assault. Both Jessie and Tank stopped to stare in astonished amusement at the miniature dachshund who was challenging their right of way with such bravado.

"Stretch, you twit—come back here. Stop that barking." The voice was low in pitch and strong in its insistence but held a note of long-suffering affection for the small tornado that held Jessie and Tank more in amazement than at bay. "Come here, dingbat."

The attractive older woman who stepped out the door of her motor home with a pleasant, if slightly exasperated, expression and followed her small, short-haired companion into the road was as tall as Jessie but tanned to a healthy glow. She wore a full denim skirt with large patch pockets and an oversized white shirt with red stripes, sleeves rolled to the elbow. The pair of reddish-brown moccasins on her feet almost matched the color of her dog, and her own hair, a salt-and-pepper blend pulled back into a heavy braid, was more dark brown than gray. Her apologetic grin was young, and her eyes sparkled with good humor as she hurried to catch the leash her dog was trailing.

"Sorry. He's pretty territorial, and when we stop in a new place he can't decide what's his and what's not. Can't really blame him—sometimes I can't either."

Jessie was caught by the vibrant quality of the woman's voice, which sang with the richness of a cello, as well as with her evident good humor.

The barking had ceased as soon as she appeared. Now the small dog stood looking up at her attentively, all wagging tail and liquid brown eyes, full of so much devotion as he beseeched forgiveness that it could have melted a glacier. Jessie, familiar with the habits of dogs, couldn't help smiling at this conspicuous bit of chicanery.

"That's okay," she assured the dachshund's mistress, holding out a friendly hand. "Hi, I'm Jessie Arnold, your next-door neighbor for the night."

"Hi, yourself," she was told in return and a lightly calloused hand with long graceful fingers, one bearing a large silver and turquoise ring, clasped hers firmly. "I'm Maxie McNabb, and this hooligan"—a nod in the dachshund's direction—"is Stretch. Yours?"

"Tank."

"An Alaskan husky, right?"

The two dogs were now paying more attention to each other than to their humans. Muzzles thrust out, noses almost touching, they circled each other and seemed to approve of what they found, for Stretch suddenly reared up and gave the husky a quick lick on the nose, then danced back and forth on his short legs in a distinct invitation to play. Tank glanced up at the watching women, then sat down with an air of tolerance, preserving face against such a frontal attack on his considerable dignity.

"You clown!" Maxie told the irrepressible dachshund, keeping a tight hold on the leash as she turned back to Jessie. "So— *they've* made friends. Can I offer you a drink? A good bottle of Irish is an excellent peace offering."

Jessie's smile grew wider. "Jameson's?"

"How'd you guess?"

"You said *good.*"

Maxie raised an eyebrow and nodded approval. "A woman with taste. Come along then."

Her motor home, Jessie noticed as she approached, was three or four feet longer than the Winnebago and had a slideout that extended a section of its width by several feet to one side, so it seemed quite a lot bigger too. Under a crank-out awning that sheltered the near side, a large piece of indoor/outdoor carpeting was spread, on which rested a padded lawn chair and small matching table. Removing the dachshund's leash and replacing it with a line attached securely to a handy ring on the side of the RV, Maxie disappeared inside for a moment and returned with a second chair, which she unfolded and placed so the table was between them.

"Make yourself comfortable. I'll get the drinks. Water? Ice?"

"Straight up," Jessie told her, finding the chair exceptionally cushy, "but I'd like an ice water with."

"Good girl! Never ruin good whiskey."

Tank lay down by her feet. Stretch's tether was long enough so that, though sensing play was not going to happen, he could join Tank, and the two were soon relaxing together like old friends.

Maxie quickly returned with their drinks and a basket of chips, which she put on the table. Settling easily into her chair, she raised a glass of similarly undiluted Jameson's in Jessie's direction. "Rose-lipt maidens—lightfoot lads."

The unexpected quote from Houseman took Jessie off guard, into an internal stillness so profound she could scarcely take the next breath. When she did, she was dismayed to find her vision awash with tears. Setting down her untasted drink, she scrubbed hastily at her face.

Maxie waited, saying nothing, till Jessie looked up to find her watching closely with a hint of sympathy and a tissue from one of her pockets in her hand. "Hit a nerve, did I?"

Jessie nodded and smiled, recovering rapidly. "Yeah. Someone I know used to say that—but he almost always got it backwards."

A chuckle from Maxie, followed by a slightly nostalgic expression that raised the corners of her mouth and narrowed her eyes. "I remember my husbands with it—good men, both—gone now."

They sipped at their drinks in thoughtful silence for a minute, remembering past lovers, but were soon talking in the interested, animated way of people who already know they are going to like each other.

By the time Jessie went back to the Winnebago, it was dark, the sky had clouded over, and a bit of wind had come up. Sometime in the previous two hours she had fed and watered Tank and been handed a plate of salad and lasagna from Maxie's galley, but what she remembered was the agreeable conversation. There had been much laughter and congenial sharing of interests. The cabin she was soon to build had been described in great detail, along with the ups and downs of her kennel business and sled dog racing. She had heard all about Maxie's travels in the motor home, the daughter married to an attorney who disapproved of her wayfaring lifestyle—*"We have an appearance to consider, you know!"*—and the son who didn't—*"Go and do whatever floats your boat, Ma. Have a great time."*

The last thing that made her smile, as she settled comfortably into her bed for the night and reviewed the pleasant evening, was the dachshund's name—Stretch. How perfect for a small, spirited dog, slung low to the ground but as full of life as his mistress. Their approach to the world reminded her of one of the mottoes she had noticed prominently displayed in Maxie's motor home: "Life's too short to drink bad wine."

C H A P T E R

The unexpected fury of the storm that swept thunderously through the Dutch Creek campground during the night had startled Jessie from her contented sleep and confused her concerning her whereabouts, but having enjoying the light show as it passed over, she had gone easily back to sleep with pleasant thoughts about what had set her on this unexpected journey and of the miles to come.

When she was jerked from dreams again sometime later, instantly alerted by a low uneasy growl from Tank, she knew exactly where she was. He had been sleeping on the floor beside her bed, but he was now on his feet, listening attentively. Padding quietly to the coach door, he growled softly again.

Slowly, silently, taking great care not to rock the motor home any more than she had to, Jessie slipped from her bed and crept forward to stand by his side. With one finger she parted the slats of the blind on the galley window and peered out into the glow shed by a campground light on a tall pole nearby. It lit up several motor homes and campers and a wide area of shrubs and grass still slowly dripping from the now departed storm, but she saw nothing move other than leaves on the trees and heard nothing but the mild wind that still tossed them gently.

Tank turned and padded to the center of open space between the door and the dinette, cocked his head, and stared at the floor. Whatever he was hearing, it was beneath them. Then Jessie thought she heard something softly scrape against the underside of the rig. An animal—perhaps a bear? Too big. It couldn't be very large if it was able to make its way beneath the motor home.

Cautiously lowering herself to hands and knees, she laid one ear against the carpet and listened intently. Under her head, something hit the floor with a small thump, startling her back to a sitting position. Something—or someone—was definitely down there.

Before leaving Knik, Jessie had considered taking along the Smith & Wesson .44 pistol that she carried on training runs and in races for protection against the moose that sometimes attacked mushers and their teams. But remembering that handguns were illegal in Canada and that most of her trip would take place on Canadian highways, she had conscientiously left it behind. Instead, in Coeur d'Alene, she had purchased two medium-size cans of pepper spray, one of which now lay within easy reach within a drawer under the galley sink—the work of seconds to retrieve.

With a stern look and quick clasp of his muzzle between thumb and fingers, she cautioning Tank not to bark, then tiptoed to the bedroom where she balanced carefully to pull on a pair of jeans and a sweatshirt and slid her feet without socks into her running shoes. Quietly collecting a flashlight and the pepper spray from the drawer, she returned to the door, Tank close beside her, and gingerly turned the deadbolt to unlock it.

She hadn't made any loud sounds, but one cannot move in an unstablized RV without causing some slight vibration. It had been very quiet, and she had the feeling that whatever was down there was waiting and listening as hard as she was. Slowly she lifted the handle and pushed against the door. As it swung open, the edge scraped very softly against the frame with the small squeal of metal against metal.

The result was the instant sound of whatever was under the floor moving quickly toward the other side. Jessie leaped out and, with Tank following, ran around the front of the rig, turning on the flashlight as she went, pepper spray ready in the other hand. She was just in time to see a dark human figure roll out from underneath and scramble to its feet.

"Stop!" she snapped, directing the light and the can both toward it. "I'll pepper-spray you if you don't."

The figure froze and, turning startled eyes in her direction, was immediately blinded by the beam from her flashlight.

It was a boy—well, sort of a boy—a young man just old enough, perhaps, to be on his own. He dropped a pack and poncho he had dragged out with him and threw up his arms to shield his eyes.

"What the hell are you doing under my rig?" Jessie demanded sharply.

"Please don't use that pepper stuff," he said. "I was just trying to get out of the rain."

"Don't you have a place of your own? Who are you anyway?"

"Rick—" He stopped, then started again. "Patrick—ah—Cutler." His voice broke on the words. He sounded young and scared to Jessie. His arms hid his face, but a shock of red hair was just visible above them.

"How old are you, Patrick Cutler?"

"Eighteen."

"In a pig's eye!"

"No, really," he entreated. "I was eighteen in March."

"I might believe that if I could see the rest of you. Put your arms down." She walked a bit closer and lowered the light from his face.

He complied and stood blinking wide blue eyes, still half blinded. His attempt not to appear frightened wasn't working well; guilty alarm made him look like a small boy caught trying out his father's pipe behind the barn. Tousled red hair hung over his forehead, and his narrow face bore a streak of dirt on one cheek, probably a result of his hasty attempt to crawl out from under the motor home. Otherwise he looked fairly clean, in jeans, hiking boots, and a black windbreaker jacket zipped to his chin with a hood that hung down his back and a tiny red Canadian maple leaf pin on the collar. Beside the poncho, a backpack lay at his feet and he was clutching a blue hat in one hand. A bell of recognition rang in Jessie's mind, but adrenaline still pumping, she ignored it in favor of her anger and questions she wanted answered.

"Anybody else under there?"

"No, just me."

"Where did you come from?"

"Wyoming."

Tank, standing alertly beside her, suddenly turned his head toward Maxie's motor home, and Jessie realized that in her concentration on her captive she had blocked out the sound of Stretch barking inside it for most of the brief interrogation. A light came on in the galley, the door opened, and Maxie, in a robe and moccasins, came down the steps onto the outdoor carpet. Stretch jumped out behind her and flew across to help Tank confront the intruder, barking fiercely from just out of reach.

"Shut up, Stretch," Maxie said in mild distraction. "What's going on?"

The dachshund stopped barking and growled instead.

"I just caught a sneak under my house," Jessie replied, looking back at the unhappy young man who was still standing in the beam of her light. His shoulders now slumped dejectedly, though he kept his chin up, watching warily.

"Interesting. What was he doing *there*?" Marie asked, as she came to stand with folded arms beside Jessie and curiously examine her prisoner.

"Getting out of the rain—he says."

"Makes sense. It was quite a rain. What's that?" She nodded to the can in Jessie's hand.

"Pepper spray. And he's lucky handguns aren't legal in Canada."

They stood staring silently at the spotlit young man beside the Winnebago. He shifted uneasily on his feet and glanced around as if contemplating escape but, looking down at the two vigilant dogs, seemed to change his mind and remained where he was, waiting and shivering. Jessie thought that it could have been nerves, but the storm had brought cooler temperatures.

"Please," he said again, and she could hear his teeth chatter. "I d-didn't mean to bother anybody. I'll just go away."

Ignoring his plea, Maxie frowned thoughtfully and turned to Jessie. "Get anything enlightening out of him?"

"He says he's eighteen, his name's Patrick Cutler, and he's here by himself—from Wyoming."

"Hm-m. What shall we do with him?"

Jessie shrugged and slowly shook her head, reflecting on the situation.

Maxie sighed and narrowed her eyes at young Mr. Cutler. "You have anything dangerous in that pack—or your pockets?" she asked.

"Just a hunting knife and some matches."

"It's too wet to burn anything. Take the knife out and throw it over here."

He rummaged in the pack till he found the knife and tossed it in her direction.

She picked it up. "Now—bring that stuff and come along." She turned back toward her motor home, amusement in the glance she gave Jessie.

"What are you going to *do*?" Jessie asked, now more interested than suspicious.

"Well—I guess the only thing to do right now is feed him. Boys always want feeding and he *looks* hungry. Are you hungry, Patrick? I can see that you're cold."

"Pat—ah—just Pat's okay," he stammered in confusion, but a hint of a grin twitched his lips as he used both hands to smooth the red hair away from his face. "*Starving!* Haven't eaten since noon—and that was just an apple, some cookies, and part of a sandwich."

"I *knew* there was something familiar about you," Jessie burst out, lowering the pepper spray. "You stole my lunch, didn't you?"

The grin now escaped his control, broke through, and transformed his dirty face into that of a cheerful, if slightly guilty, urchin with freckles scattered across his cheeks and nose.

"Sorry?" he offered. Then, bending to collect his pack and poncho, he tromped off behind Maxie toward her lighted galley.

Jessie gave up and went along.

* * *

His name was Patrick Cutler, and from the driver's license he showed them, he *was* eighteen—by barely six weeks. It also gave them an address in Cody, Wyoming.

By the time they were drinking hot coffee, Jessie, across from him at the table, was attempting to gain more information ("You owe us something for not reporting you"), while Maxie fried bacon, scrambled eggs, and tossed in a frequent question or comment, and Tank kept Stretch company on the floor. Jessie quickly learned that Pat meant to hitchhike all the way to Fairbanks to visit his "best friend, Dave" and look for a job. He had started to mention Calgary but thought better of it when she gave him a dubious frown, remembered that she'd seen his driver's license, and told the truth.

"Do you know how far that is?" Jessie asked, astonished at his optimism. "There's a lot of empty road just between towns on the highway."

"Yeah, well, I got a map," he told her cheerfully. "And people are usually real good about giving me rides. I've only hiked maybe fifty miles—so far."

The idea of hitchhiking another 2,000 miles, much of it wilderness, was mind-boggling—though he'd come quite a way from Cody already. She stared at him, appalled and dismayed by his lack of concern.

"Does your family know what you're doing?" Maxie asked calmly, one hand on her hip, a spatula in the other.

There was a hesitation and Pat's grin disappeared abruptly. They could see that some door had been slammed shut in what until then had been a fairly candid communication. "Sure," he said, a second too late for either of the women to believe him.

"Patrick," she tried again sternly, "does anyone know where you are, or where you're going?"

His grin was now firmly back in place, but it did not reach the wary unhappiness in his eyes, and the lips through which he attempted to reassure her were a little stiff. "Yeah, sure. Dave knows I'm coming."

With a thoughtful frown, Maxie turned back to her frying pan, but the force with which she slapped two slices of bread into the toaster betrayed her impatience with *that* answer.

"What gear have you got?" Jessie asked. "If you had to crawl under my rig to get out of the rain, you must not have a tent."

"I'm okay—really. I got a tarp—and the poncho."

"Why didn't you rig the tarp in a space with the other tents?"

"Ah—well, I . . ." He shrugged and stopped.

It was suddenly clear. He wasn't registered, hadn't wanted to pay the fee. Couldn't afford it?

"How much money have you got?" she demanded, as Maxie set a platter of early breakfast on the table and joined them, bringing her coffee mug.

"Plenty," he snapped back, stung. "That's none of your business." There was anger, resentment, and a hint of some other dark thing on his face. Jessie, momentarily nonplussed, backed off and began to spread jam on a piece of toast.

There was a small silence while Maxie served herself bacon and eggs, then handed him the platter.

"You're right, it's not," she agreed. "And we're not going to report you for anything, Patrick. But, you see, we've both driven this highway before and know what it's like. We're concerned that you won't be able to make it all the way to Fairbanks. You must have had enough money to cross the border, anyway."

Suspicion grew in Jessie's mind, and she wanted to ask him just how he *had* crossed the border, for she didn't believe he had the funds the Canadians would require of a young person—enough to make it all the way to Alaska. Why else would he be stealing food and not have eaten since lunch?

He shrugged casually, without confirming Maxie's assumption, looked at his plate to avoid their eyes, and began to eat, plainly trying to mind his manners and not shovel the food into his mouth.

Jessie knew she had been more than a little condescending concerning herself with his finances, but he had turned more defensive than seemed necessary. Now that she had had a better look at him in the light, she was forced to revise her initial impression of a smart-alec teenage thief. He was as reasonably clean as you could expect from someone living on the road. His clothes were of good quality, without rips or patches, and the jacket he had removed to reveal the green plaid shirt had not been purchased cheaply. The label, exposed when he tossed it onto the back of the passenger seat, indicated it had come from Lands' End—his pack, REI. It made less sense that a well-dressed kid would steal than one who was not, but you couldn't tell about kids these days—some of the most affluent wore the grungiest clothes, and vice versa.

By the time they finished eating, Patrick could hardly keep his eyes open. He stumbled to his feet and helped clear the table but was clearly all in.

"Thank you both," he said, reaching for his jacket. "I'll just be go—"

"You'll just help me make this table into a bed and crawl into it before you fall over in a heap," Maxie informed him in a voice that brooked no argument.

CHAPTER 8

The dampness left by the storm was rapidly disappearing in the next morning's early sunshine when Jessie went out for a run with Tank trotting along on his leash beside her. As they returned half an hour later, Maxie stepped out of her rig, already dressed for travel, and walked across to meet them at the Winnebago, the handles of two mugs clutched in one hand.

"Good morning," she called. "Looks like another sunny one. Coffee?"

"Already had some," Jessie told her, unlocking the door and waving her inside. "Our visitor still here?"

Maxie sat down at the dinette table. "Yes, and this coffee's an excuse to fill you in. He had a fair go at eating everything in sight for breakfast," she said with an indulgent smile. "I'll replenish the bacon and eggs first chance I get. Now he's working off his obligation over the dishpan."

"He tell you anything else?" Jessie asked from the back of the motor home, where she was collecting what she would need to take a quick shower before leaving the campground. The campground shower was handy and she wouldn't have to refill the Winnebago's water tank.

"Not much, but I'm working on it. He's going to ride with me today."

Jessie frowned at the idea. "You sure you want to do that? Don't forget he stole my lunch, and I don't think he's got much money. There was something he wouldn't talk about." It worried her that Maxie by herself might make a good mark for a quick grab and run if he was so inclined. She remembered the dark hint of something unidentifiable on his face.

"I think he's okay, actually," Maxie said. "A pretty good kid from all I can tell. But there's something bothering him, for sure, and I'd like to know what it is."

"You think he's a runaway?" Jessie came forward and sat down on the other side of the table, a towel and shower bag on her lap.

"If he is, he's old enough on paper to make his own decisions, but I think there's more to it than that. He had some kind of nightmare last night that was pretty unpleasant. I didn't get much of it—a frightened-sounding 'No, don't,' and some groaning. Maybe I can get him to talk if I go at it sideways."

They looked at each other in silence for a minute, Jessie frowning, Maxie with raised eyebrows, questioning.

It crossed Jessie's mind that people often wound up in Alaska because they were running. Either they were running *to* something—a vacation, a job, a relationship—or *away* from something—unemployment, a bad or failed relationship, a crime, or any of a hundred things people try to leave behind them in starting over somewhere else. A few, like the spouses who were dragged along when the military transferred their mates to bases in Fairbanks or Anchorage, hated the lifestyle or the winters and spent the indentured years longing to go south. A few left on their own. But many who came north were running, for one reason or another. What was Pat's reason, she wondered? Maybe it was just the adventure that was so attractive to the young—and considering Maxie and many like her, perhaps the young at heart as well.

She was not completely comfortable with Maxie driving alone with Patrick. They didn't really know him—not much more than his name, where he came from, where he said he was going, and that he was touchy about either his finances—or lack of them—or his privacy. She said as much to Maxie.

"Oh, I'll be fine," the older woman assured her. "Even in May, before the tourists fill the roads, there'll be lots of people between here and Jasper, where I'm going to stop tonight. When I pull over today, I'll make sure there's somebody around. We'll be going through national parks. I'm pretty cautious, Jessie—have to be when you travel as much as I do. I'm also a decent judge of people."

Acknowledging that Patrick seemed a nice enough young man—even if he did snatch lunches—Jessie knew it wasn't up to her and swallowed further protest. They had just agreed to look for each other on the road and to meet that night at Whistler's Campground in Jasper National Park, when Patrick came knocking, with Stretch on his leash for company. Tank went to the door to greet his small new friend.

"Hi," Pat said, peering through the screen. "Dishes done, Maxie. You want me to unhook the water and electric?"

"You can help. I'm coming in just a minute."

"Come on in," Jessie told him, taking a sip of the rapidly cooling coffee to validate Maxie's excuse for her visit. "Sleep okay?"

From the grin he presented as he shut the screen from inside and turned to face her, she would never have guessed he had anything to hide that could frighten him into nightmares.

"Better than under this place. Especially with you threatening to pepper-spray me out of there," he teased. "Maxie tell you she's offered me a ride? I really appreciate it, Maxie."

"Yes, she did." Jessie gave him a very straight and level look. "You'll behave yourself—right?"

"Sure," he agreed easily.

Sure seemed to be a word he used a lot—along with that cherubic smile, she thought. She wondered if there wasn't a certain amount of calculated charm mixed with his appealing red hair and boyishly freckled face.

She wasn't sure—not sure at all—and couldn't help speculating.

* * *

Shower taken and checklist of things to do before moving the motor home completed, she left Dutch Creek half an hour behind Maxie and was soon cruising the highway between the retirement communities and tourist attractions that continued for twenty miles to the popular town of Radium Hot Springs. There she stopped long enough to fill the gas tank, but didn't see the Jayco motor home and went on up the road to Golden.

Tank was once again snoozing comfortably in the passenger seat when she turned east on the cutoff to the Trans-Canada Highway and was almost immediately following the folds of the mountainside as the road snaked upward, high above a river full of whitewater rapids in a gorge far below. There was a fair amount of traffic, and except for pulling over once to take a picture, she paid more attention to her driving than to the scenery through this area. Soon they were once again headed downhill into a valley defined by sharp peaks that could only have been carved by the slow frozen passage of ice-age glaciers, toward the entrance to Yoho, the first of the Canadian Rocky Mountain national parks.

A few miles past it, beside a wider and more peaceful river, she came to the town of Field. Pulling into the parking lot for a visitors' center that was situated between the highway and river, Jessie almost laughed with pleasure at the sight that confronted her. A low flat bridge spanned the stream, and the small village that rose from the opposite bank, set against towering peaks that made it appear very small, had a distinct air of fantasy about it. A handful of streets climbed the first low hill, one above the other like steps parallel to the river. A cottage with mullioned windows and an extremely steep roof that framed its front door stood at the top of one cross street, adding to the European flavor. A square stone building that had once been a railroad station stared stolidly across the remaining tracks through windows so symmetrically placed that they formed a face, with a stone stoop for a smile below the nose of a door. It tickled Jessie's sense of humor. It was like Brigadoon, she thought, entranced by the idea. It almost seemed reasonable that if she were to return the following day the village would have disappeared for a hundred years. Impulsively she decided not to drive across the bridge; her impression of Field was too engaging to spoil by seeing the town up close.

She walked Tank, gave him water, and made a quick visit to the visitors' center to buy a large-scale map of Jasper National Park, which she would reach that afternoon. Making herself another ham and cheese sandwich reminded her of the one that had gone missing the day before, and she wondered where Maxie and Patrick were as she ate it. She placed the second half of a can of tomato juice in a cup holder next to the driver's seat, along with one of her favorite Snickers bars, and, with one last delighted glance at Field, moved the Winnebago out of the parking lot.

She waited for a truck and three cars to pass before swinging back onto the roadway, headed northeast.

*　　*　　*

During the afternoon, Jessie thought several times of Maxie and wondered how things were going in her attempt to break Patrick's reserve. But this route was all new to her, and the scenery as she left British Columbia for Alberta was soon so overwhelming that she all but forgot to be concerned for her new friend's welfare in her own attempt to absorb all she was seeing.

The Icefields Parkway, which runs 143 miles north through the Rocky Mountains, connecting Banff and Jasper National Parks, is one of the most scenic highways in the world. The earth's continents are huge rock plates that float on the semi-molten core of the world and are therefore in motion like rafts on a pond. Some, like the Pacific plate, lie under oceans, but they still move. Millions of years before Jessie began her drive along the parkway, the Pacific and North American plates collided, and the thicker, heavier North American plate forced the lighter, thinner Pacific plate to slide under it, as it continues to do. This, of course, happens so slowly it can be difficult to measure, but enormous pressures resulted from the collision, causing parts of the North American plate to buckle and rise in folds and crests until they finally became the magnificent Rocky Mountains, backbone of North America—the Continental Divide.

These mountains were at first much broader and higher, but the ice ages that followed created glaciers thousands of feet deep, which ground over and through them, carving off gigantic swaths of rock before they retreated to reveal sharp peaks and wide, sweeping valleys.

Nowhere along their length do the Rockies present themselves more majestically than on the Icefields Parkway, and Jessie was soon enthralled with the incredible views. Everywhere she looked there were mountains that seemed to hold up the sky, walls and cascades of stupendous peaks that parted to reveal even more in the distance. Large glaciers still flowed between some of them, and many smaller ones hung high among the ridges, their ice compressed to pale blue colors that glowed like jewels in the sunlight. She was soon wearing her camera around her neck to have it handy when she pulled off the road, stopping at two or three of the dozens of viewpoints.

Before she knew it she had traveled almost half the parkway and arrived at Bow Summit, 6,785 feet above sea level, the highest point on this section of the road. The parking area faced south and was crowded with people milling about—some absorbed in spotting the bighorn sheep that were taking a midday lie-down among the rocks high above the road, too far away for pictures, others gazing down at the road that drew a narrow line from one end to the other of the glacial bowl of an impossibly wide and graceful valley.

From this vantage point high on a mountain, Jessie watched an eagle circling in the air below, riding the thermals to stay aloft without flapping its wings. It seemed odd to look down to watch him soar. At this height the air was cool and brought the pleasant scent of evergreens and new spring grasses warmed by the sun. Fluffy white clouds moved slowly above a few of the peaks, but most of the sky was a remarkable clear blue.

She wished there was less traffic so she could listen as well as look for birds, but vehicles passed regularly on the parkway and many of them pulled in to take advantage of the views, so there was always the sound of some car, truck, or RV in motion nearby. Though most of the hundreds of people who drove the Icefields

Parkway each year went no farther than British Columbia, a significant number, lured by the mystique of the far north, used the
parkway as a route to Dawson Creek, where the Alaska Highway
officially started. From past trips Jessie knew she would
undoubtedly see some of them more than once as she traveled
the long road home, becoming familiar with the sight of them on
the road and in campgrounds. It was a friendly kind of thing that
she enjoyed about the trip, but at the moment she wished she had
less company in this particular spot.

As Jessie was aiming her wide-angle lens toward the valley, a
group of four people in their twenties, two couples, walked up to
a car parked just behind where she was standing at the guardrail.
She couldn't help overhearing their conversation as they paused
and opened the trunk to get soft drinks from a cooler, though
after a quick glance she pretended to ignore them and just listened.

"But what'd he want?" one of the women asked.

"Some kid they were looking for."

"It's pretty easy to see who's stopped here, isn't it?"

"Not just here—somewhere along the parkway."

"Hm-m. Little kid? Lost?"

"Naw—a teenager. Hitching, or hiking. I told him we hadn't
seen him."

"How'd you know that? What's he supposed to look like?"

"Seventeen or eighteen years old," he said. "About five-
eleven, red hair."

Jessie's attention was instantly caught by this description of
Patrick Cutler. Could it be anyone else?

She listened more closely as the woman's voice rose to
declare, "But I *did* see a kid like that."

"Where?"

"At that place we stopped for gas—you know, the one where

we got the postcards? He was getting into a motor home with an old lady."

"Yeah?"

"Yeah. I noticed because she had a cute little wiener dog on a leash."

Sure that Maxie would not have been overjoyed at the designation of *old* and the offhanded dismissal in the young woman's voice, Jessie had to grin, remembering that everyone over thirty seemed old to someone that young. But this expanded account told her it had to be Patrick.

Interested now, the second young man joined the conversation. "Who was looking for this kid—and why?"

"Those two guys I was talking to—the ones in the cowboy getup. They said he was hiking and they were supposed to pick him up along the parkway."

"Pretty casual way to arrange it. There's a hundred and fifty miles of this road."

"Yeah, well—they're gone, and it sounds like he got a ride anyway. Let's go back to Banff—I'm hungry and it'll be time for dinner when we get there."

As he closed the trunk and went to unlock the car, Jessie turned to watch them leave. She caught the eye of the young woman who had seen Patrick with Maxie, who smiled thinly and shrugged. "Whatever," she said, and climbed into the car with her friends.

They backed out and turned south on the parkway, leaving Jessie to stare after them, frowning.

The incident confused and concerned her as she returned to the motor home and prepared to leave the viewpoint. How many red-haired young men of eighteen could there be on one 150-mile stretch of parkway? Especially young men who were riding with an *old* lady in a motor home with a dachshund? But why would two men be looking for him seriously enough to ask strangers if they had seen him? Too late, she wished she had asked what these two men looked like—perhaps Patrick would have known who they were. She'd like to have been able to describe them and see what he had to say.

She pulled away from Bow Summit still pondering what she had heard, seen, and felt. Even the sight of the huge Athabasca glacier below Mount Columbia, the highest point in Alberta at 12,294 feet, did not distract her for long, perhaps because she was used to seeing glaciers in Alaska, though they were not often so close to a well-traveled highway. So, anxious to reach Jasper for several reasons and with questions that needed answers, she bypassed the Columbia Icefield Centre's busy parking lot and tourist facilities overlooking a remnant of the great sheet of ice that had once spread across most of Canada, and drove steadily north to meet Maxie.

CHAPTER 9

Whistler's Campground in Jasper National Park was enormous, with hundreds of spaces for motor homes, campers, and tents arranged in loops within a road that circled the perimeter. Pulling up to the kiosk at the entrance at almost four o'clock, Jessie wondered how she would ever find Maxie, but soon learned that her new friend had booked adjoining spaces, with one in Jessie's name, and had left her a map with clear directions.

Driving slowly around the outer road, she was pleased to see that it was more like a park than a campground and was surprised to see an elk placidly grazing close to the road near two campers. The velvety brown female didn't seem to notice or care that two people with cameras stood only a few yards off, clicking away—didn't even raise her head as Jessie passed in the motor home, tires loudly crunching gravel. In half an hour, with a quick stop at a sani-station to fill her water tank and empty the wastewater holding tanks, she had found loop 64 and the spaces Maxie had reserved.

As she stopped and for the first time prepared to back the Winnebago into its space, the older woman stepped out of the Jayco and came to help direct the maneuver. Standing behind and to one side, she semaphored directions until Jessie had successfully parked and made sure the rig was as level as possible.

"Good job," she commented with an approving nod as Jessie climbed down from behind the wheel.

"Used to drive a school bus."

"No wonder you do well."

Few national parks have hookups for RVs, and Whistler's was no exception. The stove, refrigerator, and furnace ran on liquid propane gas and the lights on battery power, but to run any appliances that used AC power required a generator.

Jessie remembered this when she heard one running noisily nearby. Maxie noticed her attention.

"I thought about starting mine to make coffee but decided I'd rather put my feet up and make sure that Jameson's isn't going bad in the bottle. You okay with that?"

"Absolutely. But I have gin and tonic and some brandy," Jessie offered. "We drank yours last night."

"Honestly, I'd rather have Irish, if you don't mind. You have any cheese and crackers?" She grinned. "Patrick had mine for an afternoon snack."

She didn't mind at all, and they were soon seated in Maxie's chairs, sipping contentedly between bites of Jessie's favorite Double Gloucester on saltines, while Tank and Stretch rolled in the grass at the lengths of their tethers.

"Where *is* Patrick?" Jessie asked, for she had expected the young man to step out of the motor home to greet her.

"Hiked off somewhere to take a shower. He'll be back pretty soon."

* * *

Late afternoon shadows from tall trees flickered between bright bands of sunshine on the windshield of a brown-and-cream-colored pickup driving slowly around each of the loops that connected to the outer road of Whistler's Campground. Inside, two young men, one blond, one dark, carefully scrutinized everyone they passed.

"We're never gonna find him in all these people, Lew. There're hundreds of campsites."

"If he's here, we'll find him. If he's not, we'll try the other campgrounds and all the Jasper RV parks—like I said. He's gotta be around somewhere." The dark-haired boy's exasperation was evident in his tone and the impatient look he directed at his travel companion.

"But that old lady may not have stopped here at all."

"Look, Kim, she's not gonna drive a motor home all night, is she? She'll stop and go on in the morning. Old people don't like to drive at night."

"Why not?"

"Because their eyesight isn't good anymore, stupid," Lew snapped. "Now shut up and keep looking."

Both boys were tired and discouraged after a long day of searching for Patrick Cutler and too much of each other's company. Kim had once again begun to exhibit uneasiness with the whole idea of trying to find their friend, and Lewis, tired of Kim's complaints and apprehension, was growing more stubbornly determined with every pessimistic whine and beginning to wish he'd come alone.

He sped up slightly as he steered the pickup around a curve of the outer road and turned into one of the last campsite loops. As they passed a restroom and shower building, Kim suddenly sat up and pointed out his open window in excitement.

"*Stop.* There he is—right there."

The brake Lew abruptly applied jerked both boys forward and halted the vehicle in the middle of the road.

"Where?"

But Kim had already opened the door and leaped out. "Pat. Hey, Patrick!"

*   *   *

Much part of the campground lay in the shadow of a tall mountain that rose immediately to the west, blocking the late afternoon sun, but the air was still comfortably warm. Voices could be heard among the tall birch and cottonwood trees, and here and there flames flickered in metal fire pits and barbecue grills. Someone was cooking steak, and the tantalizing smell that wafted through the air reminded Jessie that she had taken some chicken from the small freezer and put it in the sink to thaw as she drove. Maxie agreed to sharing dinner and volunteered to make a salad.

Hoping to finish before Patrick returned from his shower, Jessie quickly related the conversation she had overheard at Bow Summit concerning the two men who were looking for a red-haired boy. When she finished, Maxie frowned and remained thoughtfully silent for a moment or two before asking, "You didn't find out what they looked like?"

"No, I didn't think about it until the woman had already gone."

Maxie stood up and walked across to untangle Stretch's tether from Tank's.

"Well, I agree that it could hardly be anyone else, though

odder things have happened. There could be another redhead." She came back and sat down to sip her drink.

"Did he say anything today that would give you a clue about who those two might be?"

"Not a word, and not a sign that he's aware anyone's looking for him. I wonder if he knows they are. I did get a little more from him about his friend in Fairbanks. They went to high school together and were evidently pretty good mates until this Dave moved to Alaska two years ago."

"Anything at all about his family?"

"He wouldn't say, except that his father died when he was nine years old. There was something about a stepfather that he doesn't like, so his mother must have remarried. But I got a feeling that she's gone as well—and recently, I think—because he seemed upset and changed the subject rather too quickly. He talked a fair amount about computers and the internet—sounds like he's pretty good with them."

"Dammit, I don't like this at all. What *can* that kid be up to that he's not telling?" Jessie sat up and glared in irritation.

Surprised at the outburst, Maxie gave her a searching look. "Jessie?" she asked mildly. "Why are you so suspicious and angry at Patrick?"

"I'm not."

"Yes you *are*," she said gently. "And you have been, right from when he crawled out from under your rig. Think about it."

"I'm . . . It's not . . . It's the situation that . . ." Jessie stammered, taken aback at the idea. She stared in confusion at Maxie, who waited calmly for her response.

Turning her attention inward, she examined her own feelings and detected the knot in her stomach, the tension of her body, and the frustration that wrinkled her forehead.

"I *am* angry," she said, eyes wide in self-discovery. She

flopped dispiritedly back into her chair, and some of the ice water she was holding splashed over the edge of the glass.

"Yes," Maxie nodded. "I think you're partly angry at the things we don't understand that he won't talk about. But another part of it may be some unresolved issues of your own. Is that possible?"

It certainly was, Jessie realized. So busy she had been almost overwhelmed with all that had happened in the last few months, she had neglected to notice that there was a lot of anger floating around undetected, along with everything else.

She was still intensely angry at the loss of her cabin—the arson that had destroyed almost everything she owned and held dear. Each time she remembered something else that had been consumed in the blaze, her anger had grown till there was now an inner conflagration of unexpressed exasperation and rage. And there was anger and indignation at the friend who had betrayed her.

Then there was the loss of her relationship with Alex Jensen, almost three months before. More sad than mad, she recognized that there was still a spark of passionate anger in that disappointment, too—anger that he had thought she might give up the sled dog racing she loved, anger that he had actually left when she refused. And she was angry with herself for letting it upset her.

Both these angers were mixed with this current animosity. But why should she be so angry with Patrick? Not a stolen lunch, for God's sake—not his crawling under her motor home to get out of the rain. Was she jealous that he was riding with Maxie, not with her? No, she was relieved. There! That was close. She turned the idea over in her mind and realized that to feel that kind of relief she had to resent the very fact of his being there. He was a disruption, the puzzle of his presence an unwelcome distraction from her pleasant anticipation of this trip, her enjoyment of driving cheerfully alone up the long road north. She wished he, and whoever was looking for him—if they were—would just go away and leave her out of their problems.

As quickly as these realizations came, most of the anger faded. In a way, she still wished she had never heard of Patrick Cutler and been able to head north in the cheerful mood in which she had started. But knowing that he wasn't the ultimate and only cause of her frustrations made her more tolerant. He really wasn't a bad kid, she supposed—though she still wondered what was going on with him and if he were really being followed. But she would leave that alone and enjoy his company for the time being. Most likely he wouldn't be around long anyway. If she knew anything about young men his age, it was that they liked company their own age, and he would probably want to take off on his own soon.

She turned to Maxie, ready to share her thoughts, and found her smiling.

"You're a big girl. I thought you'd figure it out."

Jessie decided to let that go as well and was glad she had when she looked up to see Patrick coming around a corner of the Jayco, hair still damp from his shower, wearing clean clothes.

"Hey, Jessie," he grinned. "You made it."

She wondered just how much of the conversation he had overheard.

For the rest of the evening Jessie relaxed and asked no leading questions, and Patrick said nothing to indicate that he had been eavesdropping. The three ate dinner together and talked about their separate trips along the Icefields Parkway. Patrick showed off some postcards he had "picked up" at the gift shop in the Columbia Icefield Centre, and though shoplifting flitted through her mind, Jessie dismissed the idea and told him they were good choices.

Maxie had been impressed by the white mountain goats they had seen licking minerals along the side of the road at one viewpoint. "I've been through here twice and never seen any before. There they were—a herd of—how many, Patrick?"

"Six—three little ones, two ewes, and that one huge male. They were a lot bigger than I thought they were from pictures. I'd like to have one of their skins with all that white wool."

"I doubt they'd stand still for skinning," Maxie commented dryly.

By ten o'clock they were all ready for a rest, tired by a day of sightseeing. Patrick seemed especially tired. Yawning, eyes drooping sleepily, he once again agreed to stay with Maxie in the Jayco.

Jessie locked the doors to the Winnebago's cab and coach and closed the curtains and blinds so that she could pad around inside wearing only the oversized T-shirt in which she slept and a pair of socks. With a cup of tea and an apple, she settled against a pile of pillows on her bed to read for a while, with Tank snoozing contentedly in what was becoming his customary spot, the floor beside her. Through the ceiling vents and half-open window next to the bed, she could still hear soft voices in the distance—some harmonious group singing around a fire pit—and a person or two passed on their way to the restrooms not far away.

In half an hour she had found mountain goats in the *Rocky Mountain Nature Guide,* learned more than she wanted to know about the predaceous diving beetle, and was reading that the diverse-leaved cinquefoil stops "bleeding and dysentery in both man and beast," when she fell asleep with the book spread open where it had come to rest, under her chin. Roused quite some time later by the sound of vehicle tires passing slowly over gravel, she laid the book aside, turned off the light, and slid quickly back into dreams.

When a voice at the window spoke almost in her ear and startled her awake, it was still dark.

"Jessie? It's Maxie. Will you let me in?"

"Yes, of course. What's wrong?" But the older woman had already gone to wait for the door to open.

Throwing back the covers, Jessie pulled on the jeans she had worn the day before and turned on the galley light as she went past the switch.

Maxie's face wore a frown as she stepped in and sank to a seat at the table. "Patrick's gone."

"Gone where?"

"Just gone. I woke when I heard the door open, and he went out without turning on a light. I didn't get up—thought he probably didn't want to wake me by using the toilet in the rig and was going to the restroom. I must have gone back to sleep, thinking I'd hear him come back, but he *didn't*. A little later I got up and turned on the light. This note was on the stove." She handed over a lined rectangular piece of paper that had obviously been torn from a small notebook.

"Thanks for everything, Patrick" was all it said, in slightly uneven, youthful handwriting.

"He's gone," she repeated. "With all he owned—his pack, jacket, hunting knife—everything."

They stared blankly at each other across the table.

"Sorry, Maxie, but I've gotta say it," Jessie said, shaking her head and running the fingers of both hands through her sleep-tousled hair. "*Like a thief in the night!* I know it's just unfounded suspicion on my part, but did anything of yours go with him?"

Maxie looked down at the table with an oddly embarrassed expression. "Nothing as far as I can tell, except—a package of cookies, two bananas, half a loaf of bread, a jar of sweet relish, and a can of tuna."

The giggle started out as a single almost silent chuckle, but tears of mirth were soon running down Jessie's face.

"He stole—*your* lunch," she managed to get out between whoops of glee.

C H A P T E R

For the next two days of the journey Jessie's wish for solitary travel was granted. She drove, explored, and stopped for the night with only Tank for company.

Leaving Whistler's Campground early, they said good-bye to Maxie and Stretch, who were headed straight for Prince George, 234 miles west, where they planned to stop overnight to visit a friend. Jessie, on the other hand, drove into Jasper to fill the Winnebago's gas tank and couldn't resist investigating some of its appealing attractions.

The north side of the single long street was lined with small shops and restaurants, while the railroad station dominated the side to the south. Reminiscent of a Swiss village, many of the commercial buildings were decorated with balconies and gingerbread trim below steep roofs. With views of the towering Rockies to the southwest and plenty of room to park along the street, it was a pleasant place to wander along window-shopping with a trickle of tourists that by June would increase to a flood. Bypassing the gift shops full of T-shirts and postcards in favor of the Jasper Rock & Jade shop, she browsed through cases and bins of stones and minerals, bought a honey-colored quartz crystal with gold threads running through it, a moss agate that supposedly inspired peace of mind, a small bluish sphere of ocean-picture agate that looked like a globe in miniature, and a piece of green jasper, simply to remember the town.

As she left the shop, treasures in hand, calling a final thank-you over her shoulder to the shop owner, she almost collided with a man at the door who had apparently been on the point of entering when he changed his mind and turned abruptly across her path.

"Sorry," he mumbled as they bumped shoulders, and without looking back he walked hastily away to disappear around the corner.

Restoring her balance with a hand to the wall, Jessie continued down the street and soon discovered a small bookstore, where she was delighted to find a short biography of Edith Cavell, a British nurse who smuggled Allied soldiers out of Belgium to Holland during World War I, was captured and executed by the Germans, and for whom one of the highest of the beautiful local peaks was named.

A glance at her watch told her she shouldn't take much more time if she was to reach the campground she wanted that night, so she headed for the tourist information center that sat in the center of the town's grassy park for a quick look at their offerings. Armed with a handful of pamphlets and maps, she couldn't resist buying a small square bell for Tank's collar that made her smile because it was humorously intended to discourage bears with its tiny tinkling. For any of the grizzlies she had ever seen, a cowbell would have been a better choice.

Now seriously in a hurry, she was moving toward the door when a half-familiar figure suddenly turning away caught her attention. At first she thought it was Patrick Cutler because of the hooded black windbreaker jacket, sunglasses, and blue hat he was wearing, but it was a baseball cap with no floppy brim, and his profile showed a ragged fringe of mustache below a slightly hooked nose. She realized he was familiar only because, turning away in a similar fashion, he had almost knocked her down at the rock shop. Embarrassed, she guessed, or just rude. Well, it was a small town and she'd seen other people more than once on the street. Dismissing both incidents, she returned to the motor home, where Tank was patiently waiting.

Before leaving Jasper she made a quick stop at a liquor store for her own bottle of Jameson's and another at a grocery for supplies to fill her depleted larder. There she found the produce section filled with fresh spring vegetables. Many of these went immediately into her shopping cart—tomatoes, carrots, broccoli, mushrooms, onions, cucumbers, and more—with plans for the salads for which she was winter-starved. As she picked out huge purple grapes and several apples, she thought again of Patrick and wondered where he was and, thinking of Maxie, tossed in two cans of tuna. Several things she'd never seen in Alaska also joined her collection—brambleberry jelly and canned raspberry juice, an unfamiliar kind of sausage, Scottish breakfast tea, and a very British-looking pastry or two. It was fun to pick out food for no one but herself, but she added a bone for Tank, a gift from the friendly butcher.

At ten o'clock, when she had packed everything away and was driving back through town, she saw the ill-mannered man once more, standing on the street watching her motor home pass with the rest of the traffic. Things certainly come in threes, she told herself and forgot about him as she headed west toward Prince George.

She was listening to an upbeat CD of tunes from the Broadway Show *Fosse* when she reached the Yellowhead Pass fifteen miles out of Jasper and crossed from Alberta back into British Columbia. A little "Steam Heat" might be welcome soon, she thought, for the day was less sunny and bright than the one before. A dark bank of clouds rolling in from the west had already covered half the sky. The top of Mount Robson, at 12,972 feet the highest peak in the Canadian Rockies, was too obscured in the mist for pictures when she turned off for a look. In a few minutes she had seen what was visible, taken Tank for a short walk, and was back on the road.

Tête Jaune ("yellow head") was the name given by French voyageurs to an Iroquois trapper and guide who worked for the Hudson's Bay Company in the early 1800s. Thus did the Yellowhead Highway receive its name, as did Yellowhead Lake and the town of Tete Jaune Cache farther west, which Jessie cruised past on the long, gently curving road. It was pleasant driving, much of it through forest that had been logged and replanted and valleys that eventually spread out into ranching country. At one point she pulled over to watch a herd of bison grazing next to the highway—a surprise she hadn't anticipated. Bridges with glimpses of rivers and lakes flashed past, and though the sun disappeared behind the clouds that soon filled the sky, only a few sprinkles of rain fell before she arrived in Prince George, population 76,500.

It was the first sizable city she had seen since leaving Coeur d'Alene, and it seemed awkward and confining to have to follow a map through streets crowded with traffic and look for signs to guide her to the junction with Highway 97, which came through Prince George from the west coast on its way north. Satisfied with the grocery purchases she had made in Jasper, she hesitated at a shopping center only long enough to fill the gas tank and grab a hamburger and a chocolate shake from a Burger King. Then, as traffic finally thinned at the outskirts of town, she was on her way toward the real start of the Alaska Highway, Dawson Creek. With 250 miles to go until she reached it, the afternoon would be long, but she had no desire to linger in the midst of such blatant civilization. Burger King indeed!

From Prince George, the landscape flattened into farming country without the attraction of mountain scenery or even much in the way of rivers. It rolled gently away into fields divided by fences or thin lines of brush and trees, with little to break the sameness.

It started to rain—first a few drops hitting the windshield, then a steady drizzle. Jessie, already driving with her lights on, hunted out the wiper switch and turned it on. The rhythm of the blades sweeping across the window in front of her was slightly hypnotic, and she began to sing in time to the beat—a series of old camp songs from her girlhood, each one reminding her of another. By the time she had shouted, "John Jacob Jingleheimer Schmitt," for the third time, Tank had gone to sleep in spite of the noise and her voice was growing hoarse, so she drifted into silence and thought about Maxie instead, whom she planned to meet farther up the road.

Her new friend reminded her a little of Dallas Blake, originally from Texas, whom she had met on a trip from Skagway to Seattle a year or two before. Though Maxie was more than ten years younger than Dallas, they had a similar confidence and adventurous spirit.

As soon as the new cabin is finished, I should invite Dallas to come up for a visit, Jessie thought. And that reminded her that she must tell Vic Prentice that she wanted a ramp built from the yard to the front porch so that Dallas, crippled with arthritis, could move easily in and out in her wheelchair.

Maybe Maxie would like to come sometime too and park her Jayco next to the dog yard. Jessie had to smile when she thought of short-legged Stretch in the company of her kennel full of Alaskan huskies. What a contrast.

There was something about Maxie besides her independence that Jessie liked and hadn't quite been able to identify. It had to do with the live-and-let-live way she accepted her surroundings and most of the people in them. Dignity? Tolerance? She seemed to watch everything, then acknowledge or ignore, accept or reject, without relinquishing her own solid sense of self or wasting unnecessary time and energy. She let people answer their own questions and gave little advice, even when asked. Wisdom was a good word, but Jessie thought it would make Maxie laugh. She loved Maxie's laugh. It was as throaty as her voice, and when something amused her she held back nothing, threw back her head and let it go—a laugh that turned heads, intoxicating and delightful. That wonderful sense of humor was part of what appealed to Jessie. Whatever it was about Maxie, she liked it, and maybe she could figure it out when they had spent more time together. Tonight she would spend pleasantly alone, but tomorrow evening she hoped to park her Winnebago next to the Jayco again, in an RV park in Fort Nelson.

Thinking of all the places Maxie had traveled and planned to visit in the future, Jessie found herself a little envious. Most of her life had been spent growing up in Minnesota and later in Alaska. All her time at the kennel was pretty much focused on raising and training sled dogs for the races she entered. It would be fun to see new places, meet people who weren't mushers for a change. It was something to think about.

Where would she like to go, if she could go? Pictures of the desert country of the southwestern United States had always appealed to her, seeming very similar with its spare lines and vast distances to the west coast of Alaska in winter, Nome for instance. Both whispered in her mind of purple sunset shadows and treeless landscape. The extreme difference in temperatures might be part of the attraction. It was interesting that icy beaches on the edge of the Bering Sea could look so much like immense, barren reaches of desert—one locked in ice, one seared by the sun. For a few minutes she longed to spend time in Arizona or New Mexico. Was she limiting her life too much? Was her focus too narrow? There was a whole world out there that she had never experienced—tempting.

At almost six o'clock Jessie reached Dawson Creek. She had seen the marker that designated Mile 0 of the Alaska Highway on earlier trips, and rather than drive to see it again, especially in the rain, she turned toward the campground she had chosen for the night, another seventeen miles up the road. She had pictures she could look at of the distinctive white 0 marker with flags flying, taken where it stood in the center of town, 1,523 miles from Fairbanks, Alaska, where a similar monument marked the terminus of the highway.

The Alaska Highway had been built in eight months and twelve days, from March 9 to October 25, 1942. When Pearl Harbor was bombed by the Japanese in December 1941, Alaska had been considered at substantial risk for invasion. Forging an agreement between the United States and Canada, President Roosevelt authorized the U.S. Army to begin construction on a highway from Edmonton, Alberta, to Fairbanks, Alaska, along a route determined by the existing airfields of a Northwest Staging Route that was used to ferry war planes from Montana to Alaska, then on to Russia as part of the Russian-American Lend Lease Program. In a massive undertaking of men and machines, working from both ends with several construction camps in between, thousands of military and civilian workers lived in tents and scraped frozen ground at below-zero temperatures, endured the torments of black flies and mosquitoes during the summer months, and felled millions of trees to hack a passable road over the Rockies, across wild rivers, through muskeg and swamp. When the Japanese *did* invade the Aleutians, the project gained urgency. On September 25 the road crews finally met each other at Contact Creek, and it was almost immediately possible to drive from one end of the highway to the other, though the trip remained treacherous and sometimes deadly. It was not for the faint of heart—a difficult passage indeed.

The dangerous reputation of the Alaska Highway had long outlived its actual conditions, for its complete length was now paved, and except for work that was always being done in one place or other to repair, improve, or widen sections, it was a safe and satisfying if lengthy adventure. Passing through some of the world's most awesome scenery and last wilderness, it had been named an International Historical Engineering Landmark. Most of it had been straightened, so it was shorter, which created some discrepancy between actual and historical mile markers, and bridges had been replaced. In fact very little of the original highway existed or could be driven.

Though there were campgrounds in Dawson Creek where she could have stayed, Jessie had no desire for a windy in-town RV park without trees and with other people parked so close she would be able to hear them talking. She also knew that she was heading for one of the places she had put on her wish list for this trip.

The rain had, if not stopped, at least hesitated by the time she reached the turnoff she was looking for, and she was delighted to discover that the access road on which she was soon traveling, mostly gravel but with some pavement left, was part of the original highway. It wound downhill a short distance into a steep gorge, then suddenly she was driving onto the sweeping curve of a bridge eighty-seven feet above the Kiskatinaw River's rocky banks.

She knew from reading that this was the only original timber bridge on the Alaska Highway that was still in use, and that it had been completed in June of 1943. A 531-foot-long structure of creosoted British Columbia fir that had been shipped in from the coast, it curved a full 90 degrees and was superelevated, or banked, with the outside of the curve higher than the inside—distinctive enough to have made the *Guinness Book of Records.*

Turning the Winnebago around on the far side, she stopped and got out to take a look but decided to wait till morning to use her camera, hoping that the overcast would clear and give her better light for pictures. Driving back across the wooden planks of the bridge, she turned down into the Kiskatinaw Provincial Park and found a space among perhaps two dozen in which to park her rig—surrounded by spruce and poplars, with the river only a few steps away. Stepping outside she could hear the soft sounds of running water and birds in the trees—a terrific break from wheels on pavement.

Taking Tank with her on his leash, she hurried to have another look at the bridge from below before it started to rain again. Finding a path from the campground road to the river, she walked along its bank, clambering over rocks, until she stood looking up at the huge wooden structure between her and the sky. In the half-light it seemed higher than it had from above. The dark heavy timbers crisscrossing each other were bolted together at each intersection, forming the triangles that were its secret strength. Curving from one side of the gorge to the other, it loomed overhead in an ominous crescent against the gray clouds still heavy with rain. Jessie hoped again that a clear morning would give her a different impression of this original piece of the highway, for in the gathering darkness it seemed to lean menacingly toward her.

On her way back along the campground road she was surprised to meet the same green Suburban she had seen in the Dutch Creek campground. Once again it was proceeding slowly and she could see that the driver in his western hat was looking carefully at each camping space, including hers. This time he turned his head away from her as he passed, so she didn't get a look at his face, but swinging around to look after the vehicle she saw that it had a Wyoming license plate. Coincidence? Probably. Still, it made her wonder.

By the time the light was completely gone, she had eaten dinner, cleared up the galley, and settled happily at the table with her evening cup of tea and a book about the highway that she had saved for just such an evening. It was raining again, creating a quiet liquid drumming on the roof, though the gorge was a shield against all but a light breeze. She could have been completely alone, for the other campers were all inside their shelters, RVs, or tents, and the only audible evidence of their presence was the infrequent sound of feet passing on trips to the restrooms that lay a few spaces toward the bridge on the loop of campground road.

Tank did not settle so easily but wandered back and forth for a few minutes, sniffing at everything and listening intently to every unfamiliar noise, including the gas-operated furnace, which Jessie had turned on low as the motor home grew chilly. He needs a good run, she thought, but gave him the bone from the morning's grocery store trip instead. Soon the only things to be heard were his teeth crunching his treat, the rain on the roof overhead, and a page turning now and then.

The camping space just across the road had been empty, but Jessie was soon distracted from her reading by the sound of someone walking around there on the gravel, making just enough noise in setting up camp to attract her attention. Curious, she peered out the front window of the Winnebago between the curtains she had drawn for the night but could see no vehicle, just the silhouette of a bicycle with saddlebags. An attached trailer reflected small points of light from the flashlight of its owner as he worked hurriedly to put up a small tent.

What a pain, she thought, to have no real retreat from the rain and have everything you carried damp for days if it continued. Glad to be inside where it was warm and dry, she went back to her book, only to be startled in a few minutes by a knock on the door.

CHAPTER 11

Craig Severson was soaked to the skin, cold, and thoroughly tired of riding in the rain by the time he let his loaded bicycle and trailer coast down the access road from the highway to the Kiskatinaw Provincial Park and found an empty space in which to set up his one-man tent, eat yet another cold sandwich, and crawl into his sleeping bag for the night. Maybe starting off to travel the Alaska Highway this early in the year hadn't been such a good idea after all. If it didn't stop pouring water over him soon, by the time he reached Fort Nelson to meet up with his cycling partner, he would be ready to pack it in and go home to Prince George, preferably not on two wheels.

In three days of peddling he had worked hard for mileage on narrow roads with many hills, crossed the Rockies at Pine Pass on the second day, and camped twice, the last time at East Pine Provincial Park near Chetwynd. But most of the trip had been done in some amount of rain, and even when it wasn't raining it had been so overcast and damp that nothing ever quite dried out. His sleeping bag was only slightly clammy, wrapped carefully in plastic, but he did not relish the idea of getting back into it. Rain—he hated rain. And worst of all, today there had been a head wind that drove it constantly into his face. His back ached and he could feel the tension in his neck, shoulders, and arms from leaning forward, trying to keep from being blinded by the water but forced to raise his head enough to see where he was going.

Waterproof rain gear kept sweat in as effectively as it kept rain out, and clothing worn under it while riding was soon soaked. Instead he wore partially waterproof shells without the slicker and let them get wet. Usually peddling kept him warm enough as long as he kept moving. He kept clean clothes in large plastic bags, zipped tight to keep them dry, but he had now worn everything but a single cotton T-shirt. Should have stopped in Dawson Creek, he thought regretfully, but hadn't wanted to take the time to find a laundromat, then wait for his few clothes to wash and dry. Stripping off his skintight poly-shirt, he hurriedly pulled on the dry T-shirt and a rain slicker over it.

Dragging the tent, wet from last night, from the trailer, he began to work with cold hands to set it up. Everything was heavier when wet and the tent was no different. It stuck together as he opened it and sagged slightly on its supports when he finally had it secured. Into it he tossed a self-inflating air mattress and the sleeping bag. Slightly damp or not, it was all he had and would be warmer than nothing, if not particularly comfortable.

Weighing in one hand the sandwich he had made and put into a plastic bag at noon, a can of vegetable soup in the other, he considered the difficulties of heating soup on his Whisperlight stove in the confines of the tent. He longed for something hot to help warm him up and wished he had heated it and filled his metal thermos at lunchtime. But getting out the stove, putting it together, pumping to pressurize, then lighting it was suddenly more than his tired mind and body would accept.

In the space just across the road from him was a motor home with its coach lights still on. Though the curtains were drawn and the blinds closed, he had seen a woman looking out in his direction a few minutes earlier. Closing the trailer cover and saddlebags, he took the soup and sandwich, reticence overcome by the idea of something hot to eat, and walked quickly across the road to knock on the door before he could change his mind.

Jessie, startled from her reading by the knock, got up to answer it, Tank by her side. Turning on the exterior light and peering out, she saw the cyclist from across the road and opened the door to see what he wanted. He was wearing a yellow slicker and was tall enough so that, though he stood below her on the ground, he didn't have to look up very far to meet her questioning assessment. With his can of soup and sandwich, he reminded her of a small boy with an empty bowl out of some Dickensian orphanage.

"Hi," she said and couldn't help smiling.

He was shivering slightly without the exertion of peddling to keep him warm. "I was just wondering if I could beg the use of your stove long enough to heat this soup and some water to wash in. I know it's an imposition, but—"

He looked harmless enough and clearly in need of warmth of some kind. Jessie made a quick decision and interrupted. "Why not? Come on in." She moved back to give him room to come up the two steps, closing the door behind him.

"Hey, I really appreciate this." He set the can of soup on the table and held out a cold wet hand. "I'm Craig Severson."

Jessie introduced herself and Tank, wiped her damp hand on

her jeans, and picked up the soup. "I'll have this hot in a minute or two."

"I can do it. Just loan me a can opener and a pan."

"Already got it covered. There's hot water, soap, and a towel in the bathroom. Go ahead and wash. You'll feel better—and warmer."

"Thanks," he sighed gratefully, stripped off the rain slicker, and went to do as instructed.

When he returned, combing his wet hair back with his fingers, scrubbed face glowing, Jessie had already poured the steaming vegetable soup into a bowl on the table, set a hot cup of tea next to it, and was in the process of making a toasted cheese sandwich. Some of the grapes from the Jasper market and an apple lay close by in a bowl.

"Help yourself," she told him. "This's almost done."

Carefully laying the dry side of the slicker over the bench cushion, Severson sat down and started hungrily on the soup.

By the time he had finished eating everything but the apple, thanking her more than once, and was working on a second cup of tea, Jessie knew all about his planned trip. But she wasn't surprised when the hot food and the warmth of the motor home began to make him sleepy.

"Sorry," he said after a particularly large yawn. "It's been a long day."

"Come for some hot coffee in the morning," she invited him, as he pulled the slicker back on and stepped out the door.

"Thanks again," he told her. "I won't say no to that, if you're sure you don't mind."

"Not at all."

Back in the tent, Severson shed his clothes, wriggled into the clammy bag with a shiver as its chill came in contact with his skin, and turned off the flashlight. His body heat slowly warmed the bag as he drowsily considered tomorrow's ride, which with a little luck would take him to Wonowon, maybe farther. In three days he would be in Fort Nelson, where he and his friend Leo would reconsider the wisdom of such an early trip to Alaska. Yes, they certainly would.

Rolling onto one side, he rubbed at his aching neck, moved his feet into the warmer corner of the bag, and gradually slid off into sleep.

•   •   •

The rain had all but stopped again when a thunderous pounding on the door of the Winnebago woke Jessie from a dream of desert country. Zipping jeans on under the oversized T-shirt she turned on the galley light and padded barefoot to join an already alert Tank at the door.

"Who is it?" she asked cautiously, considering the pepper spray.

"Severson," his familiar voice called in a decidedly desperate tone. "Do you have a cell phone? There's a guy badly hurt under the bridge."

Flipping on the exterior light, Jessie opened the door to find the cyclist, once again in his yellow slicker, eyes full of anxiety. She motioned him in.

"What's wrong?"

"Somebody fell off the bridge and he's on the rocks down there—hurt real bad. Do you have a cell phone? There's an RCMP detachment in Dawson Creek and they *gotta* get somebody out here."

Astonished and horrified at the thought of anyone taking such a fall, Jessie shook her head. She had considered bringing her cell phone but knew that for most of the wilderness parts of the trip it would be out of range and unusable. Close to any town it was doubtful that she'd need it anyway.

"Even if I had one, it wouldn't work down here in the gorge, would it?" she asked. "The campground people should have a phone—you know, that cabin up nearer the bridge?"

"*Where?* It was dark when I came in." So agitated and upset he could hardly stand still, he started back out the door. "Where is it? *Tell me.*"

"It's easier to show you." Grabbing her raincoat and stuffing her feet into running shoes, Jessie tied them quickly, jumped outside, leaving Tank behind, and headed off at a run, Severson trotting at her side.

"What happened? How could someone fall off in the middle of the night?" she asked him between deep breaths of cool damp air.

"Don't know. Might have been drunk, I guess. But—"

"What was he doing up there?"

"Don't know. I was going to the head when I heard a car on the bridge and then he fell—or jumped. I guess he could have jumped. I didn't see it—just heard . . . Dammit, I heard him hit . . . the rocks. I saw . . ." Severson stammered, shuddering as he remembered.

"You went down to look?"

"Yeah—kept hoping it might be garbage someone had tossed off—but I knew it wasn't. He made a sound on the way down. Garbage doesn't scream. Oh God." Without warning, Severson turned aside, stopped, and bent over to vomit into the brush by the road. "He's dead," he managed to get out between convulsions. "I saw."

•   •   •

He was—very. If he had fallen in the river, shallow but running fairly high from late thaw and rain, he might have had a chance.

But the body lay on the rocky bank under the northern end of the bridge, and there was no doubt at all that he had died instantly, his head horribly crushed, face first, against one of the large rounded boulders that lay half buried in the muddy bank. Jessie's stomach contracted in nausea, but she swallowed hard at the taste of acid in her throat and managed to keep from losing it by walking a few steps away, while she, Severson, and the couple that were caretakers for the campground waited for the authorities to arrive.

What gave her the sick shakes was finding that there was no chance this person had made a suicidal leap or fallen accidentally. His wrists and ankles were tightly bound with duct tape. Someone had intentionally dropped him over the bridge railing, for he could not have climbed it himself.

After cursorily checking the body for any sign of life, the caretakers went back up to the road to await and direct the police, but Jessie and the cyclist stayed near the body in an unspoken agreement that, whoever he was, he shouldn't be left alone, even—perhaps especially—in death. Jessie stayed partly because she didn't want Severson, distressed and shivering, to be alone either.

Neither of them said much as they waited. He didn't seem to want to talk, and the details of what he had heard, then found could wait for the police. Jessie sat near him on a log a dozen feet from the body, backs turned to death, keeping silent company while he nervously, and uncharacteristically for a cyclist, smoked cigarette after cigarette, carefully depositing the scorched filters in his slicker pocket, shivered, and stared out blindly across the dark waters of the river.

The image of what she had seen would not leave her mind. After a while she got up and walked back to shine her flashlight on the still form spread-eagled on the rocks, to make sure of what she thought she had seen and to prove or disprove a horrible suspicion that was slowly growing. In the beam of light she could see that the dead man was wearing jeans, hiking boots, and a black windbreaker jacket. The hood of the jacket had flopped forward over the uncrushed back of the head. Heart pounding, she hunkered down next to the body, cautiously reached, and slowly, holding her breath with anxiety and dread, lifted the edge of the hood just enough to see the color of the hair it covered.

Brown. Oh, thank God, it was brown—not the red she had been terrified she would find. It was *not* Patrick Cutler. A gasp of relief escaped her, and tears flooded her eyes till everything blurred as she released the fabric and stumbled back to her feet.

"What?" Severson asked without turning.

"Nothing." She started to turn and walk back to where he sat, but something new caught her eye.

Separate from all the bright blood that had run down over the wet rock and soaked into the damp sandy ground, on the collar of the black windbreaker was another bit of brilliant red— a tiny maple leaf pin. Hand to her throat as it contracted, she stared at it.

This person wasn't Patrick, was it? But he was not just clad in similar clothes—the jacket on the body *was* Patrick's. The realization was so appalling that she couldn't mentally process it, could do nothing but gape at the pin in confusion and disbelief. When she couldn't look anymore, she sat back down next to Severson and tried her best to think rationally.

It didn't make sense. How could Patrick's windbreaker be on some stranger? And why? He was supposedly traveling alone. Could this be one of the men who had been looking for him? Would they have switched jackets? No, not only jackets—weren't the boots also similar to Patrick's? The combination was too close to be a coincidence, wasn't it? And the pin was the clincher. She could not imagine a circumstance that would explain it, but there were a lot of things she didn't understand and that she was beginning to question.

Had Patrick really been who he said he was? A driver's license could be faked or stolen. What was she going to do with the disjointed pieces of information that were churning out more questions than answers? None of it sounded credible, even to her. How could Patrick Cutler be involved with this death? This *murder*—she made herself call it what it was. Could this cyclist, Craig Severson, who said he had *found* the body, be involved somehow? She didn't think so, but if the dead man had screamed loud enough to be heard on the campground road, why hadn't the caretakers heard it, too? Maybe they been asleep, as she had been. That was possible, of course—especially since their house was higher on the hill and thickly surrounded by trees. Or could they be involved? Suddenly everyone was suspect. It all went round in a confusing mix of thoughts that made her stomach turn over again.

Jessie rested her head in her hands, elbows on her knees, and gave up, trying not to think about any of it but not succeeding. For a long time she and Severson sat, still and silent, until at last she heard the faint wail of a siren and raised her head to listen, thankfully.

It was beginning to grow light in the east, and the hint of dawn was just enough to reflect from the ripples and eddies and make the river visible, when the Royal Canadian Mounted Police arrived with an ambulance close behind. Five men came clambering hurriedly from the dark shadows between the trees of the campground and down to the river's edge, two of them bearing a stretcher and medical cases, which Jessie knew they wouldn't need.

While the two RCMP constables with flashlights examined the body, the area around it, and the top of the bridge for clues, Jessie sat listening to the inspector in charge, one William Webster. A small, clear-eyed, watchful man wearing a dark raincoat, he took Severson through an account of what he had witnessed and made brief jottings in a small notebook that the growing daylight just allowed him to make out.

"You didn't *see* anyone—just heard them?"

Severson nodded numbly. "Right. I was going to the head when I heard the car—"

"How do you know it was a car?"

"Well, an engine then. From where I was hearing it—down on the campground road—it might have been a pickup, but it wasn't a heavy engine. I can tell because I hear a lot of different kinds on the road as they pass me on my bike."

Inspector Webster scribbled in his notebook, then looked up and asked attentively. "Then what happened?"

"I could hear the rumble of the tires on the planks go part of the way across the bridge—then it stopped, but the motor was still running. There was nothing for a minute or two, then I heard . . ." His voice thickened and he sat up straighter as if to brace himself for the rest. "I heard him scream as he fell. It was awful. It startled me so much I stopped walking to listen, and then—then I heard him hit the rocks."

"Did you hear the vehicle leave?"

"Yeah—it went on across the bridge and up the north access road till I couldn't hear it anymore. I went down to the river under the bridge. You know—to see if I could do anything, but . . ." He waved a hand toward the body in mute explanation.

There was a moment of silence while Webster jotted in the notebook.

"You didn't touch or move him?"

"No. It was obvious there wouldn't be—ah—a pulse. His head was all . . . broken. I went back up—for help—to find a phone."

"Did you know this man? Had you ever seen him before?"

"No, I don't think so. You can't . . . really tell, can you?"

"But you didn't recognize anything about him?"

"No."

"How about you, miss? Did you recognize him?" Webster turned to Jessie, who was glad to be honestly able to say no as well. Just answer what he asks you, she told herself, remembering past advice. Don't volunteer. Still, not telling him that she had recognized the coat bothered her. She would have told an Alaska state trooper, but this wasn't a trooper, or Alaska. However close to Alaska, or the Lower Forty-Eight, it was a foreign country, and she didn't know this man—or whether she could trust him.

"Did you hear him fall?"

"No," again. "I was asleep."

She told him about waking up to Severson's frantic pounding on her door, their trip to the caretaker's cabin and from there to the riverbank. Still conflicted, she hesitated about the coat and the pin. Then it seemed too late. She knew she would have trouble trying to explain what she knew and how she knew it—that it would complicate everything and might not help—so she kept her knowledge to herself, wondering if she would regret it.

"Did you two know each other before this?"

They shook their heads, and Severson explained that they were camping in spaces across from each other.

"So neither of you has any idea who this might be?"

They shook their heads.

"Anything else you can tell me?" He gave each of them a level, searching look, one that lingered a second or two on Jessie.

"No? Well then . . ."

The inspector took both their names, checked their identification, and asked detailed questions about where they were going and how long they would be in Canada, before sending them back to the campground. Letting them know that he could locate them by notifying the RCMP on up the highway, he said he would not delay their travel, then asked them both to check with a post in a day or two, in case he needed more information.

But when Jessie glanced back as she left the rocky part of the riverbank and went into the trees, she saw Inspector William Webster still sitting on a rock next to the log, staring after them thoughtfully, with his notebook on his knee.

At the Winnebago she found she had neglected to lock the door, but hadn't the mental energy to be concerned, knowing that Tank would have repelled any intruder with barks and growls. He had never bitten anyone in his life, but no stranger would know that.

At her suggestion Craig Severson followed her inside and sat slumped, staring wordlessly at the table, while she turned on the furnace to warm the place up and quickly made a pot of coffee. Filling two mugs, she sugared them liberally and poured a stiff slug of brandy into each before sitting down across from him.

They drank the first mug in silence. Jessie was beginning to be concerned about him when, accepting a refill, he finally looked up with an inquisitive expression.

"You saw something you recognized down there, didn't you? What?"

"Nothing," Jessie told him. "For a minute I thought it might have been someone I knew—but it wasn't."

"Why did you think it was?"

"Just a mistake in the dark." If she hadn't told the inspector what she knew, she certainly wasn't going to tell anyone else, especially a stranger.

*   *   *

Inspector William Webster remained sitting on the rock by the river for a long time after he sent the two witnesses back to the campground, writing once or twice in his notebook, mentally organizing his impressions of the interviews. Focused on his own deliberations, he scarcely noticed the flashlight beams of his men, on the bridge and around the body below it, as they grew paler and less distinct in the increasing dawn light, though as usual he was aware of everything around him and recorded it for later reference. The watery rush of the river beside him covered any sounds his men made and left him alone with his thoughts.

His efficient second in command eventually came down from the bridge to report scuff marks on the railing that could have come from the boot soles of the victim. Placed as they were, they indicated that a struggle had probably taken place—resistance that could prove he had been alive when he was lifted over and dropped. These marks would have to be retrieved and held as evidence, and Webster assigned him the responsibility.

"Tire marks?"

"Nothing identifiable."

"Anything to identify the vic?"

"Nothing in his pockets. No wallet. Nothing on the body or clothing. The labels might make him American—western shirt—green."

But they both knew that many Canadians crossed the border periodically on shopping trips to the United States, and American-made clothing was also sold in Canadian stores.

"Age?"

"Young—eighteen to twenty. Have to wait for the doc's report."

"Well—keep at it."

"There's an Alaska-bound trucker pulled over to sleep at the south end of the access road. Too far away to have seen or heard anything, but he might have noticed the vehicle coming down."

"Wake him up and check. Get some identification."

The constable left, and Webster went back to his interview analysis. It wasn't totally impossible, but he doubted that the cyclist, Severson, was in any way involved. His shocked state and the fact that he had reported the death and stayed to tell what little he knew made that possibility very slight. Hard to fake that kind of emotional upset.

But the woman, Arnold, held his attention. It was not in what she had told him, for he thought she had told exactly what happened, as she knew it—but something in what she didn't say. Something had moved behind her eyes when he asked her if she recognized the dead man. Perhaps he should have rephrased the question and asked it again. Either she had been holding something back and hadn't been completely comfortable with it, or she was uneasy being caught up in the thing at all—perhaps both. She had not been as disturbed by the situation as Severson, but that in itself meant little. People responded with different intensity to murder, and with different timing. She might be one of those who maintained calm during an event, whose emotional reaction came afterward. But he had a feeling she was simply stronger than Severson when confronted with violent death and wondered what in her background had prepared her.

He briefly considered following her back to her motor home in the campground and pushing a little to see if he could come closer to deciphering her reticence but decided to let it go for the moment, doubting that the result would be different or positive. She had for some reason decided to keep her thoughts to herself. In time she might change her mind. He knew where she was going and could always find her later. Right now he needed to make his own examination of the scene, for his impressions of that were even more important. With more rain on the agenda soon, they would have little time before vital clues could be washed away.

Webster stood up, pocketed the notebook, and stretched his shoulders, which were slightly stiff from his all but motionless stint on the cold rock. As he started back toward the body under the bridge, he felt the first few drops on his face and, glancing toward the river, saw small splashes in the smooth water of an eddy near the shore. Shrugging his collar up around his neck, he trudged on along the rocky bank, pigeonholing his thoughts about Jessie Arnold for later examination, returning his focus to the gruesome reality of the responsibility at hand.

CHAPTER 12

For the first time in a long while Jessie broke a personal rule and invited someone she didn't know well to ride with her. It was 250 miles to Fort Nelson, rain was once again hammering on the roof of the Winnebago, Craig Severson's state of withdrawal was worrisome, and she felt uneasy leaving him alone. What he had heard and seen during the night had evidently hit him hard and he seemed to be still struggling to come to terms with it. Perhaps, she thought, they could both use the company, having shared the rest of the dreadful experience. She still felt a nagging sense of guilt over what she had not shared with the inspector, on which she didn't want to dwell. Conversation would make that easier.

Exhausted and withdrawn, Severson accepted her offer without argument and packed up his gear while she cooked breakfast for them both. The familiar work seemed to return him to a more positive mood. Still, he pushed eggs and sausage around the plate with his fork, not eating much, then seemed to realize what he was doing, rapidly cleaned his plate, and looked up with a twisted half-grin.

"Thanks for this and for dinner last night. You've no idea how much I wanted something hot." He told her about his debate with himself over the can of soup.

"Well, there's plenty of hot water," Jessie told him generously. "Take a shower if you want."

"You really wouldn't mind?"

She wouldn't, so he did, even shaved off three days of stubble, and emerged from the back of the rig wearing his last T-shirt, cleanest cycling pants, and a pair of crew socks she had offered him, seeing that he was about to put on dirty ones. An almost shy, grateful smile had replaced most of the introspective look that still haunted his gray eyes.

"I owe you big time, Jessie Arnold." He hesitated and she watched recognition dawn on his face. "Arnold? Jessie Arnold the Iditarod musher?"

"Guilty," she admitted, and the word jolted her conscience.

"Hey, I bet you know the Streepers from Fort Nelson."

"Sure." Jessie was glad to see some enthusiasm on his face. "Everybody who races dogs knows them."

"My friend Leo is one of their handlers sometimes."

She wasn't surprised to find that they almost had an acquaintance in common. Many racing people traveled from Canada or the Lower Forty-Eight to events in Alaska or the Yukon. Alaskan mushers sometimes drove the other direction to races—the Minnesota Bear Grease, for instance, or the Rocky Mountain Stage Stop—finding the long highway trip less expensive than air freight for their sleds and dog teams. The world of top-level sled dog racing was a fairly small one, and the races and racers were few enough to be known to each other, at least by name and reputation.

Shutting off the propane at the tank and getting the rest of the motor home ready to roll, Jessie put Tank's rug on the floor between the driver's and passenger seats. He would have to forego his view of the landscape for the day, his seat preempted by her human passenger.

Together she and Severson loaded his gear, the bicycle, and the trailer into the coach of the motor home, where it took up most of the available space and stood dripping on a blue plastic tarp he had unfolded and spread on the floor. He wiped it all down with paper towels till most of the rainwater was gone, then hopped out at the garbage bins on their way out of the campground to leave the soaked paper with the rest of Jessie's trash.

Making a right turn at the entrance to the campground, Jessie noted that the police had gone, undoubtedly taking the body of the dead man with them. Driving across the wooden bridge again, she saw Severson glance down into the gorge. She was relieved that because of the railing and the angle it was impossible to see the spot where the man had landed and died. She followed the road up a hill on the other side and was soon stopping the Winnebago at the highway, where a trucker had pulled over and had the back doors open on the trailer behind his Peterbilt tractor to adjust his load. She looked both ways, swung out around him, and headed north toward Fort Nelson.

For almost an hour they rode without talking and enjoyed a collection of Celtic harp music that Jessie had picked out in Coeur d'Alene to replace a favorite that had been destroyed in the fire. The music was soothing and they listened in a companionable silence until it ended and the only rhythm was again that of the windshield wipers.

"I only saw one other dead person before," Severson said after a while. "My grandfather—at his funeral. But that wasn't so . . ." He hesitated, searching for a way to express many feelings at once.

"Shocking—brutal," Jessie supplied. Inadequate, but it might help.

"Yes, and violent and horrifying, among others. Sickening—intolerable—outrageous. There isn't one word, is there?"

"No." She shook her head, remembering a man she had met and liked, who had washed up on an island beach in Kachemak Bay. But that death had been a drowning, clean and lacking the abomination of the purposeful bloody ruin of a human being. She recalled one of her dogs caught in the sharp, tearing teeth of a steel trap and her sense of violation and panic on its behalf and her own. "Not *one* word. Every death needs different ones, I think. But this one just about used all mine up."

"I can't stop thinking how he must have felt as he fell—knowing he was going to die."

"Maybe he didn't know." She tried to hope it was true.

"He knew. He screamed," Severson reminded her. "I keep hearing that sound."

Jessie felt her skin contract in goose bumps and was selfishly glad she didn't have that cry permanently recorded in her brain—that he had heard it, and she hadn't. It reminded her of what she knew about the dead man's clothing, but she didn't want to consider that again at the moment.

"Tell me about distance cycling," she suggested, abruptly trying to change the subject. "People think sled dog racing is a punishing sport, but cycling in this kind of weather? I'll stick to my mutts and sled, thank you."

But Severson wasn't ready to give it up. Once started, he

couldn't seem to stop talking, and all Jessie could do was listen as whatever came into his mind tumbled out in words.

"My cycling buddy in Fort Nelson? Leo—the guy that's going to do the highway with me? His father was RCMP and got shot by some drug pusher in Prince George—while we were still in school. It broke Leo up pretty bad. I can sort of see now why he wouldn't talk about it. I never really thought about how awful it must have been—all that blood and . . . I mean he didn't see that, of course—but somebody did. I couldn't do that paramedic stuff. How the hell do they stand it? You ever see anyone dead before?"

Jessie had, and briefly related who and how. She had also been shot once, and told him about that.

"Good lord! And I'm whining over seeing what happened back there?" He was quiet for a minute or two, then, as requested, started talking about various bicycle trips he had taken in the United States and Canada.

Jessie watched the rain pouring onto the highway and was glad to be driving. Besides being inside, dry and warm, it gave her something to do—and she needed something to do. She listened and asked a few questions to keep him going, but soon Severson's words became a sort of background to her thoughts, and she didn't notice they had stopped until she glanced over and saw that he had fallen asleep, exhausted by the events and upheaval of the night at Kiskatinaw. He had leaned up against the door in an uncomfortable-looking position, but she didn't wake him, deciding that a stiff neck was probably little to pay for a few moments of oblivion.

She drove on through the morning, aware of how both her mood and the weather had changed since the first two days of this trip. Though still enthusiastic about traveling, her delight had been markedly diminished in ways she didn't want to consider. The even, well-paved road and the attention required to drive a big rig were soothing to her nerves, and as mile after mile rolled by with very little to see, she began to feel that she was standing still and everything was moving around her like an old black-and-white film. She relaxed and let it be, and when her thoughts began to slip back to what they had found beneath the bridge at Kiskatinaw, or the puzzle of Patrick, quietly told herself stories, sang songs, or recited humorous poems without waking her passenger.

Tank snoozed between the two seats, rousing periodically but not for long, used to sleeping in his box in the kennel when it rained.

*   *   *

It rained all day—through Fort Saint John and Wonowon (Historical Mile 101), past far-off Pink Mountain (hidden in the mist), down into and up out of the deep canyon that held Sikanni Chief, stopping for gas and lunch at the Buckinghorse River Lodge. The strip of road with its yellow center line that could at times be seen for miles across long rolling rises (more or less following the north-flowing Prophet River) finally led into Fort Nelson, the last of the flatland communities on the highway.

After their lunch stop, Jessie had talked Severson—who kept drifting off to sleep in a combination, she thought, of weariness and denial—into taking a real nap on the bed in the back of the motor home, knowing it was illegal not to be wearing a seat belt but feeling his obvious need for physical and emotional rest was more important than official safety regulations. Tank had immediately reclaimed the passenger seat, though there was not much to see from the window. The cyclist had slept all afternoon, waking when she slowed the Winnebago to accommodate the speed limit on Fort Nelson's long main street. Then he maneuvered past his bicycle and equipment to stand behind the passenger seat and direct her to the house of his friend.

"He's at work, but there's a key. He's not expecting me for another day or two."

"Are you going on up the road?" she asked as she helped him unload his gear in the empty driveway of the cottage in an eastern residential section of Fort Nelson.

"Don't know. Leo's pretty set on this trip. But we'll have to see what the weather report says and think about it."

"Well," she told him thoughtfully, "I think you should if you can. Put last night behind you. Maybe we'll see you somewhere on the road."

"Not at the speed we go. You'll be in Alaska before we make Watson Lake."

He returned her socks and thanked her profusely for the ride. Then, without warning, she found suddenly herself engulfed in such a huge hug that she couldn't decide if he was grateful or clinging.

"You're okay, Jessie Arnold. Stay well—and safe."

Sweet guy, she thought, and was glad that in her confusion she had not let him know she had wondered if he might possibly be involved in the bridge death.

He waved again as she turned the corner and headed for the RV park that she knew was somewhere at the northwest end of town, next door to a museum of some kind. Seeing a service station, she stopped to fill the fuel tank, eliminating the need to do it before leaving the next day. She was tired, ready for dinner and an early bedtime, but also anxious to see if Maxie and Stretch had arrived from Prince George.

•   •   •

They had not. The Westend RV park was less than half full of campers and motor homes when Jessie checked in, and Maxie's Jayco was not among them. The parking spaces were arranged in two concentric wheels with an access road around the perimeter of each. By taking the outer road Jessie was able to pull the Winnebago directly into one of the spaces without having to back up and would be able to pull out into the inner one when she was ready to leave the next day. She chose a space as far as she could get from the traffic of the entrance, though it was also farthest from the laundry and restrooms, and asked to have the empty space on one side of her held for Maxie, hoping she would show up soon.

After hooking up to water and electricity and turning on the propane, she donned her raincoat and took Tank for a quick walk. Towel-drying him so he wouldn't drip water on everything, she locked him in and hurried off to take a quick shower and wash her hair. But the hot water felt so good that she fed the meter extra quarters and spent almost half an hour shampooing and scrubbing away what felt like a week of travel grime which she knew had a lot to do with the psychological foulness of last night's murder and the contamination she was feeling from her involuntary involvement. Glad to be clean and to put on fresh clothes from the skin out, she used her towel to partially dry her hair, brushed it into its usual waves and curls, and trotted back through the rain to her house on wheels.

As she was unlocking the door, tires rattled gravel behind her and she turned to watch Maxie park the Jayco next door. It was so good to see her new friend that she found she was almost in tears and realized that her own shock at the Kiskatinaw incident had gone deeper than she thought, had been diverted in her concern for Severson.

"Come over for a drink," she told Maxie through the open driver's window, before the older woman could even get out. "I have a lot to tell you."

"And I have some interesting things to tell *you*!" Maxie said, with an intent and questioning examination of Jessie's white face. "Let me walk Stretch and I'll be right there."

In less than ten minutes she was climbing into Jessie's Winnebago, wriggling travel companion under one arm. The dachshund, much relieved by his short, rainy walk, greeted Tank with enthusiasm. His mistress sank into a seat at the table, drank off half the shot of Jameson's that Jessie had already poured for her, and smiled wearily at the glass.

"Ah—you fair beauty," she told it with a grateful sigh. "Thanks, Jessie."

Then reaching for a cracker and a slice of the summer sausage Jessie had also put on the table, she asked, "What's wrong? Bad drive in the rain?"

Jessie was reminded of Severson's earlier jumble of thoughts and words as she tried and failed to shape her tale of the last twenty-four hours into some kind of reasonable form. Feelings she was only now beginning to identify kept getting in the way, and she had to go back and fill in details several times in her effort not to leave anything out.

Maxie listened carefully, but a frown had deeply creased her forehead by the time the flow of words slowed. When they stopped, she asked an obvious question.

"Didn't this dead man have a wallet with identification?"

Open-mouthed, Jessie stared across the table at her. It was such a glaring oversight on her part that she couldn't understand why it hadn't occurred to her on the riverbank. Though she wouldn't have searched the body for it, she might have asked Inspector Webster.

"I don't know," she admitted, feeling foolish. "I only checked to see if his hair was red."

Maxie stared out the window for a minute in silence, thinking. Her frown relaxed, but an uncertain and worried expression took its place.

"It might have been helpful to know who he was," she said finally. "Last night, while I was asleep in my friend's house, someone broke into the Jayco. Now these two things may not be connected, but if they are, I think we just might have inadvertently gotten ourselves tangled in something very unpleasant. At the very least it makes me uneasy and glad to be a good way up the road from both places."

Her story of the break-in was quickly told. The driver's door of her motor home had been jimmied sometime during the night and the inside trashed in a thorough search, though nothing seemed to be missing. She had been late leaving Prince George because she had to put her motor home to rights and make a report to the police, who had been less than encouraging about the possibility of finding the criminal.

"They left black fingerprint powder all over the place, but all they found were mine, Patrick's, yours, and a few they couldn't identify that could have been left by friends in New Mexico before I left."

"How'd they know which were mine—and Patrick's?"

"The glasses we used for drinks in Jasper were still in the sink and your prints were on one of them. The one that wasn't mine had to be yours. Patrick's were mixed with Stretch's nose and paw prints on the passenger door." She couldn't suppress a quick smile, remembering that they'd had no trouble telling which were human. "Maybe whoever broke in wore gloves. If so, they'll never make an arrest. I'm just glad nothing was damaged or stolen—but bugger if I know what it was all about. They were looking for something they evidently didn't find. Odd."

There wasn't much more to be said and too many unanswered questions to even begin to understand either incident. Neither woman felt like cooking, and Maxie's rig was not yet hooked up to power and water, so they used it to drive six blocks back into Fort Nelson and had dinner at a hotel near the other end of town. On the way back they made a quick stop for groceries and gasoline for the Jayco.

"Thanks, Maxie," Jessie said when they were back in the RV park and had finished the hooking-up process for the Jayco. Since both were physically tired after a long day of driving in bad weather and mentally tired from their separate traumas, Maxie suggested that they to go to bed and meet for breakfast.

Jessie willingly agreed. "I'm going to sleep like the dead tonight," she said with a sigh and immediately wished she had phrased it any other way.

C H A P T E R

After filling the water tank and emptying the holding tanks in a drizzle of rain, Jessie drove the Winnebago from the Fort Nelson campground and made a left turn onto the highway, with Maxie right behind her. In less than a mile she was flagged down by an RCMP constable in a broad-brimmed rain hat and slicker, who was stopping northbound traffic on the edge of town. For the minute or two that she waited while he talked to the driver of another car, her heart was in her throat. But the trouble she was soon apprised of was of a completely different nature than what she feared.

"Sorry, ma'am," the constable said, coming up to her open window. "There's a mud slide about ninety miles up the road that's completely blocked the highway. No one's getting through from either direction, so you might want to stay in town for now."

"How long till it'll be clear?"

"Hours, I should think, but we really don't know."

Jessie climbed down from the cab and trotted back through the rain with a map over her head to speak with Maxie. Stretch barked a greeting at the constable, who had followed and listened while Jessie repeated his information.

"Must we stay here?" Maxie asked him.

"Oh no. You can go on if you want. But you'll have to wait at Summit Lake until the road's clear if you do. There's a lodge with a restaurant and a campground up there."

Maxie nodded. "I know the place. There's a pretty little lake at that campground. Let's skedaddle on up the road, Jessie. The weather can't be worse there than it is here."

The highway leading away from Fort Nelson curved gently through farms and thick stands of first growth white spruce, poplar, and aspen, some of which were in the process of being cleared for fields and pastures. Spray flew up from passing vehicles to be swiftly cleared from the windshield by constantly working wipers, and fog drifted in periodically to further obscure visibility.

Jessie saw the dark shapes of buffalo in one pasture, all lying down contentedly resting, oblivious to the rain that soaked their thick coats. The fog grew thicker as they reached foothills where the road began to climb gradually upward toward Steamboat, and it was hard at times to make out other traffic in either direction. At one point she slowed even more to allow a moose to amble across the road on long gangly legs and disappear into the mist.

The road grew steeper, and around one long sweeping curve two cyclists materialized out of the gloom ahead of her. She recognized one as Severson, pumping hard. His friend Leo must have talked him into going on immediately, though the rain had not lessened, and they must have started early to make it this far already. She hoped he had recovered his emotional equilibrium, but there was no place to pull over and say hello, so she honked one instead and caught a glimpse in the rearview mirror of his wave as she passed.

In just over an hour the two motor homes turned into the parking lot of the Steamboat Café, where they parked one behind the other.

"Was that the cyclist who found the boy's body at Kiskatinaw?" Maxie asked as Jessie climbed hurriedly into the Jayco to get out of the rain, leaving Tank behind in the Winnebago.

"Craig Severson," Jessie told her. "He must be feeling a lot better to start off again in this weather, but he slept most of yesterday, so he must be okay."

"I wish we knew what happened to Patrick," Maxie said a bit plaintively, "and if that really was his jacket you saw. I can't stop wishing I'd found out more about him."

"Me too," Jessie confessed, wiping at her wet face with one hand. "When that policeman stopped us, I thought maybe it had something to do with Kiskatinaw or your break-in."

"That crossed my mind as well."

There seemed little more to say about it.

"Let's go in for coffee," Maxie suggested.

"There's a trash can out there," Jessie said, noticing a lumpy plastic bag near the door and picking it up as she was about to go back to the Winnebago. "Want me to get rid of this for you?"

"Yes, please. But wait a minute. There's another thing or two to go out as well."

She collected two damp paper towels from the counter next to the sink and bent over to pick up a magazine from the floor under the table where it had fallen from the bench.

"What's this?" she asked in a hesitant tone of voice and straightened up, holding a small bottle that she had retrieved from far back under the table. Her obvious confusion became concern as she turned the bottle so Jessie could read the label.

It was a bottle of brown hair dye.

"This isn't mine," Maxie stated flatly. "What's it doing here?"

"*Patrick.*" Jessie breathed, eyes wide with dawning apprehension and anxiety. Her mind was racing—then stumbling. She had a vision of the dead man's brown hair as she had seen it upon lifting the hood of the black windbreaker—and Patrick's own red hair.

"Oh God. Do you think . . ."

They stared at each other in distress. Then Maxie, without speaking, took a new plastic bag from her cupboard and put the hair dye bottle inside carefully, without touching it any more. "Let's go in and talk about this before we go on," she said through tight lips.

Dropping the trash in the parking lot barrel, they ran through the rain to the café and were soon settled, deep in conversation, with coffee and a huge cinnamon roll, which they divided.

•   •   •

Half an hour later, Butch Stringer pulled his rig into the parking lot at the top of the long winding grade from Fort Nelson, shut down the Peterbilt, and swore to himself as he trotted through the downpour to the Steamboat Café. It had rained for most of the 860 miles he had driven from Seattle. He was tired of being drenched every time he climbed from the cab for fuel or food, and fed up with the constant monotonous rhythm of the windshield wipers.

From past trips he knew that to the northwest the landscape fell dramatically away from 3,500-foot Steamboat Mountain to the Muskwa River Valley far below, making tourists catch their breath when the weather allowed them a look at the treetops hundreds of feet below. Oncoming traffic always bore watching, for flatlanders nervously hugged the inside of their lane, made skittish by the drop, and sometimes wandered across the yellow line. At almost nine on this morning, there was nothing to see but a layer of dark sullen clouds that clung to the summit, obscuring one of the most spectacular views on the long run to Anchorage.

Tall and angular, tough as rawhide, wide through the shoulders and narrow at the hips, at forty-six Stringer was beginning to develop a bit of a pot belly, which lowered his belt buckle an inch or two and which he sucked in when he thought about it. There wasn't much physical exercise in sitting behind a wheel hour after hour, for ten hours or five hundred miles a day.

Some people are born with the natural grace of athletes or dancers. Butch Stringer seemed born not just to drive but to choreograph the movement of big trucks. He wheeled the Peterbilt and trailer with the effortless assurance of an exact knowledge of their capabilities. Instinctively he almost *wore* the tractor, employing its power to ease a heavily loaded trailer deftly through traffic or reverse into the tightest of spaces against a loading dock, playing the gears and peddles like a musician, with rhythm and efficiency.

For the fifty-one miles from Fort Nelson, hard rain and thick bands of fog had created hazardous passing conditions as the scattering of oncoming headlights barely pierced the curtain of mist before the vehicles became visible. Taillights headed cautiously west had appeared with no little or no warning, and Stringer had been thoroughly frustrated by a senior citizen behind the wheel of a mammoth motor home who had slowed to a scaredy-cat crawl in the poor conditions and stubbornly refused to pull over to let him by. It had cost him speed and forced him to wait impatiently for miles before a *slow-moving vehicles keep right* lane finally appeared and allowed him to pass.

Damn dim-witted dawdlers shouldn't be allowed on the road. Why couldn't they take a ferry up the Inside Passage and leave this singular road route to commercial traffic? Between the RVs, local vehicles swinging out of side roads, and the weather, he was losing more time than he liked.

With a quick pat and a "Hi there, Boots" for the black-and-white spaniel who greeted him just inside the door of the café, Stringer whacked his baseball cap against a thigh to rid it of rain and held out a hand to the younger man who came to the counter from the kitchen, a spatula in one hand, in response to the bell that rang when anyone entered. "Hey, Al, you order this shit?"

"Not me. Where've you been hiding, stranger? It's a couple of months since we saw your ugly face."

"That construction section the other side of Muncho Lake must be slop. What's the weather doing up there?"

"You're looking at it." The younger man scowled and shook his head.

"*Damn.* Tomorrow?"

"Weather report says more of the same. Coffee?"

"Ah—yeah, I guess."

Taking the steaming mug Al handed him, Stringer turned to find a place at one of the small tables. Except for two women sitting by a window, who had looked up as he came in, there were no other customers. They were probably driving the two motor homes parked outside, so he intended to sit a good distance away, drink his coffee, and leave before they could pull out and slow him down some more. But the younger of the two nodded and spoke.

"Weren't you at Kiskatinaw night before last? I think I saw your truck on the road as we pulled out in the morning. That's a good-looking Peterbilt."

A little surprised at a woman who could tell one eighteen-wheeler from another, he paused, then, curiosity overcoming reluctance, walked across and dropped into a chair at the table next to theirs.

"Yeah, I was up above on the access road, trying to get some sleep. But it was tough with the cops coming to ask questions. Nasty business—the kid going off the bridge like that. Were you in the campground?"

"*I* was," Jessie told him. "A guy in a space next to mine heard him fall. I went with him to see if there was anything we could do and waited until the police got there."

Maxie was listening with a thoughtful frown. Now she joined the exchange. "Did you happen to notice any kids in a pickup turn off the highway and go down to the bridge?" she asked.

Stringer gave her a long look of appraisal and took a sip of his coffee before he answered. "There *was* a pickup," he said slowly. "Camping gear in the back and three kids in front."

"One with red hair?"

"It was too dark to get a good look, but the one on the passenger side had on a western hat."

"You're sure there were three?"

"Yeah, I'm sure. Seemed a bit crowded in the cab."

Maxie and Jessie stared across the table at each other, both wondering if the boys this man had seen were the ones who had been looking for Patrick on the Icefields Parkway—and if Patrick really *had* been with them.

"It would explain his leaving in the middle of the night," Jessie commented.

Maxie nodded. "But how did one of them—if it was one of

them—wind up dead under the bridge? Where is the other one—and Patrick?"

As they talked, Stringer had scooted his chair up to their table and set his half-empty coffee mug on the edge of it. "You knew that boy?" he asked in a more interested tone.

"No. Well—we knew *of* him—met someone who may have been *with* him," Jessie told him.

"What do you mean?" he demanded.

Maxie sighed and shook her head in frustration. "It's confusing," she told him. "You see, we were camped next to each other just below Radium Hot Springs in British Columbia when Jessie—this is Jessie Arnold, by the way, and I'm Maxie McNabb—found this red-haired boy under her motor home in the middle of the night."

The details of everything that had happened tumbled out as they took turns telling their own bits of what had transpired. Stringer interjected a question or two as the tale progessed.

"Unbelievable! And you told all this to the cops at Kiskatinaw?" he asked Jessie, when they had finished.

"Ah—no." She shook her head and frowned. "You see I didn't get back together with Maxie until Fort Nelson. Then we put some of the pieces together. But it's all speculation. We don't really know anything but what Patrick told us. The rest is just guesses."

"I think you should tell them the whole thing. They may be able to fit it together with what they know or have figured out since Kiskatinaw."

"I think you're right," Maxie agreed. "My cell phone will work here, I think, but this would be hard to explain on the phone. I'd rather talk to someone in person. We're over halfway to Summit Lake, and with the slide, there should be someone there."

"Good thinking," Stringer agreed.

Jessie nodded, slowly. Inspector William Webster, who had come to Kiskatinaw, was now over three hundred miles away in Dawson Creek, the Prince George police at least six hundred miles. They could go back to the RCMP detachment in Fort Nelson, but Summit Lake was closer—they could be there in an hour. It seemed important now to get in touch with the police.

With a scrape of chairs they pushed back from the table and headed for the door, Stringer jamming his hat back on and yelling a good-bye to Al, who had vanished back into the kitchen.

Stringer pulled out of the parking lot first. But in a few minutes the two women were also back on the highway, heading carefully down the long grade into the Muskwa River Valley behind an early-in-the-season bus full of tourists who would rather ride than drive, though there was little to see through swirling fog and depressing rain.

As she drove, Jessie wondered about the hair dye bottle. The night Patrick had disappeared his hair had still been red, but it would seem from the bottle of dye that he had intended to dye it brown. If he had joined up with the two young men who had been looking for him, he could certainly have obtained more hair dye in Jasper or Prince George. Maybe the RCMP at Summit Lake would be able to answer some of the questions that troubled her. She thought of the night below the bridge and how sure she had been that the dead man was not Patrick because of the color of his hair. Now she was anything but sure.

CHAPTER 14

The rain had momentarily stopped, though the clouds still hung threateningly low and dark. Jessie, with Tank at her feet, stood looking out across Summit Lake from the campground space in which she had parked the Winnebago. They were waiting for Maxie and Stretch to come out of the Jayco parked next door and join them for a walk. The highway continued in a curve around the right side of the small lake, and from where Jessie stood it was possible to watch earth-moving equipment working to clear away the wall of mud that had slid down a gully in the rocky cliff, buried the road, and continued on to the edge of the lake.

At 4,250 feet, Summit was the highest point on the highway and so rugged that early building crews had been forced to blast a space between cliff and lake to create the roadway. A line of vehicles stretched along the highway from the site of the slide all the way back to the campground, parked where they had been halted by a flagman, waiting to get through as they had been for hours. The first few cars of a similar line were just visible beyond the slide, snaking back to disappear where the road began to descend in the distance. Rather than join the line of impatient people, Jessie had followed Maxie as she drove into the campground and parked where they would be able to see when traffic was able to move again.

Maxie soon came out wearing a blue raincoat and carrying an umbrella, locked the Jayco, and taking Tank and Stretch, they walked together from the campground to the lodge with its small store and restaurant, in search of an RCMP officer. But law enforcement was nowhere to be found, having departed for their usual duties in Fort Nelson. "They didn't have time to stick around here," a woman behind the counter in the store told them. "We'll let 'em know when it's open. Be a while though." She agreed to ask the police to contact Maxie or Jessie if they came back before the slide was cleared.

When they came back out into the parking lot, the clouds had parted slightly and a ray or two of sunshine lit up the area. The tour bus Jessie had followed away from Steamboat was parked outside, and its passengers, mostly senior citizens, were stretching their legs in the lot, some heading for the restaurant. With only a few tables, it was already jammed with people from the line of cars—a diversion as they grew hungry and tired of watching the work on the slide slowly progress—so the seniors were in for a wait.

"Glad I have my own kitchen." Maxie sighed as they walked slowly back toward the campground. "Shall I make some more coffee?"

Jessie nodded, distracted by a truck that was parked at the end of the lot nearest the campground. The driver was bending over beside the trailer to check its tires.

"There's Butch Stringer," she said and they both began to walk in his direction.

Finished with the chore, he straightened, raised his face to the sun, and closed his eyes. Sticking his thumbs in the pockets of his jeans, he rocked on his heels and half-smiled to himself in the thin warmth. The expression wiped a concerned frown from his face and changed him from just another irritable person unwillingly held up by the slide to someone who could take pleasure in the small things in life. Hearing the gravel crunching under their feet as they approached, he opened his eyes, turned his head, and his smile grew broader.

"Hi, again." Jessie nodded to him and paused, attracted by his expression of appreciation. "Nice change, isn't it?"

"Sure is. It's been rain all the way from Seattle. But this break in it won't last long."

He squatted as Stretch trotted across under Tank's leash, stopping just close enough to inspect him.

"Hi there, fella. Who're you?"

"That's Stretch," Maxie told him with a grin. "He thinks you need his permission to park here, arrogant galah that he is—or he might just want to piddle on your tires."

The big man chuckled and held out a hand for the dachshund to sniff. "Great name! Long and low, like a limo."

Stretch evidently approved of the scent of the proffered fingers, for he padded forward and allowed his ears and throat to be stroked, leaning into the gentle motion of the large hand on his smooth coat.

Tank, now sitting quietly beside Jessie, watched intently.

The trucker glanced up to meet his look. Tank blinked but didn't move.

"Nice-looking husky. Sled dog?" the trucker asked.

"My lead dog," Jessie told him.

"You one of those Iditarod mushers?"

"Yes," she said, smiling at the gleeful grin he gave her as he rose.

"Hey, you know, I think I saw you leave the gate in Anchorage on the first Saturday in March a year ago, but you look different—much slimmer—without all that cold weather gear."

They smiled at each other, remembering the same race.

"Looks like we're gonna be here awhile," he commented with an impatient gesture in the direction of the slide and line of vehicles.

"It does. Pretty grotty weather," Maxie agreed.

The look he gave her was quizzical and amused at the same time.

"Aussie?"

"No, but my husband was. I picked a bit up from him, I'm afraid. Some of it stuck."

"Crowded in there?" Stringer nodded in the direction of the restaurant.

"You could say that. But if it's coffee you're after, I'm about to make a pot and you're welcome."

He accepted Maxie's offer, and the three walked together to her rig in the campground, where Stringer's robust presence seemed to fill most of the available space.

Before the coffee had finished perking, the clouds had once again filled in the gap and the sun disappeared. Stringer sighed as he looked out the window. "Well, at least we know it's still up there. I think that . . ." He paused, his attention caught by a brown-and-cream-colored pickup passing on the campground loop road. "Hey! There's those kids again—the ones I saw at Kiskatinaw. There's only two of them now."

Jessie craned her neck to see and was instantly on her feet headed for the door.

"Maxie, I think that *was* Patrick," she called back over her shoulder as she jumped out and took off running. Thinking quickly, she did not chase the pickup but turned in the other direction, hoping to cut it off as it completed the loop. Reaching the entrance she paused, but not seeing it coming toward her, trotted on around the loop, expecting it to appear at any second.

She had seen a flash of red hair as the passenger leaned out the open window, looking back toward the line of vehicles waiting to move north. Could it really have been Patrick? If it was, she wanted to know. Not only that, there were a lot of questions she was no longer content to leave unanswered.

The campground was not large, and in just a few minutes Jessie had jogged halfway around the loop that connected its parking spaces. It was also fairly flat and had few trees, so she soon saw that the pickup had parked in the space farthest from the entrance. Picking up her pace, she ran up to it and looked in. Empty! Where had they gone? Glancing around she noticed a hiking trail that appeared to curve along the lake opposite the construction and off into a small grove of trees. She glimpsed someone moving quickly away from her along the trail and without hesitation hurried after them, not bothering to turn at the sound of another vehicle sliding to an abrupt stop, throwing up gravel on the loop road behind her.

As she trotted along, the trees grew thicker and the hiking trail twisted and twined through them, obscuring the way ahead. It had grown darker, and as she felt a few drops of rain she realized that she had left her raincoat in the Jayco, and Tank as well. She would soon be soaked if she didn't go back, but she quickly discarded that thought: she was not about to quit trying to catch up with the boys ahead of her, whoever they were. If it wasn't Patrick, she wanted to know. If it was—well, she wanted to know that even more. And who was with him?

Her feet pounded along on the already muddy path, which was becoming wetter and more slippery by the minute as the rain increased. The trail was uneven and full of roots and rough spots. On one sloping section a foot went out from under her and she fell to one knee, scraping it painfully. Ignoring the hurt, she jumped up and started on, but not before she thought she heard someone else running behind her. Who else would be foolish enough to run on this muddy trail, and why? Was this other person also chasing the boys or . . . A new thought leaped into her mind—they were following her? Maxie, perhaps, or the trucker? She hurried on, intent on the objects of her pursuit.

A sharp turn around a tree, and the hiking trail divided, one section continuing to follow the lakeshore, one heading uphill into the trees. Which direction had they gone? She remembered a sign with a diagram of the hiking trails in the area and wished she had bothered to read it. Even in the rain this was evidently a popular spot, for there were footprints in the mud of both branches of the trail. Now what?

As Jessie hesitated by the tree, the sound of running feet behind her grew louder. Frowning, she turned to see who was following but was too slow. All she saw was a dark shape that burst from behind the tree and sprang at her, one arm raised. Something hit her head hard, she felt an intense flare of pain, and she was falling, partially aware that the figure had leaped over her and away, down the lakeside section of the trail.

For what seemed a long time Jessie lay with one side of her face in the mud, fading in and out of awareness, and couldn't make her body move to get up. The back right side of her head hurt like fury, and she scrabbled ineffectively with the fingers of one hand, digging them into the wet ground. Then she began to feel the cold rain pouring on her hair and the pain grew a little less fierce.

It took all her remaining strength to pull herself carefully to a sitting position, where she held still for a minute or two, afraid she would be sick. Concentrating, she raised her muddy hand, touched the back of her head, and found a lump and her hair sticky with blood. Fingering the swelling created another agonizing flash of pain, but it faded again to a sharp ache that made her clench her teeth and grimace, and the sound that escaped her lips was a sort of half whine, half grunt.

It seemed to take forever to regain her feet and stand wobbly and sweating, determined to keep her balance. Her shoes, jeans, and shirt were caked with mud, and something was running down her neck out of her hair—either rain or blood. Who had hit her? Why? What the hell was going on? For the moment she didn't much care but knew she had to get back to the campground and find help.

Slowly, cautiously, she started back the way she had come. Every one of the first few steps cost her, jarring her head and making the trail beneath her feet seem to recede, then come closer, but gradually it grew easier and less painful to retrace her steps. She had made it almost halfway to the campground when she heard a thumping, swishing sort of sound on the trail in front of her and a voice called out something she couldn't quite hear for the ringing in her ears.

Oh God, was it her attacker again? But he had gone the other direction, hadn't he? Staggering, she turned to look for somewhere to hide, but the trees had thinned out and there was nowhere, unless she ran—and she simply could not run. Defensively she braced her feet, faced the new sound, and waited.

In a moment there was motion from the small stand of trees

closest to the campground. Then out of them came a man on a bicycle pulling a trailer, with another man close behind him. Jessie stood staring dumbly. *Severson!* It was Craig Severson and his friend—Lee? No—Leo. With the delay caused by the slide, they must have caught up. Her legs gave way and folded under her, and she sat down suddenly on the muddy trail, relief flooding through her at the sight of someone she knew.

"Jessie? What the hell happened?" The cyclist stopped in front of her, leaped from his bicycle, and dropped to his knees in the mud beside her. "Did you fall?" He noticed the blood, now soaking the shoulder of her shirt. "Let me look at that."

His friend Leo came with a compact first-aid kit, but Jessie waved him away. "Just help me back to my rig, will you? I've got more stuff there. I don't think this is as bad as it seems."

They insisted on checking her injury and decided the cut could wait the short time it would take to get her in out of the rain. Jessie stood up again and with Severson's support was soon leaving the trail for the loop road in the campground. There they met Maxie and Stringer, who, worried when Jessie didn't return, had come out to find her.

Then it was a jumble of voices in a small space, as all five of them crowded into Maxie's Jayco, the uninjured four all asking questions Jessie couldn't answer and expressing concern at once. Stringer and Leo, both trained in first aid, soon conferred and declared that the cut was small and would not need stitches, but she might have a mild concussion. They applied first aid and an ice pack to Jessie's head. Tank came to lie at her feet and would not be moved. She made them leave him there, knowing that he sensed something was wrong and would be uneasy anywhere else.

She was beginning to feel overwhelmed with attention when

Maxie remedied the situation by announcing that it was time for the three men to leave. "You blokes have all had a gander and she's going to be fine, but she needs to rest now."

In minutes they were gone—Severson to collect his bicycle from where he had left it on the trail, Stringer to nap in his truck after an admonition to wake him if they needed anything. Leo—his last name was Taylor, they had learned sometime in the hub-bub—mentioned pitching a tent, for they had decided to stay till the next morning and start early. Before they left, remembering how miserably cold and wet Severson had been in the rain at Kiskatinaw, Jessie offered the two cyclists her Winnebago for the night, which they gratefully accepted.

Maxie had insisted that Jessie stay in the Jayco, where she could keep an eye on her for the time being and feed her dinner later. So, patched up and clean, in warm socks and her oversized T-shirt, Jessie crawled into the bed made up from the dinette table and sighed in relief over a cup of hot tea.

"Was it Patrick?" Maxie asked, when everything had settled down.

Jessie started to shake her head but quickly thought better of it. "I never got close enough to see who it was before I got hit."

"And you didn't see who hit you."

"Just an impression of someone in dark clothes. But was he chasing me? Or the boys?"

"Well, it doesn't matter right now. Get some rest and we'll talk about it later," Maxie told her, but her forehead was creased in concern and puzzlement. "Some loony, perhaps."

But Maxie didn't believe that and neither did Jessie, who drifted off to welcome sleep still wondering about the incident and wishing she could think straight.

She slept the rest of the afternoon, woke enough to eat a light dinner of hot soup Maxie brought her from the restaurant, then went back to sleep again. Maxie woke her once in the night to make sure she wasn't comatose. After dark, Tank jumped up and settled down close to her at the foot of the bed, which he never did unless she was sick. Though the blankets belonged to Maxie, Jessie let him stay, feeling comforted and safe with him there.

CHAPTER 15

All night long it rained, and it was still raining when they woke early the next morning to the sound of engines and found that, though there had been a second smaller slide, it had been cleared, the road was finally open, and lines of traffic were slowly moving along below the raw cut in the rocky cliff. Mist hung close at the summit, obscuring the hilltops and dulling the colors of the landscape.

After an early breakfast and some Advil, the headache that had accompanied Jessie into consciousness subsided enough for her to declare herself fit for driving, tired of the drizzle, and ready to see some new country. After checking the lump and redressing the cut on Jessie's head, Maxie suggested that they make it a short driving day and only go as far as Liard Hot Springs Provincial Park, ninety-seven miles away and another place Jessie had on her wish list.

"Soaking my aches away in the hot water of those pools will be heaven," she said. "Even if it's raining."

Cyclists Severson and Taylor had put the Winnebago back to rights after their night of dry comfort and again expressed their gratitude for the loan of it. Packed up and ready to travel, they rode away leaving Jessie waving from the door. Stringer, who had stopped to check on her and agreed that she wasn't concussed, just battered and bruised, pulled out right after them, with a blast from his air horn as he swept past the campground on the highway.

"What a nice man," Maxie, who had eaten dinner with him in the restaurant the night before, commented.

She was filling a thermos and Jessie was folding blankets and making the bed back into a dinette table when there was a rap on the door of the Jayco. Maxie opened it to find two men standing outside, one of whom identified himself as an RCMP inspector.

He looked up at her with rain dripping from the hat he tipped rather than removed. "The clerk at the store said that you were asking for the police. I'm also looking for Jessie Arnold." He gestured toward the Winnebago parked next door. "Would you happen to know where I might find her?"

"She's right here." Maxie moved aside to make room for him to step in, followed by his slightly taller companion. Stretch hopped down from the bed in the back and came barking at strangers invading space he knew didn't belong to them, but hushed immediately at a word from Maxie.

Jessie, the table raised back into position between the two benches, had just picked up the bedding to put it away when she recognized the voice at the door and turned to greet Inspector Webster from Dawson Creek. But her eyes widened in surprise at the sight of the man who came into the Jayco behind him, and she backed away till she ran into the edge of the table and froze, staring. There, in the same black windbreaker and blue baseball cap, was the man with the mustache she had seen three times in Jasper.

He nodded to her as Webster introduced him, taking note of her reaction. "Detective Dan Loomis from Cody, Wyoming. You've met?"

"No," the detective answered quietly, assessing Jessie's reaction with half a smile. "But we sort of ran into each other in Jasper."

Maxie raised a what's-this-about eyebrow but said nothing, though his mention of Cody rang warning bells in her mind.

"You were following me." Jessie found her voice, but Webster broke in before Loomis could answer.

"We have some problems we need to straighten out, Miss Arnold, and you may be able to help. May we sit down?" The request was directed to Maxie, who nodded.

She poured the coffee back out of the thermos into cups at the table, and the four settled, women on one side, men on the other.

The inspector turned to Jessie with a questioning look, but she raised a hand before he could put it into words.

"Before we start, I need to know." She gave Loomis a suspicious frown. "Were you following me in Jasper or not?"

He nodded slowly. "Yes, I was, actually. But it wasn't you I was looking for. It has to do with a case I'm working on—with the inspector's help." He nodded courteously toward Webster, establishing that the RCMP was in charge, that it was Webster's territory and responsibility after all. "I'll explain later, but let the inspector start with the things he needs to know first—okay?"

She agreed, because it wasn't the only thing on her mind.

Why would these two show up together? Did it have something to do with the death at the Kiskatinaw bridge? She reluctantly waited and let him speak, anxious for information.

The inspector began by directing an unexpected question to both women. "Patrick Cutler. That name mean anything to either one of you?"

They stared at him, astonished. "But that's what we wanted to talk to the police—to you about," Maxie said with a puzzled frown. "We met the boy at Dutch Creek."

"I saw him earlier than that," Jessie reminded her.

"That's right," Maxie agreed, thinking back. "But that's where you found him under your rig and we really met him."

"But it all started when he stole my lunch at Fort Steele," Jessie began, and went on to tell the two attentive policemen all she could remember about Patrick, from Fort Steele until he disappeared in the provincial park. Maxie listened, adding a comment or two in her low, gravely voice but mostly watching the two law enforcement officers closely for their reactions.

"Okay, let me see if I've got it straight." Webster looked up from the notes he was once again making in his book. "You're sure it was Cutler you saw at Fort Steele?"

"Yes, definitely—he admitted it."

"How'd he get there?"

"Hitchhiked, from what he told us."

"You know," Maxie broke in with a sudden realization, "I think I saw him on the road between Fort Steele and Dutch Creek with his thumb out. I don't pick up hitchhikers so I went on by. He must have caught a ride to Dutch Creek."

"There's no record of him at the border. Do you know how he crossed and where?"

"He never said and we didn't ask," Jessie told him.

"He came close once," Maxie mused, remembering that

middle-of-the-night conversation. "When you asked him how much money he had and he avoided the question. We thought he couldn't have had very much."

"From all we know, you're probably right," Loomis said. "So he must have slipped across illegally somehow. Wouldn't be too hard for a smart kid."

"Then you caught him under your motor home in the middle of the night." Webster addressed Jessie, striving to be sure he was correctly interpreting what she had told him. "Trying to keep dry."

"And he would have run, but I got there first with the can of pepper spray."

"So you didn't report him—you fed him." Loomis grinned at the thought.

Maxie nodded, encouraged by his sense of humor and the note of sympathy she recognized in his tone. But Jessie was remembering the bedraggled sight of Patrick as he crawled from beneath the Winnebago with his dirty face and chattering teeth, the little they had learned about his background, and what she had heard on the next day's drive.

"Were you looking for him on the Icefields Parkway?"

A question passed between the two men in a glance. Loomis set down the cup he had been about to drink from and straightened himself on the bench. "Why do you ask?"

She told him about the conversation she had overheard concerning two men looking for a red-haired boy.

"Secondhand information—you didn't see these two men, right? Then he disappeared sometime during that night."

"He left a thank-you note," Maxie volunteered. "But it went out with the trash." She repeated its brief contents.

Webster, who had been watching the exchange, turned slowly toward Jessie, leaned one elbow on the table, centered on her alone, and carefully asked what had been on his mind for two days.

"Something was bothering you at Kiskatinaw. Will you tell me what it was?"

She stared at him for a long minute, hesitating, and felt a lump of guilt rise in her throat that had to be swallowed hard before she could speak—sorry now, as she had been afraid she would be, that she hadn't voiced her confusion and suspicion at the time.

"I think the dead man was wearing his jacket," she said simply and felt immediately relieved. "I didn't tell you then because I had decided it wasn't, but at first I was afraid it *was* Patrick."

"Why would you think so?"

"The jacket was the same—and there was a maple leaf pin on the collar that I recognized—or thought I did. He was wearing one like it at Dutch Creek."

"But you changed your mind?" He had not taken his eyes from her face, not jotted a note in his book.

"Yes—after I checked and saw that the dead man's hair wasn't red—it was brown."

The horror of lifting the jacket's hood came suddenly back to her. She shuddered slightly, and though she turned her gaze to the waters of the lake beyond the window, she saw none of it, her inner sight focused on what she disliked remembering. "But I think that jacket *was* his. I've seen a lot of those pins, but how many could there be, worn in exactly the same place on a similar jacket?"

There was a moment of silence as they all considered the complexities involved in the puzzle. Then Maxie told them about finding the bottle of brown hair dye in the Jayco at Steamboat, got up to get the bottle she had saved, and set it on the table. "This is what made us wonder if Patrick had dyed his hair—

made us decide to tell the police what we'd found. We were afraid that . . ."

". . . the dead man could have been him after all," Webster finished for her.

"Yes." She sat back down.

Turning the bottle over in his hands to read the label within the plastic bag, Loomis said to Webster, "This is interesting, considering the other one. Same brand."

"What other one?" Maxie asked sharply.

But before either man could answer, Jessie's original fear got the better of her and she turned to Webster, deep disquiet in her voice as she asked, "*Was* it Patrick—under the bridge, I mean? Please—was it?"

"No, Ms. Arnold," the inspector told her. "I can assure you that it was not Patrick Cutler. But it *was* one of the two boys who were looking for him on the Icefields Parkway."

Hardly hearing the rest, Jessie sat back with a sigh of relief, feeling tension melt from her whole body as she realized just how much she had wanted it not to be Patrick. How odd that seemed, when at first she had resented the interruption of his presence to the point of anger. This had certainly not turned out to be the calm, pleasant trip she had envisioned.

Maxie, on the other hand, forearms on the table, was leaning toward the two men with more questions.

"What other bottle?" she asked again, directing the question to Loomis. "And who are, were . . . oh, hell—who were the two on the parkway? Why were they looking for Patrick?"

Loomis glanced at Webster, and she could see that the two officers were agreed in their disinclination to divulge information about their investigation.

"Ms. McNabb," Webster began, "we really can't—"

"Look," she said in a determined tone that told him she had

little patience with foolishness and considered his close-to-the-chest attitude in that category. "I understand your reluctance to tell us everything. You don't know us, but we're not total ningnongs, and there's a lot going on that seems to keep catching us up in it. It's clear as a crow in a bucket of milk that Patrick was running from something he wouldn't talk about—something that frightened him badly. It bothers me that he disappeared so suddenly, with nothing more than a note, that Jessie was accidentally involved in finding a dead man that you say was someone who was looking for Patrick Cutler, that this wagon was broken into in Prince George, and that Jessie was conked on the head yesterday when she was chasing someone who might have been Patrick. All you do is ask questions. How about some answers? I think we deserve to be trusted with a little more about whatever the hell is going on. We *might* even be able to help you with some of it."

A momentary silence followed her outburst. Then Loomis's sense of humor surfaced again—lightly. At least he smiled, if a bit grimly.

"That's two things we didn't have on *our* list—a break-in and an injury," he said to Webster. "I think maybe she's right, and we'd better barter some parts of our information for theirs."

Inspector Webster nodded slowly, the corners of his mouth twitching with a smile he couldn't quite suppress. "You don't have a tendency to say what you think, do you, Ms. McNabb?"

Startled, Maxie stared at him for a moment, began to grin, then threw back her head, and the richness of her uninhibited laughter filled the confined space of the motor home so completely that any remaining tension was dispelled and they all had to chuckle with her.

By the time a second pot of coffee was made and gone, the two men had been told everything they didn't know before they arrived—in exchange for some background information of their own.

"A woman was killed in Cody," Loomis had begun.

"Patrick's mother," Maxie stated flatly.

"How could you know that?"

"He mentioned her once when he was riding with me that day. There was something in the way he spoke—something painful in his voice. But he changed the subject very quickly."

She and Jessie then learned that not only Patrick but two of his friends and his stepfather had disappeared in Wyoming. The dead man at Kiskatinaw was one of those friends, a nineteen-year-old named Lewis Jetter. The two had evidently run off after Patrick intending some kind of help, found him, and continued north on the highway in their pickup. Webster and Loomis didn't know who had dropped Jetter from the bridge. The other boy, Kim Fredricksen? Patrick himself? The stepfather, McMurdock? Someone completely unknown?

"But we think, from what you've told us—and from this, of course"—he lifted the dye bottle in its plastic bag—"that Patrick *may* have dyed his hair brown, as you thought, and that Fredricksen may have dyed his red. He must have lost this under the table and not noticed when he left. But he could easily have bought another. We found another bottle in the abandoned pickup in this campground. It had been used, and the remains of the dye in it were red. By switching personas, they may have thought that young Cutler would be safer. Wouldn't work for long, or up close, with anyone who knew them both. But if no one was looking for Jetter and Fredricksen, and they crossed the border legally . . ."

"You thought you saw Patrick yesterday?" Webster broke into the tale to ask Jessie. "Before you were hit?"

She closed her eyes to concentrate on what she had seen. "I saw a red-haired man on the passenger side of a passing pickup who was about the right age, but I didn't see his face."

"So it *could* have been Fredricksen—or someone else entirely?"

"Yes, I guess it could. They left the pickup and took off on the hiking trail. I never got close enough to see them."

"And you didn't see who hit you?"

"He ran up behind me," she told him, raising a hand to the lump on the back of her head and fingering it gingerly.

"May I look?" Loomis asked.

He lifted the bandage carefully and peered at the cut. "Hmm, something with an edge from the look of this. I've seen handguns do this kind of damage. You may have been lucky, Jessie." He laid a hand on her shoulder. "It could have been a lot worse."

*   *   *

It could have been, she thought later, as she drove away from Summit Lake. It was good to be traveling toward Liard Hot Springs, and she was relieved to be leaving the campground, policemen, lost boys, and she hoped, confusion. She'd had enough—had never asked to be involved in any of this unexpected and unpleasant situation.

Glancing in the mirror, she could see Maxie's Jayco behind her coming out of the campground and was not unhappy to have company, but a low-key depression clung stubbornly to the edges of her thoughts. She could hardly wait to arrive, get settled, and hike the long boardwalk out to the pool at the hot springs, where she could immerse herself up to the neck in hot water and let the tensions of the last few days float away.

What she wanted was for all the excess people and problems

to go away and leave her alone. What she needed was some calm, peaceful solitude.

What she couldn't know was that she wasn't about to get calm—and definitely not solitude—and that some of the people with whom she was about to come in contact would be most unwelcome company.

CHAPTER 16

Jessie led the way as she and Maxie turned onto the highway and soon passed the spot where the slide had buried it so successfully—twice. The pavement was still coated with mud, and large rocks falling from the cliff had broken it in several places, but a crew was already at work repairing the damage. A workman in rain gear leaned on his shovel and saluted Jessie with his hard hat as she steered the motor home slowly past him, rocking over the rough road.

Tank sat up to look out the window from his place in the passenger seat. She reached across and gave his ears a quick rub.

"I'm glad I brought you along, guy."

She caught a last glimpse of Summit Lake in the rearview mirror as she started down the other side of the pass. The highway went around several bends, where smaller slides had brought rocks and mud to the edge of the pavement, then to the north a group of erosion pillars—hoodoos—appeared in the distance, just visible through the rain. Below them, near the road, a solitary caribou picked its way across an open space with no regard for passing vehicles.

The highway wound down into a steep limestone gorge, and four miles from the summit she drove into a turnout, leaving room for Maxie's rig behind her, and stopped for a minute to watch a small herd of stone sheep meander along the rocky hillside until they disappeared over a ridge. Back on the winding road, she was soon looking down into the broad expanse of MacDonald Valley, where the creek of the same name snaked its way in loops and bends along the flat bottomland. She passed 113 and 115 Creeks, named for their distance from Fort Nelson, which had been Mile 0 when the highway was begun.

Twenty miles from Summit Lake, the road ran into a narrow valley with spectacular cliffs of folded sedimentary rock. She drove beside the Toad River and was pleased to see some sunshine light up its unusual blue-green water like turquoise. The valley began to wind upward, and the sunlight seemed to follow along until, leaning out to look up, Jessie saw that half the sky was clear. Some of her depression began to roll away with the clouds that were moving swiftly to the east, and she noticed that the rain had washed the windshield as clean as the world outside, which was now Technicolor instead of gray and white.

Before she was ready for it she was headed down into the Muncho Lake basin and onto a section of the highway cut into the steep cliffs looming over its eastern shore, so close to the water that it almost seemed to float. Copper oxide leaching into its waters gave the lake a color so deep and intense that even the ice that froze over it during the winter months was green. In the sunshine it shone like an emerald in a perfect setting of dark conifers that clung under towering gray stone cliffs and ridges.

At the far end of the seven-mile lake and up a steep hill, Jessie stopped in the large parking lot of a viewpoint for a last look at the lake far below. She and Maxie took their canine friends for a short walk and watched the shadows of a few tardy clouds crossing over the green water, which glowed again as they floated away and disappeared over the hills.

A red pickup was parked to one side of the lot, and two men sat on the guardrail eating sandwiches and passing a bottle of water back and forth between them. One of them turned his head to watch the two women pass with such different dogs. He nodded a greeting and grinned as Tank paused to sniff at a guardrail, then trotted back to his place at Jessie's side, forcing Stretch to scamper after him, working his short legs so fast they were hardly visible. The other man stared out at the lake and ignored them completely.

"Lunch?" Maxie asked as they headed back to their respective rigs. But Jessie elected to wait until they reached the hot springs and could relax over food. "It's only another thirty miles."

The rough military road that had been punched through to Alaska in eight short months had been possible to drive on in 1942 but not in regular passenger vehicles. Later it was widened, sections of it paved, and though hair-raising tales of nightmare trips littered with flat tires, shattered windshields and headlights, broken axles, and window-deep mud kept most from attempting its length, courageous people were drawn to see for themselves the wilderness through which it passed and began to return with glowing accounts of the country, if not the treacherous roadway.

The section of the winding road that followed the Liard River from Muncho Lake to the Liard Hot Springs and then continued for a few miles north was one of the last to be modernized and was still under construction, so it was slow going for a few miles until Jessie reached Liard River and the only remaining suspension bridge on the highway, crossed it, and was soon turning into the provincial park where they would spend the night.

French-Canadian voyageurs had named the area for the poplar (*liard*) trees that lined the banks of the river, which the highway parallels for another 135 miles, as far as Watson Lake. The provincial park campground was spread around a large loop, parking for RVs and tents placed well apart with plenty of trees and brush between them, giving most of them an agreeable degree of privacy and a feeling of camping in a grove of pine, poplar, paper birch, and trembling aspen.

It was still early in the day and there were many choices left, so Jessie parked the Winnebago in a space just across the road from Maxie's Jayco, on the back side of the loop near a trail that would take them to the hot springs on a boardwalk. Since the park provided no hookups, there was little to do but turn on the propane and open vents and windows to let fresh air sweep through the rig. The soft breeze was now pleasantly warmed by the sun, which cast light and shadow through the bright green of spring leaves like a moving curtain. Jessie stepped out and walked across with Tank on his leash to greet her friend, who had also climbed out and stood smiling, her face turned toward the source of light like one of the sunflowers they had seen along the road.

"Ah-h-h," Maxie said with a contented sigh. "This is more like it, yes?"

"Definitely an improvement," Jessie agreed. A weight of worry and concern seemed to have suddenly lifted from her mind, but when she stretched to relieve an aching stiffness in her back, there was a sharp reminder of her encounter and fall on the hiking trail. She winced, and Maxie noticed.

"Why don't you go soak some of the soreness out in the hot springs while I rustle up something for a late lunch?" she suggested.

Jessie thanked her, glad to agree. Collecting her bathing suit and a towel, she left Tank to keep Stretch company and hiked off toward the parking lot that she knew lay at the near end of the long boardwalk leading to the springs. She passed several camping spots occupied by people in motor homes and campers—one with a tent that would have held a whole family. Two children stood outside it, poking sticks at a small fire in the pit provided in each space, and waved at her as she passed. She was reminded that several trails ran in shortcuts through the brush and trees when she heard someone running on one of them beyond some bushes, but she stayed on the loop road until she reached the parking lot.

It was almost empty. By the middle of the summer it would be full and Liard Hot Springs almost constantly busy with people coming and going from the two hot spring pools perhaps a quarter of a mile away in a woodland setting. On this early afternoon in May there were only two cars near the boardwalk, with three people standing between them talking, and a pickup parked at the other end of the lot. One of the women by the cars had wet hair, so she had already been to the pools, and the license plates were British Columbian, so they could be locals, many of whom came year-round to bathe in the luxurious heat of the sulfurous waters.

A bear warning was posted near the start of the boardwalk. There were always a few bears in the area, and park officials were careful to let campers and bathers know that they should not feed them. "A fed bear is a dead bear," the sign read in bright red letters. In the over fifty-year history of Liard Hot Springs, there had been only one incident that involved a bear, and unfortunately it had happened at the nearest pool. The black bear that had attacked three people, killing two, had been sick and a complete deviation from the norm. Jessie knew that black bears had more curiosity and less fear of humans than browns or grizzlies, but they were usually cautious, easily frightened away, and avoided direct contact with people. Though often seen in this park, they were no real threat if you stayed out of their way and left them alone. Garbage-seeking bears were quickly darted and moved to faraway locations in the hope that they wouldn't find their way back.

Strolling along the boardwalk was enjoyable. At first it crossed a section of swampy ground created by overflow from the springs, where the warmth of the water encouraged early grasses and small flowers to bloom before they would elsewhere and sometimes in unusual combinations. Jessie stopped once to examine a few violets and white strawberry blossoms and a perfect spiderweb suspended between two tall cattails, raindrops still clinging to the delicate strands like dew.

She went slowly, pausing again to watch a school of minnows swimming in shallow water in the shadow of the walkway, and finally, after the way led into a grove of trees, came to a bend in the walk from which she could see the bathhouse next to the lowest pool. Just before reaching it the boardwalk divided, one section leading away to the left toward a trail that would take bathers to an upper pool, but Jessie was content to use this closer one and moved quickly onto the deck that held the bathhouse and three flights of steps with handrails that descended to the pool itself. She could hear the soft rush of water falling into one end of the pool and out the other, but no voices or splashing. *Great,* she thought, *I'll have it all to myself for a while,* and hurried into the women's half of the bathhouse, where she quickly put on her bathing suit, and returned to the pool.

Steam rose from the hot water, drifting over its surface in the light breeze, but it was clear enough to see pebbles on the bottom as she went down the middle flight of steps. Water from the spring, farther up the hill, was too hot to tolerate where it flowed into one end of the pool but cooled as it slowly drifted toward a small dam that had been built at one end to contain and deepen the water. A submerged stone bench rested on the bottom in the center opposite the steps, and Jessie headed toward it, knowing from past trips here that when she sat on it the water level would come to just under her chin and cover her shoulders. It smelled sulfurous but felt wonderful as she sank onto the bench, resisting her body's tendency to float.

Sunlight fell through the trees around the pool, making bright, sparkling lines across the water. Resting on the bench, she closed her eyes against the glare and leaned back, allowing her sore muscles to relax and the heat to permeate her whole body. A squirrel chattered somewhere off in the trees and a few birds chirped in the branches. Ah-h, this was even better than she had imagined. It reminded her that the last time she had been here she had thought how nice it would be to have a hot tub at home in Knik, where all winter long she could soak away the aches and pains suffered in wrestling a sled and driving dogs. When she got home she thought she would talk to Vic Prentice about it—see if it would be possible to include one in her plans for the rebuilding of her cabin. Saunas were fine too, but there was something about immersing herself in hot water that she liked much better. Maybe she could have a hot tub on the side of the new cabin nearest the yard, so she could watch her mutts while she enjoyed the heat. Might even be good for some of *their* sprains and strains, cuts and bruises.

It was very calm and peaceful. How terrific that there were no children splashing about, or crowds of people, some of whom would also want to sit on *her* bench. The quiet allowed her to clear her mind as she eased her physical hurts. After ten minutes or so, she yawned and realized she was feeling sleepy and limp all over. Time to get out for a few minutes and cool off.

Standing up, she started to move toward the steps but noticed something half floating, half resting on the lip of the dam, as if it were about to wash over into the stream that flowed away on the other side. It looked rather like a peeled log of some sort. How inconsiderate of someone to toss a log into the pool. As she moved in slow motion through the resistance of the water and came closer to the floating object, it began to look less and less like a log—but what was it? Curious now, she did not climb the steps but waded past them and peered toward the dam. It was hard to see in the contrast of sun and shadow, but slowly her vision adjusted.

There was a moment of utter mental stillness when she didn't think at all—as if her mind had shut down and refused to interpret what it saw. Her body went still as well, and she stood staring at the body that bobbed gently in the small waves she had created in moving through the water toward it. The log she had thought she was seeing had transformed itself into an outstretched human arm, shoulder, head, and neck that hung over the lip of the dam. Now she could see that the rest of the body floated just below the surface of the pool. In the water the hair looked almost brown. But it was not brown really. It was dark—and red.

As Jessie stared the squirrel chattered, and she was again aware of the rush of water splashing over the dam to her right. Then she could move. As fast as she could, against the resistance of the waist-deep water, she waded close enough to lay a hand on the shoulder of the person who floated there and leaned to see if he was breathing. He was—in short, shallow breaths that hardly seemed to draw in enough oxygen to sustain him. She could see that it was a boy—but not Patrick, though the hair was red. His skin was very pale, almost blue-looking around his mouth. Pressing her fingers into the angle of his jaw, she could discern a pulse, but it was not as strong as it should be.

Accidents were not uncommon in the sled dog races Jessie participated in each year. In anticipation, she had made sure she was well trained in both first aid and CPR, but she knew she couldn't help the boy in the water; he must be pulled out and onto the deck. She tried to raise his body back over the dam and found he was too heavy for her to lift, let alone carry up the steps. Resting as he was over the edge of the dam, he was not in danger of drowning, so the best she could do was make sure he would not slip off, then go and find help. She wished now that she had not been in the pool alone. She didn't like to leave him by himself, but she could not be in two places at once. There was a park ranger station near the entrance. Someone would be there—had to be.

Frightened and feeling desperately alone, she quickly climbed the steps to the deck and ran around the bathhouse onto the walkway. There, perhaps fifty yards away and heading directly toward her, was a park ranger.

"Help me," she called to him. "Someone's almost drowned in the pool."

The man began to run, and in seconds she was showing him the boy who lay on the dam. At the opposite end of the pool was a building for park officials. He ran toward it, shouting back, "Keep his head out of the water. I'll get my equipment."

Jessie waded back in and over to the boy, where she was joined almost immediately by the ranger.

"Let's get him up on the deck."

Together they lifted and carried the boy up the steps, but by the time they laid him down on the boards of the deck his breathing had stopped. Feeling again for a pulse, Jessie felt no rhythm at all under her fingers.

Without hesitation the ranger pulled out a mask from his case of first-aid equipment, made certain the boy's airway was clear, positioned the mask, and began breathing through it into the boy's mouth.

"You trained?" he asked Jessie, between breaths. "Good. Start compressions."

Kneeling beside the boy, she began the basic five-count rhythm of the CPR procedure while he maintained artificial resuscitation. Between breaths he used his radio to request help from the park staff.

They worked together efficiently until three park people showed up at a run and took over. Then Jessie slumped to a seat on one of the deck's wooden benches and watched until suddenly, with a couple of gasps, the boy began to breathe on his own. They halted the procedure while one of them felt again for a pulse. He nodded. "It's there. You can stop." Not long after that the boy was breathing shallowly but regularly, his chest consistently raising and lowering.

"You found him?" the ranger asked Jessie. "How long had he been there?"

"I don't know. I was in the pool for ten minutes before I noticed him, but I have no idea how long he was there before that."

"Who is he?"

Jessie hesitated slightly before saying, "I don't know that either."

It was true. She knew that he wasn't Patrick Cutler, but was it Patrick's other friend, Kim Fredricksen, one of the two who had come north from Wyoming to find him? If so, where was Patrick?

She felt the same way she had at Kiskatinaw, when she had withheld information from Inspector Webster, but short of trying to explain the whole unbelievable story, she could see no way to speculate on this boy's identity. He was alive, breathing, and what was most important was keeping him that way. An ambulance was on its way, probably police as well. She would wait till they arrived and make a decision then whether to try to explain or to make an attempt to reach Webster.

She didn't think his near drowning had been accidental, for in the midst of CPR she had seen that his neck was badly bruised. What appeared to be the finger marks of someone who had held him from behind were evident around his neck. Who?

"Can I go change clothes, please?" she asked the ranger.

He nodded but asked for the number of the space in which she had parked the Winnebago. "I'll find you if we have any more questions."

Retrieving her clothes from the bathhouse, she started slowly along the boardwalk toward the parking lot, feeling so tired, physically and mentally, that she could hardly move or think.

Just before the end of the boardwalk, she passed an older man and his wife headed for the hot springs and realized she had seen them before—in the parking lot at Fort Steele.

"Something wrong?" the man asked, turning to look after her.

"Someone almost drowned," she told him without stopping.

"Come, Mother." His words to his wife were the last Jessie heard as she moved away from them. "Let's go back to . . ."

What could have happened to the boy in the pool? Could it have been an accident? She didn't think he had drowned by himself any more than the boy at Kiskatinaw had jumped from the bridge. Who had held him under long enough for him to float like that? She remembered the dark red of the wet hair and her stomach lurched with apprehension. Oh God—not again.

CHAPTER 17

Maxie finished making a tuna salad and put it in the refrigerator to wait till Jessie came back from her soak in the hot springs. It was too fine an afternoon to sit indoors, so she settled comfortably in one of her padded lawn chairs with a tall glass of iced tea on the table beside her. Lacing her fingers behind her head, she leaned back and listened drowsily to the rustle of leaves in the light breeze and the chirping of the many small birds among them. Though it had been pleasant in Arizona, it was lovely to feel spring in the air again and especially nice that the rain had stopped. Periodically a car or motor home went by on the loop road, looking for a camping space, but resting peacefully, she didn't bother opening her eyes to see them pass.

On her trips up and down the highway, she had come more than once to the Liard campground and was fond of it. Later she would go out to the springs and spend some time in the pool herself, but not yet. It was enough simply to sit in the sun and think agreeable thoughts of the summer to come. For the moment she refused to consider what she had learned about the Wyoming case from the two law enforcement officers earlier in the day.

When she reached Anchorage, she planned to stock up on groceries and gardening supplies before heading on down the Kenai Peninsula to her house in Homer. Once they knew she was back, some fisherman pals of her first husband, Joe, would undoubtedly stop by with fresh halibut or salmon, as they had every year since his death. Though it was a welcome addition to her dinner table, she appreciated their gestures of friendship more than their fish.

She looked forward to cleaning her deck of whatever leaves and detritus the winter had left and to giving it a new coat of weatherproofing stain. There would be gardening to be done— she would need bedding plants to fill the flower beds around the yard. She had created a garden overlooking the bay, on the sunny southern side of the house, so her perennials would be up and growing well when she arrived. With long hours of Alaskan daylight, in July she could look forward to the deep blue of tall delphinium and a host of orange tiger lilies in bright contrast against them. This year she thought a basket or two of blue lobelia and white petunias might be attractive hanging from the edges of the roof over the deck.

Stretch, on his lead, had been snoozing contentedly on the indoor/outdoor carpet that she had laid down before setting out the chairs. He suddenly sat up and barked at the trees behind the Jayco. A squirrel chattered from among the limbs of one of them and Maxie shushed him. "Too quick and high for you, galah."

She leaned back in the chair and started to close her eyes again, but the determined dachshund was up and moving. Reaching the end of his tether, he barked again, and this time she heard something larger in the brush that separated her parking space from its northern neighbor. The bushes rustled loudly, and Stretch set up his usual complaint against intruders.

"Hush, you twit," she told him, listening carefully and with the beginnings of concern.

Whatever was in the brush, it was coming directly toward them and fast. A bear, frightened by someone else in the park and making a speedy getaway, would make this much noise. Thinking it might be wise to be inside the motor home, she quickly grabbed up Stretch, unclipped his lead, and moved toward the door. Before she could reach it, the source of the noise burst into the clearing, stumbled over the fire pit, and fell to his hands and knees on the ground.

It was a near-naked boy—barefoot and wearing only a pair of underwear shorts—a boy she recognized, though his damp hair was brown, not red. White-faced and plainly terrified of something, he stared up at her, mouth and eyes as wide as if he had seen a ghost. "Maxie?"

"*Patrick?* How did . . . What's the matter?"

Shoving Stretch into the Jayco, she stepped toward him as he scrambled frantically back to his feet, gulping in ragged breaths the air he had lost in his apparent effort to escape whatever had panicked him.

His body was scratched and dirty from his dash through the brush and roll on the ground. Wild-eyed and practically hysterical, he limped toward her on a foot he'd apparently injured in his flight over rough ground, and panted out a plea. "Please—hide me. He's *here*! He got Kim and he's—after me. *Please*, Maxie. I've gotta *get away*—gotta *hide*."

There was more crashing in the bushes through which he had come, as someone followed, in a hurry.

Without hesitation Maxie whirled and held open the door to the Jayco. Patrick leaped in and crouched on the floor below window level as she followed him and locked the door behind her.

Stretch was frantically barking again. With one hand she grasped his muzzle and held it closed. "No. No barking." When she let go he remained quiet, though alert and wary.

Listening intently she heard someone dash from the brush behind the motor home, pause, then start around it to the door. Patrick cowered on the floor in a huddle, hidden between two seats. Quickly Maxie backed into the shadows beyond the galley and out of sight from the open windows.

A sharp knock rattled the door in its frame. "Hey. Open up," a gruff voice she did not recognize demanded. "Anyone in there?" Another knock, then a hesitation. Feet moved on the outdoor carpeting, on dirt and gravel. She listened as they went around the rig. Then she could see the shape of a person peering in through the window opposite the door, but not well enough to identify him.

This encroachment was more than Stretch would tolerate. Flying onto the bench nearest the window, he barked aggressively into the face of the person looking in, startling him into a backward step or two.

"*Shit!*" Maxie heard him swear. "Just a goddammed dog!"

Motioning Patrick not to move, Maxie froze where she was, allowing Stretch to deal with the intruder in his best defensive style, though she was thankful that he was inside and his size not so obvious.

There was a long moment of silence. Then she heard footsteps walking away toward the loop road. Leaning out of her hiding place, she looked out and saw a man in jeans and a dark jacket disappear from sight beyond the sheltering trees. With a sigh of relief she stepped from the shadows and, finding her knees a little weak, sat down abruptly on the bench and took a deep breath, laying a hand on the dachshund's head.

"Good boy, Stretch. Good dog."

Turning to the boy, still huddled on the floor as small as he could make himself, she stared at him in astonishment. "Who the hell was that? Why was he chasing you?"

He looked up at her, tears of fright and anguish running down his freckled cheeks, still terribly pale.

"*That*," he told her, bitterness and distaste twisting his mouth, "was my bastard stepfather. Oh God. He's going to kill me, too. What am I going to do?"

Maxie frowned, considering the obvious extent of his anxiety and her own confusion. The adrenaline that had stimulated her heart to a pounding against her ribs dissipated slowly, leaving her limp with relief.

"I believe the first thing you'd better do is tell me what's going on. Then we can decide what to do about it. Get up off the floor while I find you a towel and something to put on. Then I'll get us both some iced tea."

"But he can see me if I get up."

Maxie looked cautiously out all the windows again and shook her head. "He's gone—at least for now—and all the doors are locked. I'll close the blinds so no one can look in."

She did so, then went for the towel and a shirt. Patrick, still trembling, climbed awkwardly to a seat at the table, put his elbows on it, and buried his face in his hands for a minute.

"Here," Maxie said, handing him the things she had brought, setting the liberally sugared tea in front of him, and sitting down across from him. "Drink that now and tell me."

He looked up at her, tears still running, and choked as he tried to speak. She waited patiently, and when he finally found his voice the words spilled out in a flood.

"I don't know how he found us. After he caught Lew, we drove to Summit Lake. When he showed up there we ran and hid, then we hitched to here—thought we lost him. We went out to the hot springs and got in with some other people—but they left and it was just us out there. I got out for a minute, but Kim was still in the pool. I came back from the dressing room and saw that bastard jump into the pool behind him and grab him around the neck. He pushed him under the water—and held him down—for a long time—till he quit fighting. I was really scared. I just couldn't move—didn't know what to do 'cause—he's really big. Then I started to run—to get away—to get somebody to help. But he heard me. He turned around and saw me running. I don't think he knew it was me—but he knew I'd seen him drown Kim. I mean—I think he thought Kim was me. That's why he jumped in the pool, see. Kim looked like me from behind because—"

"Because his hair was red," Maxie finished.

"How did you know?"

"Never mind that," she said anxiously, getting up from the table. "There's a lot more I want to know from you, but first we've got to go tell someone about your friend in the pool. He may not be dead, you know. But he's at least hurt and needs help as soon as we can get someone out there, so I've got to tell the park people."

Patrick shook his head and shrank against the wall by the dinette bench. "No, Maxie. I know he drowned Kim. I saw. I can't go out there. He'll be watching—he'll get me."

"You stay here, then."

"But what if he comes back? I tried to run and hide, but he found me before." He was shaking harder now, and she could see he was about to panic again, so she spoke quietly to calm him.

"It'll be fine. I'll leave Stretch, and with the blinds closed no one can see you in here. I'll be back as soon as I can—okay?"

"I guess so." But he clearly didn't like being left alone.

Maxie grabbed her keys, went to the door, and opened it to look carefully before getting out, but saw no one. From the ground she turned back to ask a last question.

"Jessie went out to the pools. Did you see her?"

"No. There wasn't anyone at the pool or on the boardwalk when I ran."

"You must have just missed her. I'll find her. You stay out of sight and keep the door locked."

* * *

Several park workers were hurrying back and forth along the boardwalk toward the hot springs pool when Maxie reached the parking lot, so she knew that someone had already found Patrick's friend Kim. Perhaps a dozen others—campers, or those who lived nearby and had come to use the pools—were standing in a ragged group close to the near end of the boardwalk, talking together in low voices full of tense curiosity. She didn't see Jessie anywhere, but a short man in a park uniform stopped her at the boardwalk.

"Sorry, ma'am. You can't go out, there's been an accident."

"I know. Is the young man alive?"

"I couldn't say. They're working on him now, and an ambulance is on its way, but it didn't look good."

"Have you seen a tall woman with short blond hair? Her name's Jessie Arnold, and I'm looking for her."

"I think she might be the one who was doing CPR on him, ma'am. She's still out there with them."

Maxie was about to tell him that she must see Jessie right

away—that it was an emergency—but looking up saw her coming toward them on the boardwalk. She was still wearing her blue bathing suit and carried her clothes and towel. Her expression was troubled, and she looked very tired. She was not walking with her usual easy stride but moved as if she was taking care how her feet found the walkway. She raised a hand to let Maxie know she had seen her waiting, but did not increase her moderate speed. As she reached the two who watched her, she shook her head unhappily.

"He's not dead," she said in an odd clipped voice. "He finally started breathing, but it's not good. The RCMP and paramedics are coming. They'll take care of it. Let's go back to the rig, Maxie." To the ranger, "The other ranger has my space number if you need me for anything else."

He nodded, and they walked away. Maxie watched her closely and waited until they could not be overheard before telling her, "Patrick's in the Jayco. Says his stepfather tried to kill that boy—one of those friends of his that Loomis mentioned—Kim something."

"Kim Fredricksen?" Jessie abruptly stopped walking and turned to stare at her with a confused frown. "Patrick? I was afraid it was him when I found that boy in the pool!"

"*You* found him?"

"Yeah," she admitted, almost in tears remembering. "After I'd spent about ten minutes soaking without even seeing him. He was floating right there by the dam. Maybe if I'd seen him sooner . . . How did Patrick find you?"

"Accidentally fell out of the brush and into my space—all scratched and bruised from running through the woods. He was almost hysterical—scared to death. His stepfather was right behind him. We hid in the Jayco and he pounded on the door till Stretch barked at him, and he went away."

Jessie's shoulders drooped and she gave Maxie an exhausted look. "What the hell do we do now? I'm not inclined to try explaining all this to these people who don't know anything about it, are you? It's more than I'm worth right now. Besides, there's Patrick to think of. He shouldn't be there if his stepfather comes back."

"Somebody has to tell them something. We can't let that boy just . . . be nameless. You didn't tell them who you thought he was, did you?" She stopped, but Jessie knew what she meant—the boy Kim needed to be identified and proper care taken to notify his family in Wyoming. He was somebody's son, after all.

"Loomis—and Inspector Webster—should be here. It's their case. Can we get hold of them?"

Maxie stood thinking for a minute, then nodded emphatically.

"Yes, but wherever they are it's going to take them time to get here. I think we should get Patrick out of here—on up the road somewhere. How about this? Why don't you go on back, get dressed, and take care of Patrick—see if you can find him something to wear besides that denim shirt of mine. Get your rig ready to go, and we'll take off just as soon as I get back. I'll find a phone and give the Dawson Creek RCMP a jingle—find out where Webster and Loomis are and how soon they can get here—talk to one of them if I can. But you'd better not tell Patrick that I'm calling the police. We don't want him to do another runner. He thinks his friend Kim is dead, so be sure to tell him that he's not."

"Where shall we go?"

"As far as we can, I think. Got any suggestions?"

Jessie thought a minute about the route ahead and what she remembered. "It's about three hours to Teslin. There's a place called Dawson Peaks Resort just this side of it, right on the lake, where we could get both motor homes out of sight from anyone passing on the highway."

"Works for me. You?"

It worked fine for Jessie, though the thought of three more hours of driving would not have been her first choice. Still, she agreed that it seemed wise to take Patrick somewhere else. There were a lot of questions she wanted answered—just not right now. It all seemed too much to handle, and more than anything she wished she were home in Knik—even if home was only a tent until her new cabin was built. But there was also a red-hot spark of anger at everything that seemed to be closing in around them.

CHAPTER 18

Maxie found a phone outside the park entrance by the highway and called the RCMP in Dawson Creek, reasoning that since Inspector Webster's office was there, they should know where and how to find him. The dispatcher, hearing the facts of the near death at Liard and Maxie's connection with Webster at Summit Lake, told her what she had anticipated—that he was out of the office, somewhere on the highway, and it would take a while to find him. But if Ms. McNabb would please wait by the phone, she would call back very soon.

With nothing to do but wait impatiently, anxious to go back to Patrick and Jessie, Maxie paced back and forth for almost half an hour within hearing distance of the phone. She saw several cars, trucks, and motor homes turn off the highway into the park. Some almost immediately drove back out, turned away, she imagined, from use of the hot springs pool.

She was considering another call to Dawson Creek when she

was surprised to see a familiar eighteen-wheeler pull into the large open lot across the highway—overflow parking for the crowds that sometimes filled the parking spaces inside the park. She had imagined him far up the road ahead of them but was very glad to see Butch Stringer climb down from his Peterbilt and raise a hand in her direction.

"Hey, Maxie. You the welcoming committee? How's Jessie?" he called, starting across the highway to where she stood.

"How'd you leave Summit before we did and wind up behind us?" she asked.

"Some of the load shifted. I had to stop at Toad River and take care of it."

He had almost reached her when the phone rang and she hurried to answer it.

The dispatcher's message was that Inspector Webster was on his way to Liard Hot Springs. He had requested that she stay in the campground so he could find her when he arrived. Would she do that?

"Well—yes, if I can," she agreed, though not really happy with staying put. "But tell him that if I'm not here, I'll be on the road north—with good reason. Is Detective Loomis with him?" she asked, and was assured that he was. "How long will it be?"

The dispatcher wasn't sure but predicted something over an hour.

As she hung up the phone and turned back to Stringer, who had been waiting near enough to listen, an ambulance drove up and turned in through the park gate. He watched it pass and a questioning frown creased his forehead, replacing his smile of greeting.

"More trouble?"

"Afraid so," she told him. "I've got to get back to the Jayco. If you'll walk with me, I'll fill you in on the way and give you lunch, if you haven't eaten."

              •   •   •

Jessie had hurried back to the Jayco, found all its blinds down, and knocked on the door.

"Patrick," she called, "it's me—Jessie. Maxie said you were here. Let me in."

There was no answer, but she could hear the dachshund pattering around inside. He whined but didn't bark, recognizing her voice.

"Patrick—it's okay," she said again, assuming he was afraid to answer her, but there was no response at all.

She tried the door handle, and to her surprise it opened easily to show her Stretch waiting inside—no one else. Stepping in she looked quickly around, expecting to see Patrick Cutler, but the motor home was empty. Two glasses stood on the table, one empty, one almost full. She picked up a towel from the bench and felt its dampness—he'd been there, but where was he now? Had something frightened him into running again? Had his stepfather come back and somehow forced him to open the door? Maybe he was hiding nearby, somewhere outside.

She stepped back out, closing the door behind her to keep Stretch inside, and called for Patrick. No one answered.

Having no idea where he'd gone she couldn't go after him, but maybe he would come back. She decided to change her clothes and wait for him or Maxie, whoever showed up first.

Knowing Maxie had the keys, she locked the coach door from inside, then let herself out the driver's door, locking it before she closed it. Walking across the road to the Winnebago, she climbed in, shutting the screen but leaving the door open so she could watch the road and the Jayco. Tank came out to greet her from under the table where he had been taking a nap, and she sat for a minute to pet him.

"You are such a good guy," she told him. "Bet you'd like to go out, wouldn't you?"

He had been so patient and good, even in the last day or two when she had been paying very little attention to him. So much had happened and she had been so focused on herself and the confusion around her that all she had done was feed and water him and take him out for short walks when necessary. Well, she would take him out now.

She had noticed the chairs by the Jayco. It would be nice to sit there for a while, and when Maxie came back they could have something to eat. She thought she might be hungry by then, though now she still felt a bit nauseous. Once she had seen the heavy bruises on the boy's arms, shoulders, and neck, she had been unexpectedly and thoroughly sick in the bushes beyond the deck.

Again she wondered where Patrick could have gone and worried about him. According to Maxie, he had been afraid of the stepfather who was chasing him and who had evidently assaulted the boy in the pool. Why would he leave a secure place inside the motor home and take off again—especially without his clothes? But she did not want to speculate—there had been too much of that. Refusing to think about it, she got up and went to dress so she could take Tank out into the sunshine. Who knew how long it would last? How long did anything seem to last on this trip? Not peace of mind, certainly.

Quickly she slipped out of her bathing suit, hung it to dry in the shower, and still feeling shaky and a little chilly, dressed in a pair of jeans, sweatshirt, and tennis shoes with socks. Thirsty after her time in the hot water, she took a can of tomato juice from the refrigerator, put a handful of dog treats for Tank and some crackers for herself in her pocket, fastened the leash to his collar, and went across to the Jayco, where she sat down in the sun to try to relax for a few minutes.

She had been there for perhaps five minutes when Tank suddenly sat up from his place at her feet and she heard the crunch of feet on gravel directly behind her. Starting to turn, she suddenly felt a hard cold metal object against the back of her neck.

"This is a gun. Don't move and don't yell," a gruff male voice told her sharply. "Just sit still and listen—very carefully."

Tank, now up on all four feet, growled and bared his teeth menacingly, alertly watching whoever was behind her, ready to spring to her defense.

"Keep that dog still if you don't want to lose him."

Still holding the leash, she pulled it up short and held it firmly. "Sit, Tank. Stop that."

Reluctantly, he did, watching the man behind her alertly.

"Now," the voice behind her said, "when I tell you, you will get up and tie that dog to the picnic table. Then you will walk across to your motor home. You won't look around and you won't try anything stupid." The pressure on her neck eased and the coldness disappeared, though she felt it was still there somewhere close. "Do it now."

Carefully, slowly, Jessie got up and did as she was told.

Holding Tank to a walk close beside her, she moved to the heavy picnic table that the park provided in each space and fastened Tank's leash to one wooden leg of it. Thinking fast, she did not tie it into a secure knot, but only looped the leash around itself once. He would be able to pull it loose if he tried, and she knew he would before long.

"Sit," she told him firmly. He sat again and looked up at her, doing what he was told but clearly not happy about it. "Stay, good dog." She walked away from him and didn't look back, knowing that at least as long as he could see or hear her he would remain where she had left him. Thank God he was so well trained.

As she walked she could hear footsteps behind her—more than enough for one person. Someone whimpered—Patrick? Reaching the road, she glanced along it in both directions without moving her head, but no one was in sight. She walked on, slowly but steadily, without hesitating, and when she reached the coach door, stopped, waiting for instructions.

"Open the screen and get in very slowly. Lean forward and put your hands flat on the table as far in front of you as you can and spread your legs." It was a position from which it would be difficult to move quickly—a law enforcement position. Patrick's stepfather was supposed to be a policeman in Wyoming, wasn't he?

Again she did what she was told and waited for what would happen next, her heart in her throat. There was a scramble, then a thump, as someone was shoved in and fell against the back of her legs. Glancing under one arm, she caught a glimpse of long bare legs on the floor—it *was* Patrick. The door was slammed shut, she heard the sound of the lock, and her captor stepped up into the coach. Abruptly he kicked hard at the boy, who grunted and cried out as the heavy boot connected with his body.

"Move," the voice said. "Get out of the way, you little shit. Get up there on that bench and be still. It's your own fault you were scared and dumb enough to open the door."

There was another scramble as Patrick complied, yelping as he was assisted forward with another kick.

Then Jessie could see him more clearly as he huddled to her left in the seat against the outside wall. The denim shirt that Maxie had mentioned covered his arms, back, and shoulders but flapped open in front, unbuttoned. He was so pale she thought he might faint, and his ragged breathing was accompanied by sobs he was attempting to suppress. Drawing up his long legs, he wrapped the tails of the shirt around them, hugging himself into as small a space as possible. His face was tear-stained and terrified as he looked up at her, but as his stepfather turned his attention back to Jessie, she saw Patrick give him a swift glance full of anger and hatred, so he evidently hadn't had quite all the resistance beaten out of him.

"Now," her captor said to her. "You will get behind the wheel, start this thing, and drive it out of here. Keep in mind that I will be right behind you with this gun aimed in your direction. You try anything and I'll shoot one of you—and I don't much care which one."

"Don't you have your own wheels?" she asked, straightening and turning to look him in the face, trying to think of something—anything she could do to keep from following his orders.

He was a big man, with muscled arms and shoulders, though he carried extra weight around his waist and stomach. As blond as his stepson was—normally—red-haired, he wore a dark jacket, jeans, and western boots. A pair of sunglasses concealed his eyes, but not his belligerent expression, or his anger.

"My truck's in the parking lot with all those goddammed people, where I can't get it," he snarled. "So we're taking this rig. Get up there and drive—*now*."

CHAPTER 19

Maxie and Stringer had gone only a few steps back into the park and she had started to tell him about the attempted drowning at the pool, when she heard a heavy rig coming from the campground loop road. Moving to the side of the road, she looked up to see a Winnebago like Jessie's coming toward her. It was moving faster than the park's allowed speed limit and did not slow as it approached, though she knew the driver had to be able to see that there were people on the road ahead. As it reached them, then sped past, throwing gravel from its tires as it swung around a bend in the road, she got a look at the person behind the wheel.

The rig wasn't *like* Jessie's—it was Jessie's—and Jessie was driving. She passed without a wave, or any indication that Maxie and Butch Stringer were anyone that she knew, staring straight ahead except for one quick glance in their direction, leaving them behind in the dust. Hardly slowing and without stopping, she swung the motor home onto the highway so fast it rocked, headed north. But her expression had told Maxie all she needed to know. Tight with stress and fear, eyes wide, every line of her face silently shouted *help!* And running full out behind the Winnebago was Tank, dragging his leash behind him.

Stringer, quicker than Maxie imagined the big man could be, leaped out and caught the trailing leash to stop the dog from dashing onto the highway. Jerked to an abrupt halt, Tank struggled for a minute, straining to keep after the motor home, but finally gave up and looked up resentfully at his captor.

"Hey, buddy," Stinger said, crouching down and pulling the animal toward him gently. "That's not a good idea, however much you want to go. Wasn't that Jessie?" he asked Maxie, in confusion. "I thought—"

"Yes," she told him grimly, a tide of alarm washing through her. "It was Jessie—and something's really wrong."

＊　＊　＊

As they went hurriedly back to the Jayco, Maxie told Stringer about the boy in the pool, Patrick's sudden reappearance, and the man he said was his stepfather. She also filled him in on what Webster and Loomis had said at Summit Lake about the death of Patrick's mother in Wyoming.

"So the stepfather told the police that the kid did the killing," he said thoughtfully.

"That's what Loomis says."

"What does the kid say?"

"He hasn't said anything—refused to talk about it when he was riding with me, and I didn't have time to ask when he showed up here today."

"Could he have run off because he did it?"

Maxie glanced at him, disturbed at the thought. She hadn't considered this point of view seriously, but it was good to have someone who could take an outsider's look at the situation.

"I think if you had met Patrick, you might not think so, but . . ." She heard herself use the qualifying word, and a vague cloud of doubt drifted into her mind.

"Maybe not. You're right, I haven't met him—or his stepfather," Stringer agreed. "Besides, it could work just as well the other way around. If the stepfather *was* beating his wife, he could have killed her—on purpose or not. If he's a cop, and he and the kid didn't get along, who're the police going to believe? If I was Patrick, I'd have hauled myself out of there just as fast as I could, too. But why come in this direction?"

"The friend in Fairbanks, he said."

"Maybe it's time to talk to that friend. Do you know his name?"

"Only Dave something. I don't know how we'd find him."

They reached the Jayco, she unlocked the door, and they climbed in, greeted enthusiastically by Stretch, who was pleased to see Tank. But the husky seemed anything but glad. He wanted to be going after his mistress, who for some odd reason had gone off with a stranger he didn't like and had left him behind. He paced through the motor home, ignoring the dachshund, finally sitting down by the closed door, clearly hoping to be let out again.

Maxie watched him in growing concern.

"What am I going to do about Jessie? I don't know why she'd take off like that unless he came back and forced her."

"The stepfather, you mean."

"Yes. She looked desperate, and she'd never go off without Tank. I've got a terrible feeling about it, and I'd go after her right now if I hadn't promised to wait for Webster and that

Wyoming detective, Loomis. Besides, I don't know what I'd do if I found her."

"Loomis is another cop from Wyoming? One of the stepfather's cronies?"

It was another idea that had not seriously occurred to her. Was Loomis, hunting Patrick because he wanted to help or hurt him? Could he actually be in league with the stepfather, Mac—something? She wished she could remember his name. "Dammit. Am I as senile as my daughter thinks I am?" she burst out in frustration and anger at herself.

"Hey." Stringer laid a hand on her arm and gently swung her around to face him. "How would it be if I headed on up the road toward Watson Lake and looked for Jessie on the way? That rig of hers'll be pretty easy to spot if I can catch up with her—she was moving pretty fast. If the stepfather's with her, he's probably got her *and* the boy—two hostages, so I won't try anything, just see if I can find them and see where they're headed. You stay here and wait for the cops. The closest RCMP unit is in Watson Lake. The inspector can let them know she's coming their direction. Do you know her license number?"

Maxie shook her head. She had never noticed, though it had been there right next to her for several nights. But his idea was sound, and she told him so with relief. He would also be more help to Jessie than she could, if it came to that. "She may be going too fast for you to catch up."

"If she's not being forced to drive but had some other reason to leave, there's no problem. She'll slow down and I'll catch her. If she is being forced, she's no dummy. She knows we saw her go out the gate. If it were you, wouldn't you expect somebody to follow you? And wouldn't you go as slow as you could to give them a chance?"

She agreed that she would, and in seconds he was gone, without the lunch he'd been promised, but neither of them remembered or cared. Tank tried to get out of the Jayco with him but was restrained by Maxie.

"Better keep close track of him or he'll take off on you. That's one loyal dog," Stringer observed, and jogged off in the direction of his Peterbilt.

Knowing Stringer would shortly be speeding up the highway with his eyes open for Jessie's rig allowed Maxie to feel a little better about waiting for Webster and Loomis, but it seemed like a very long time before they finally showed up at her door.

∗   ∗   ∗

Jessie was driving the road that followed the winding Liard River more west than north from the provincial park. She kept her eyes on the highway and a heavy foot on the accelerator, as instructed, and wondered what, if anything, she could do about the situation without getting someone hurt or killed—either Patrick or herself.

The boy had been forced to close all the blinds so that no one could see into the coach section of the motor home and was now huddled again close to the window on the dinette bench across from his stepfather, who sat directly behind the driver's seat. Jessie could almost feel the handgun, though he had kept it away from her neck. Since the speed at which he was requiring her to go made it essential to keep all her attention on the road ahead, she didn't look around.

The motor home rocked with centrifugal force as she took curves too fast, and it all but bounded from the rise of several small bridges. Finally the highway widened and grew straighter, allowing her to relax her back, neck, and arms, which were aching from the tension of her grip on the wheel and the concentration needed to keep the Winnebago on the road and in its lane. The few approaching vehicles passed in a blur.

"Do you have a name?" she asked glancing in the rearview mirror, trying to start some sort of dialogue with the man behind her.

"Just keep driving," he told her sharply.

They covered the sixty-five miles from Liard Hot Springs to the truck stop and highway maintenance camp of Fireside in just over an hour. Jessie allowed the Winnebago to slow slightly when she saw the gas pumps in front of the small restaurant and motel that were approaching on the left.

"Don't stop," he growled from behind her.

"Take a look at the fuel gauge," she told him as calmly as possible. "If you want to go much farther, we've got to get gas."

There was a moment of silence as he leaned forward to check for himself.

"Okay," he told her finally. "Do it, but don't go inside. Let them pump the gas and pay them out here, where I can see and hear you. Act normal, and remember that if you try anything, I'll use this gun—on Patrick first, then on you and whoever else may be out there. Got it?"

She climbed down slowly to meet the attendant, an older man, who walked from the office to fill the tank for her.

"Where you headed?" he asked with a friendly grin.

"Ah—Alaska." She did not return his smile.

"New Winnebago. Nice looking."

"Thanks," she told him, trying not to look frightened but finding words hard in her terrible consciousness of the hidden gunman who was monitoring the exchange.

"Turned out to be a pretty nice day, didn't it?" he said, waiting for the pump to stop.

"Yes."

He gave her a questioning look. Clearly noting her reluctance and feeling personally snubbed, he stopped trying to engage her in conversation. Finishing the job, he took the credit card she handed him, and disappeared into the office with a shrug. She waited, longing to follow him—to get out of range—to tell him to call the police—but intensely aware of what might happen to Patrick, held hostage inside the coach, if she moved in that direction. The attendant was a nice man and she felt sorry for offending him.

He came back with the receipt and she signed it. Taking the copy he shoved at her, she climbed back into the driver's seat and started the engine. He didn't wait to watch her pull the motor home back onto the highway. Glancing into the mirror outside the left window, she could see him walking away, shaking his head in disgust at the behavior of uppity tourists.

"Get going."

She took the Winnebago up to seventy on the speedometer and put it on cruise control, grateful for the wide smooth highway that allowed her to rest her foot and leg, then remembered that she couldn't allow the speed to drop unless she controlled it, and shut it off. Below the left side of the road the Liard River, now deeper and wider, made a huge bend. Beyond it she could see Goat Mountain with its distinctive flat top. Away from tall trees, she could see far across the rolling hills to a series of low mountains in the west. Fluffy white clouds were sailing across the blue sky overhead and seemed to be piling up against those hills. She hoped it wouldn't rain again.

They sped past several turnouts, including one that Jessie remembered was famous as a lookout where early outlaws waited to rob boats that floated down the river. Bridges took them across Contact Creek, where the southern sector of the Alaska Highway had been completed, and Irons Creek, where the construction workers stopped their trucks to put on winter chains, making it possible to climb the following hill.

The highway turned more to the west, and as the sun sank lower in the sky and into her eyes, Jessie wondered what to expect from this stepfather of Patrick's. She considered running the motor home off the road, but the shoulders were soft and very steep, and the result could be disastrous. As long as they were moving she felt a little safer, but they would have to stop somewhere—sometime. Then what?

She hoped Maxie would do *something*—tell someone that she had left the campground under suspicious circumstances. But what if she thought Jessie had merely taken Patrick and gone, as they planned? She could only hope her unexpected and premature exit without Tank had let Maxie know something was wrong.

If Maxie had been able to reach Inspector Webster on the phone, perhaps he would do something—call the RCMP ahead of them, maybe. She didn't know whether to feel good about that possibility or not, having a feeling that law enforcement officers would tend to respect each other's word about who was guilty, even though they lived and worked in different countries. Would her abductor be able to talk his way out of trouble if they were stopped? She decided she would rather have the opportunity to find out than to go on driving with no help at all, and hoped to see a patrol car somewhere along the road. If she saw one, could she alert them somehow? Turn on her emergency blinkers? Possibly, but they made a clicking sound that would be audible to her captor.

She had been surprised to see Stringer walking with Maxie as she drove out of the Liard Hot Springs campground. Was there anything he could do? Was he now somewhere on the road behind her in that big eighteen-wheel rig of his? She hoped so. Though he probably would not be able to catch them, the idea that he might try was a little comforting. Or would Maxie have taken the Jayco to the road after her? Wherever she was, Jessie hoped Maxie had Tank with her. It had been hard to leave him tied to the table in that camping space, even knowing he could pull himself loose. She hadn't wanted to leave him helplessly tethered but didn't want him lost trying to find her either.

Damn this monster with the gun. Where was he taking them? He must have something specific in mind. Or was he just going as fast as possible to somewhere else? According to Patrick he had killed the boy at the bridge and tried to kill the one in the pool. Would he kill two more when she had driven him to wherever he decided was far enough? There wasn't anywhere to go except farther northwest on this route. You couldn't get off this highway—you had to drive its length, from Fort Nelson to Whitehorse, before any roads took you away from it in directions that wouldn't end abruptly or simply bring you back to it somewhere else.

No, she suddenly remembered. That wasn't entirely true anymore. The Cassiar Highway connected with the Alaska Highway just fifteen miles west of Watson Lake, the next community of size. The north/south-running Cassiar had been completed through British Columbia in the early 1970s but had been such a rough trip that most travelers refused to use it, leaving it to freight and logging trucks. Though still mostly gravel, with fewer services and towns than the Alaska Highway, it ran farther to the west and was now much improved. It had a reputation for spectacular scenery, ran closer to the coast, and connected via an access road with Stewart, British Columbia, and Hyder, Alaska, communities previously reachable only by air or water. Would this man force them to take the Cassiar—hoping to escape pursuit? It was possible. In only thirty miles or so they would arrive in Watson Lake, so she would soon know. She wished she knew more about the man himself, for she had no way to judge his personality or assess his attitude. The few curt, demanding words he had spoken on this wild ride had done nothing to increase her confidence.

He had removed his sunglasses, and in the rearview mirror she had periodically been able to catch glimpses of his eyes, remote and always alert, but not clearly, for the closed blinds darkened the coach behind her considerably. He sat sideways on the dinette bench, leaning on the back of it, watching the road they traveled through the windshield.

How was the boy doing? She tried to look, but he was out of sight to the left behind her. Maybe she could get away with speaking to him.

"Patrick? Are you okay?"

"Shut it," came the immediate response from the stepfather. "He's asleep."

Jessie was grateful for that, knowing how frightened Patrick had been when he climbed into the motor home. She put her attention into driving—and watching closely for any opportunity to change the balance of power under the circumstances. The farther they traveled, the angrier she grew. It was an intolerable situation that she would do something about if she were given any chance that wouldn't put herself or Patrick in more peril than they were in already.

C H A P T E R

Arriving in Watson Lake, a community of almost 1,800 people with its businesses laid out along both sides of the highway like beads on a string, Jessie slowed to comply with the speed limit and, as instructed, cruised through the town at what seemed a crawl compared with the rate at which she had been driving. Halfway along this main street, she saw the building that housed the RCMP, a squad car parked in front, and tried to think of something she could do to attract attention. Could she swing hard enough onto the access road that ran beside the highway to knock her captor off his feet? Oncoming traffic made that impossible. Should she attempt to sideswipe a car? She thought the possibility of injuring someone too great to risk.

"Don't even think about it," the familiar voice behind her warned, and she realized she had eased back on the accelerator as she scrambled for an idea.

She could hear Patrick moving behind her and caught a glimpse of him in the rearview mirror, sitting up at the table, roused by the change in sound and speed.

They were now almost through the small town, and coming up on the right Jessie recognized a service station from a prior trip. Beyond it, across a small gravel road, lay one of the most famous attractions of the Alaska Highway, the Watson Lake Signpost Forest.

The Signpost Forest had been started in 1942 when a U.S. Army soldier who was working on highway construction nailed a sign to a post with his name and hometown written on it: Carl K. Lindley, Danville, Illinois. Through the years that followed, passing travelers put up thousands of their own signs to join his original effort, until a whole forest of tall poles arose, decorated with an astonishing assortment of notices—everything from hand-painted scraps of lumber to intricately carved works of art, from battered street signs to colorful city advertisements—anything that could bear names, origins, and dates of travel. In the middle of this forest of wayfarers were some interesting old graders and other pieces of machinery that had been used in building the highway.

Twice before, Jessie had taken time to wander through the signs and been fascinated with all the countries represented and the names of people who had left their mark in this unique way. On one of the earliest poles, she remembered seeing a sign dated 1953 with the names of a whole family carefully printed on it: George Washburn, Cynthia Washburn, David and Carol Washburn, Wilmington, Delaware. Under their names, George had written, "I helped build this road." It seemed to have been repainted at one time or another. Below this was a second sign: David and Ruth Washburn, George Washburn, Baltimore, Maryland, 1965; and under that, another: George Washburn, Cheryl Washburn, Tracy and Michael Washburn, Anchorage, Alaska, 1979, 1982, 1986, 1991.

Jessie recalled standing for several minutes, picturing George bringing his wife and children to see what he had helped to build and nailing up a record of that trip. She had imagined the son, David, and his family, adding their own record and repainting his father's original, and the grandson, named for his grandfather, doing the same as he moved to Alaska, then recording the dates of subsequent trips back and forth on the highway. She had wondered if Michael would someday add another.

As if in response to her fervent wish to have things be normal, to be able to go and see if he had, the man behind her spoke.

"Turn in there, to the right, and park behind the hotel."

As demanded, Jessie pulled off and around to the back of the Watson Lake Hotel, where she eased the Winnebago into a space beyond another motor home. Discouraged, she knew that anyone following would now be unable to see her rig and would continue on out of town, thinking she was still ahead.

"Get up slow and come back here," her captor said from the rear of the coach. "Get him something to wear. And don't try anything stupid."

She did as she was told, tossing Patrick a pair of her own jeans from the closet, which fit well enough, for they were close to the same size in height and slenderness. As he pulled them on, he gave her a fearful, dispirited look, but there was also anger in his face and she hoped he wouldn't be foolish in his panic.

"Open the door. We're going into the hotel," she was informed. "You and the kid'll go first and stand against the wall by the phone that's just inside the door. I've got a call to make, but I'll have this gun in my pocket, so don't make any mistakes. Got that?"

Jessie nodded and did as she was told. Opening the door, she stepped out into the parking lot and waited until Patrick joined her. With their captor close behind, they walked side by side along the walk. She was reaching for the handle of the door when it unexpectedly flew open and a young couple came hurriedly out.

Suddenly five people were bumping into each other in confusion.

"Sorry," the young man said, and the girl who held his hand giggled.

With two strangers between him and his captor, Patrick took instant advantage of the situation and bolted. In seconds he had reached the end of the walk that continued the length of the building and vanished around the corner at a dead run. Jessie, with people still in the way, was unable to follow and spun around to see if she could delay the man behind her.

"Get out of my way," he barked, shoving the amused girl to her knees in his attempt to push past her.

"Hey!" her escort yelled. Angrily he grabbed at the other man's arm, but missed and fell. Jessie was the only obstacle left, and without hesitating she hurled herself into his path but was straight-armed in the process and knocked down as well. With a quick change of direction, he dodged her attempt to catch his ankle and ran off after Patrick, who was visible for a moment or two as he ran into the Signpost Forest and was swallowed up among the hundreds of signs.

"What the hell's his problem?" growled the young man as he helped his girlfriend to her feet. He turned to Jessie. "Are you okay?"

But Jessie, realizing that chasing after Patrick would do no good at all, picked herself up and ran back to the Winnebago without answering his question. Climbing in, she closed and locked the coach door and made her way quickly to the driver's seat, where she had left the keys in the ignition.

Before she could drive away, she had to back up and swing wide to avoid hitting the motor home in front of her—a behemoth, larger than a bus. Clearing it by inches, she drove back around the hotel, headed for the highway, and swung the Winnebago onto it.

Between the highway and the Signpost Forest was a wide space for vehicles to pull off the road. She drove into it and between two cars and a truck with a trailer attached, looking anxiously for Patrick among the posts covered with signs. *Forest* was the right word for the collection, for the signposts were as impossible to see through as real trees with branches, obstructing vision for any distance greater than a few yards. Keeping the motor home inching forward, she kept searching. He had to be somewhere, unless he had been recaptured already, but she thought his dash had been quicker than the lumbering gallop of the gunman chasing him. He wouldn't be easily caught.

Glancing ahead to see how much room she had left in the pull-off space, she caught a glimpse of motion among the signposts, and Patrick dashed out into the far end of the space ahead of her. Her foot came down heavily on the accelerator as she simultaneously beat on the horn with her fist. Still running, he turned his head and saw her coming, glanced behind him, then swerved toward the Winnebago as she pulled up beside him and stopped. Behind him in the Signpost Forest she could see his pursuer coming fast.

As Patrick reached the passenger side of the motor home, Jessie suddenly saw that the door was locked and realized that the button to unlock it was too far away to reach without leaving the driver's seat. Jamming the gearshift into park, she leaped for the door as Patrick madly tried to yank it open from outside. There ensued a few seconds of frantic struggle in which the two worked against each other and neither was able to open the door.

"Leave it alone," Jessie shouted desperately at the boy and was finally able to pull up the button, just as the man behind him broke out from the signposts.

"Get in! *Get in* and lock the door!" she yelled, scrambling back into the driver's seat and wrenching the motor home into gear. Behind them she could hear the man shouting four-letter words and knew he would try to catch the vehicle, which was not yet moving fast enough to leave him behind. Patrick leaped in and tried to slam the door as she drove forward, speed increasing as they moved, but their pursuer caught hold of the door frame with one hand, attempting to pull himself close enough to climb in.

"*No,*" the boy screamed, and opening the door a few inches, he slammed it hard on the grappling fingers. A howl of pain was the immediate result and the injured hand disappeared. In the sideview mirror, Jessie saw him trip and fall to his hands and knees in the dirt.

Patrick solidly shut the door and locked it.

Looking back she could see that the figure was growing smaller in the mirror but was up and running after them.

"I'm going to have to stop for traffic," she warned Patrick, "and he's still coming."

He slid lower in the passenger seat as she slowed to a halt and waited for a pickup and two cars to pass on the highway. Then, with a startled cry he flinched away from the glass as the furious face of their captor appeared at the window.

"Let me in, you bitch," he screamed, brandishing the handgun he had taken from his pocket and pounding it on the glass barrier between them.

Without hesitation Jessie stepped hard on the gas and pulled out into the path of another passenger car. The driver stood on his brakes to avoid hitting them, and as she rolled past she could hear his horn blaring and see that he was shouting furiously, incensed at her seeming stupidity.

The face and handgun outside the passenger window vanished as they swung right and careened onto the road, in a cloud of dust and flying gravel. She hoped that someone would report a wild man waving an illegal handgun to the RCMP, but was not at all inclined to hang around to see if it happened. Police were seldom there when you needed them, and except for the squad car at the police building, she hadn't seen evidence of one anywhere in Watson Lake.

The satisfaction she felt at escaping their captor was nothing compared with Patrick's relief and appreciation. He watched the man disappear behind them and turned to Jessie with tears running down his face.

"He would have killed us. I know he would." He slumped back against the seat and scrubbed at his dirty face with both fists.

Jessie didn't like to have people walking around in the motor home while it was moving, but it seemed a good idea to give him something to do at the moment. Her mouth was dry from apprehension, but she was not about to stop anywhere soon in search of something to drink. She meant to keep driving until she reached the resort where she and Maxie had agreed to meet.

"Go back and wash your face and hands," she told Patrick. "There's a T-shirt in the right-hand closet if you want it—and some socks. Get whatever you want to eat or drink, and bring me something to drink—anything—from the frig when you come back."

Periodically she watched behind them and carefully examined the driver in any vehicle that passed, not trusting that Patrick's stepfather would give up. If he could steal a car, she thought he would, and might come after them. What could she do to make it impossible for him to find them?

There were a few turnoffs, but none of them led any distance off the road, and if she allowed her enemy to pass while she hunted a hiding place, he would be able to simply wait and watch for them. Without stopping, there was no way to contact the police, and pulling off the road to make a phone call could let their pursuer reach them precious minutes before the RCMP.

The Cassiar Highway. Though she had been afraid earlier that she would be forced to turn down it, *now* it would suit her purpose to do so. By heading south away from the Alaska Highway, she could disappear quickly down a road she would not be expected to take. It would mean losing contact with Maxie, but she could find a telephone later and call the resort where they had agreed to meet with an explanation of her failure to turn up. Less than fifteen miles ahead of them now, the Cassiar seemed a safer alternative, if only they could reach it first.

Patrick was soon back in the passenger seat, his seat belt securely fastened, munching on peanuts from a package he had found in the cupboard. She missed Tank and worried about him, hoping again that he was with Maxie and Stretch. In no other circumstances would she ever have left him, but there was no way she could go back for him now, or stop and wait for them to catch up. She concentrated on driving as quickly as possible to the Cassiar Highway junction.

*   *   *

With half a tank of diesel, Butch Stringer had not stopped at Fireside but had gone barreling up the road, gaining ten minutes on the Winnebago, though he had no way of knowing it. In just over two hours he had driven the 136 miles between Liard Hot

Springs and Watson Lake without a break, slowly closing the gap between himself and the motor home, going faster than he normally would have, but he was a good driver, and most of the distance lay over a road that was well-paved and wide, with plenty of room.

He cruised slowly through Watson Lake, looking for Jessie's Winnebago in the parking lot of every motel, restaurant, service station, and grocery he could see, to no avail. In the middle of town he stopped to grab a burger to go and gobbled it down at the north end while he had the tank filled with diesel at a station next door to the Signpost Forest.

Having seen it all before, Stringer hardly glanced at the display of poles and signs as he pulled out of the gas station, still looking for Jessie's motor home. A tow truck pulling a car into the station for repairs distracted him just long enough to miss a glimpse of the Winnebago, parked almost out of sight at the back of the nearby Watson Lake Hotel, so he drove off without knowing he had been within sight of it and headed out of town.

Thirteen miles up the road, almost to the junction with Highway 37, the Cassiar Highway, he was coming to a turnout with a litter barrel on the right side of the road when a red pickup with a camper hurriedly pulled away from it onto the highway, a boat on a trailer behind it, its driver stubbornly resolved to get ahead of the Peterbilt, though he should have waited for the truck to pass.

"Damn fool," Stringer muttered in disgust.

Almost immediately he caught up with the pickup, which loaded with both camper and boat was gaining speed more slowly than his truck was traveling, forcing him to apply the brakes. A blast of his air horn did nothing to encourage the doggedly determined driver to ease his vehicle to the right and allow Stringer to pass. Another blast of the horn drew a fist out the pickup window with the middle finger raised in defiant rudeness.

Stringer swore furiously. Had he not been anxious to catch up with Jessie, not knowing that she was now behind him, he probably would have let it go and dropped back till there was more than enough room to pull around. But the incident had angered him, and for one critical instant he lost sight of the fact that safety was his priority. He shifted gears, put his foot down hard on the accelerator, and swung the forty-ton Peterbilt and trailer out to pass.

Had it not been for the boat, he might have made it. He was almost even with the pickup when he saw a passenger car at the intersection turn carelessly off the Cassiar Highway onto the road and pick up speed in his direction before its driver realized the road was blocked. It was far too close for him to either complete the pass or fall back behind the pickup and the boat it was towing.

His reaction was instantaneous.

Stomping on the clutch, he bore down on the brakes with all his weight. At the same time, knowing it was impossible to bring the 80,000 pounds of truck and trailer to a halt in less than two hundred feet, he made the choice he had always been afraid he would someday be forced to make and aimed the rig for the left-hand side of the road, intending to drop it over the edge, hoping there would be enough room for both the other vehicles to clear the trailer as it left the roadway. It was too much for the stability of the rig. With a sick feeling he felt the trailer break loose in an uncontrolled slide. Its enormous weight immediately obliterated the traction of the tractor as well and propelled it forward on the pavement. Out of control, brakes smoking, tires howling in protest, it slid past the parking lot in front of the small cluster of buildings that made up Junction 37 Services on the near side of the Cassiar Highway intersection.

Instead of increasing acceleration, which would probably have saved him, the driver of the pickup had also applied his brakes and was slowing, still beside the huge truck, when the trailer behind the Peterbilt, heavier by far than the tractor, jackknifed to the right, sliding faster than the cab. It impacted the boat on its light trailer first, then the pickup, sweeping both off the road.

As the pickup left the paved section of the shoulder, it dropped a wheel into the dirt beyond and rolled over and over again down the steep embankment, finally coming to rest upside down in the ditch at the bottom. The boat, which had separated from its trailer, flew across the ditch to impale its bow in the opposite bank. The camper came loose from the bed of the pickup on its first rotation, which increased its momentum. It fractured into a twisted heap of wood and metal that rolled with the pickup to the bottom of the incline, scattering its contents over a wide area of the road and embankment—pillows, clothing, sleeping bags, frying pans, cereal boxes, fishing rods, and a thousand things almost too bent and broken to identify. The glass of its windows shattered into bits and shards that were hurled through the air in a glittering shower. The propane tank on the camper exploded, and within seconds the whole pile of tangled wreckage was on fire.

In the cacophony of screeching brakes, rending metal, and breaking glass, the car that had turned into the path of the Peterbilt from the Cassiar Highway, unable to stop, crossed the center line and slid straight under the trailer, which sliced the roof from the passenger compartment at windshield level.

From where he sat, high in the tractor of the Peterbilt, Stringer could clearly see the buildings of Junction 37 Services as he slid past them and a man who stood in front, frozen into shocked immobility, gaping at what was still happening on the highway. The trailer of the Peterbilt stopped on the Cassiar Highway, totally blocking it to traffic. The tractor slid on across, dropped over the steep edge, and hit a small tree, then a utility pole on the far side of the road. Both snapped, but the impact crushed in the left side of the tractor, pinning Stringer's legs, and threw him hard against the steering wheel. Over the horrendous noise of the wreck, he distinctly heard and felt the crack of his ribs breaking.

When everything stopped moving and grew still, he couldn't seem to get air into his lungs. By the time the first people could run from Junction 37 Services to do what they could for those involved in the crash, Stringer had passed out and slumped forward over the wheel.

*   *   *

Not long afterward Jessie slowed to pass the terrible accident at the intersection of the Cassiar Highway. A crowd of people had reached the vehicles involved and were trying to help while they waited for emergency crews to arrive, but the crumpled cab of the Peterbilt was far enough below the level of the road so that she didn't see it. What she saw was the smoking ruin of an unidentifiable pickup and camper that lay in the right-hand ditch and a passenger car that had run under the trailer and been dragged till it stopped, completely blocking the Cassiar. The sun was low in the sky, and the flashing lights of the one police vehicle that had arrived looked very bright against its fading light. Small concerned groups of people stood along the edge of the highway shaking their heads. At a glance it was clear that no one would be able to turn off on the Cassiar Highway for a long time, and to try for the attention of a single RCMP constable under these circumstances would be futile. Jessie's only option was to keep going toward Alaska, so she took it. It was better than stopping and perhaps being caught.

She was growing tired from fear and stress in addition to the driving, but making the best of things, she was determined to make it to Teslin. Going at least that far would make it safer to stop. She drove away from the scene of the accident, took the motor home back up to speed, and put it in cruise control. Now that she was on her own there was no reason not to rest herself as much as possible and still keep the Winnebago moving north at a good speed. The glare of the sun now angled directly into her eyes, making it difficult to see oncoming traffic, and she could feel the hint of a headache behind her eyes. She wished the sun would disappear over the western horizon and make seeing the road ahead easier.

The vehicles that had bunched up as they slowed to pass the wreck at the Cassiar intersection, traveling at different speeds, gradually spread themselves out, and she was soon headed west by herself again. Though she kept a close watch behind her, no headlights appeared to stay behind her for long, and no one who passed was the man for whom she watched. The sun finally set, and the sky slowly grew darker until the bright glow of the headlights on pavement was all she could see except for the silhouettes of trees against a band of light that lingered in the west. When it was gone, she could make out a star or two in the deep black of the sky.

She had intended to question Patrick extensively about everything, but a glance in his direction told her he had drifted off to sleep and she decided to leave him alone for the time being. Once they reached their destination she would cook them both a hot meal and there would be time for all the things she needed to know. So she concentrated on driving through the night toward Teslin, Yukon Territory, and let her questions wait.

CHAPTER 21

Maxie McNabb waited anxiously in her motor home for Inspector Webster to arrive with Detective Loomis, pacing back and forth and keeping an eye on the two dogs. When she had put down food for them, Stretch immediately gobbled his up as usual, but Tank refused. He drank some of the water that she placed next to him, where he still sat by the door, but ignored the dachshund's attempts to play until Stretch finally gave up and lay down close by to keep the larger dog company.

Very worried about Jessie and anticipating that she herself would want to drive north as soon as she had talked with Webster, Maxie made sure the Jayco was ready for travel, secured everything movable inside and packed up the lawn chair and table she had set out earlier. But she had been waiting for almost two hours before she heard a car approach on the loop road and pull up beside the Jayco. The two men stepped hurriedly out and came to the door. Inviting them in, she held Tank's collar tightly until the door was closed again.

"We understand somebody almost drowned up here," the inspector said as she let the dog go back to his place beside it. Both men seemed reluctant to sit down, anxious to be somewhere else, but they finally sat when Maxie offered them iced tea.

"Close. Jessie found the boy in the hot springs pool and hauled him out in time to help give him CPR," she told Webster. "What you need to know is that, according to Patrick, it was one of those friends of his, that Kim Fredricksen, and he said his stepfather did it."

"So you *have* seen the boy? Where—"

"There wasn't a name reported," Loomis broke in, surprised at this news.

"Jessie didn't know who it was until it was over and I told her I'd seen Patrick, so she didn't tell the rescue people. We decided you should know first. It was too hard to explain it all, or even know who to tell it to, and what would it do but confuse things. He was getting the medical attention he needed, whether they knew who he was or not."

"We'll take care of that," Webster said, nodding impatiently. "But I want to talk to Patrick. Where is he? With Jessie?"

"Jessie's gone, and I think he went with her." Maxie filled him in quickly about how Patrick had appeared, followed by a man she thought was his stepfather, how she had sent Jessie to take care of him while she made a phone call, the swift departure of the Winnebago from the campground, and her speculation that the stepfather might have taken Jessie and Patrick hostage. "She absolutely would not leave without her best lead dog," she motioned at Tank, tirelessly waiting by the door. "Stringer caught him running after Jessie's rig."

"Stringer?" Loomis asked, not recognizing the name.

"A trucker we met at Summit Lake—nice man. He went after them, hoping to catch up and see where they were going."

"What kind of a truck?" he asked sharply.

The question seemed odd to Maxie, who couldn't see that it mattered. But the troubled expression that had narrowed his eyes and tightened his mouth changed her mind and an uneasiness crept in.

"A Peterbilt—the cab-over kind. Why?"

The look he gave Webster conveyed distress and resignation.

"What is it? What's happened?"

Webster explained. "There was a bad wreck on the highway north of Watson Lake—a Peterbilt hit a pickup with a camper and a boat, and a passenger car. The pileup's evidently playing hell with traffic, and there's four dead and one about to be med-evaced out."

Maxie could almost hear her heart pounding. She felt as if she were drowning. "Who?"

"No idea. It just came over the radio. We're headed up there now."

"So," Maxie told them, getting hurriedly to her feet, "am I. It may be Stringer, and it might have something to do with Jessie. You're sure the Winnebago she's driving wasn't involved? Reports aren't always accurate."

"To my knowledge it was a *camper,* not a motor home."

"Well, I'm going anyway. I can't just sit here. I've got to find Jessie if I can."

"It's going to be dark before long," Webster called back to her as they went back to their car. "Don't try to get there too fast. Drive carefully. We'll watch for you and keep a lookout for her and her rig."

210 · SUE HENRY

She heard the siren on his car begin to wail as he turned onto the highway from the campground. As it faded away in the distance, she started the Jayco and pulled out of the space where she had meant to spend the night. So much for soaking in the hot springs.

But I might not have wanted to anyway, she thought, remembering the boy floating in the pool.

. . .

The sun was soon sliding down the western sky as Maxie drove, a little faster than the speed limit, toward Watson Lake. Its concentrated brightness shone directly through the windshield, half blinding her till she put on a pair of sunglasses and lowered the visor above the window to cut off the glare. It was better, but still difficult to see clearly.

Tank had abandoned his vigil at the coach door when she put the motor home in motion, evidently feeling that wherever they were going, Jessie might be there. Stretch rode in his basket hung over the back of the passenger seat, and Tank jumped up to sit below him on the seat itself, where he could see out the windows. Both dogs soon curled up and went to sleep, leaving Maxie alone behind the wheel to worry and wonder what she would find farther north.

She had almost reached Watson Lake when she heard the wail of a siren behind her and then the burp of it quickly silenced. In the sideview mirror she saw flashing lights behind her from an RCMP patrol car. Her heart in her throat, she pulled over, stopped the Jayco on the wide shoulder of the road, and waited as the constable walked forward to stand beside the window she had rolled down, hoping he was not a bearer of bad news, expecting a message of some kind from Inspector Webster.

She almost laughed in relief as the young officer, resplendent in pressed uniform and reflective sunglasses, looked up at her and said sternly, "Do you know how fast you were going, ma'am?"

"A little over the limit, perhaps?" she said, with a smile she could not keep from her mouth.

"Seven miles over, ma'am. May I have your license and registration, please? I'll have to give you a ticket, I'm afraid."

The whole thing struck Maxie as supremely ridiculous and humorous, considering present circumstances. Also, she suddenly remembered, it was Sunday, Mother's Day. Was it Mother's Day in Canada?

"Young man," she said, handing him the documents he had requested, "does your mother know where you are and what you're doing?"

"Yes, ma'am, she does," he told her, busily writing on his pad of tickets, seeing nothing at all humorous in the situation. She didn't even try to explain, just took the ticket and drove on.

By the time she stopped for gas in Watson Lake, the sun had disappeared over the horizon and Maxie had stopped laughing and was once again worried. Trying to think what she should do, she decided to go on as far as she could and park overnight in some turnoff if necessary. She considered getting something to eat, but hunger had mostly vanished in her anxiety, so she drank a glass of milk and put a package of cookies where she could reach them as she drove.

Fifteen miles later she arrived at the site of the wreck and its terrible remains—the skid marks on the pavement left by the Peterbilt, the blackened pickup in the ditch to her right, and the litter left by its exploding camper. She recognized the trailer from the Peterbilt, which had been dragged off the road and into the parking lot of the Petro-Canada service station at the Cassiar intersection, next to a car with its roof missing. She pulled in beside the trailer, and though she had hoped it would not be Stringer's, there was no doubt in her mind that it was, but there was no sign that Jessie's motor home had been part of the tragic accident.

As she sat with the motor still running and her heart pounding, wondering what could have caused such a disaster, Loomis suddenly appeared at her window, startling her. She rolled down the window to hear what he had to say.

"Hey, I've been watching for you—figured you wouldn't stop for the night in Watson Lake," he told her. "Webster went on to Teslin, because Jessie had to go that way—the Cassiar was blocked. Can I catch a ride with you?"

"Yes, of course. But please—do you know anything about the man who was driving the truck? Is he alive—hurt—what?"

"He was lucky—the only one who survived. They took him out by helicopter."

"Thank God," Maxie whispered to herself and began to breathe again.

The dogs were evicted from the passenger seat and Loomis climbed in with a paper bag in one hand. An unmistakable aroma of hamburger and french fries immediately filled the cab, and Maxie at once realized that she was starving—learning that Stringer had survived the crash and Webster was searching for Jessie had lifted a little of the tension and allowed her appetite to return.

"May I assume there's tucker in that bag?" she asked. "My stomach thinks my throat's cut."

He grinned and handed it over. "I've already eaten," he confessed. "Thought you might not have. Want me to drive?"

"Not now—maybe later. Just give me a minute to appreciate this."

*　*　*

It was very late and Jessie was very tired when a sign for the Dawson Peaks Resort appeared on the left, then a driveway with poles on barrels blocking it, indicating that the resort was not yet open for the season. A few yards farther on there was another driveway to the same resort, with the same kind of barrier of poles and barrels, but she had had time to take another look down the dark hill, notice how little she could see, and think about it. Without lights in the yard below, no one following would be able to see the motor home if she parked there. Assuming that she couldn't have turned in at a closed RV park, they would probably go on down the road toward Teslin.

Patrick woke as she slowed the Winnebago to a stop at the second set of barrels, so she had him get out, move the barrier, and put it back when she had driven through.

"There's nobody here," he said as he climbed back in.

"The place isn't open for the summer yet," she told him. "We'll drive on down there and take a look."

The road curved down and the lights of the motor home swept first across an area that was divided into spaces for RV parking, then around the front of the main lodge, which was covered with yellow signs with red lettering: YOU BET WE'RE OPEN, COME ON IN FOLKS, RVS 15/30 AMP, TENT SITES, CABINS, CANOES, FISHING, RESTAURANT, BAKED GOODS. A large sign over the door read DAWSON PEAKS NORTHERN RESORT WELCOMES YOU. REGISTER HERE. There was no evidence of caretakers and no lights of any kind.

Jessie turned the Winnebago around and headed back toward

the RV parking area, looking for a place that would not be visible from the highway that ran above them on the hillside. As she drove into it, the headlights revealed a single-lane dirt road that ran between the parking spaces, then curved to the left. She followed the curve, and the narrow road dropped farther down the hill, which put the lodge between it and the highway. It ended in a turnaround, where the headlights lit up three small, new-looking cabins nestled in the trees. Beyond them Jessie could just make out a beach and the edge of Teslin Lake.

As she guided the motor home around the loop, its headlights revealed two canvas tents on platforms and another cabin, under construction judging by the absence of a door and the chain saw and toolbox someone had left on the small deck that extended in front of it. These told Jessie that the place was not as empty of people as it had first appeared, for someone had to have been working on that cabin to have left the tools. Nobody would leave tools out to rust through a northern winter. Someone would be coming back soon, probably in the morning, to use them. A crumb of optimism crept into her thinking and remained. Having someone else around wouldn't hurt a bit.

She pulled over and stopped next to one of the tents, where they couldn't be seen from the highway, even in the morning, and the interior lights would be blocked by the lodge. She couldn't put the tent completely between them and the lodge because the motor home was slightly longer, though they were the same cream color. Part of it would extend beyond and probably be visible from the lodge tomorrow if someone came down to it and looked closely, but it wasn't likely their pursuer would do that.

Feeling relieved and much safer, she had Patrick switch on one galley light, then turned off the engine and the headlights.

Slipping outside, she turned on the propane so she would be able to use the stove. It was definitely time for hot food of some kind. There was a package of frozen lasagna in the freezer compartment of the refrigerator and vegetables for a salad. Though it would take the better part of an hour to bake, she intended to have it for dinner before they went to bed.

When it was heating nicely in the oven and she had made a salad, she poured herself a shot of Jameson's and sat down at the table with Patrick, who had opted for hot chocolate.

"Soon," she told him, "I want you to tell me the whole story—how this thing started and everything you know, right up to now. But we'll wait until after we've eaten because I need to just sit here for a while and rest. Okay?"

He gave her a small grin and nodded, a little of the self-confidence that she recognized returning. "Okay." Then he frowned. "Will Maxie know where to find us?"

"She knows, but I don't expect her to show up until morning. We'll stay right here, though, until she does."

He sat up straighter and sighed, relaxing.

"Thank you, Jessie," he said. "You saved my life. I'll tell you anything you want to know."

In the end, however, when Patrick was yawning and she found that she too was almost asleep over her food, she deferred hearing his tale until morning, when she would be rested enough to concentrate.

But she couldn't help thinking about the man they had escaped in Watson Lake. Was he gone for good? Teslin was only a dozen miles up the road beyond this place. Would he find transportation and return to hunt them—or just keep going? Would he be able to find them if he did? There were only so many places to hide along this highway, and he would have the rest of the night.

She decided not to worry about it now, having done the best

she could at evading him and hiding. She refused to allow her fatigue to let fear, anger, and frustration creep back into her outlook. It was unlikely they could be found by anyone but Maxie—or perhaps by Webster and Loomis if they had been told where she was headed. Nevertheless, she had already made sure the motor home was securely locked.

CHAPTER 22

It was 163 miles from Watson Lake to Teslin, and all of it would be night driving. Her eyesight not as good as it used to be, Maxie hated driving in the dark and avoided it when she could. In a short time she switched places with Loomis and let him pilot the Jayco up the highway toward the village with a population of less than four hundred that had originated as a trading post in 1903 and was located at the confluence of the Nisutlin River and Teslin Lake.

She knew that Teslin had a large native population and that many of its residents supported themselves with hunting and fishing, others with traditional crafts and woodworking—the building of sleds and canoes. There was a resort and RV park next to the bridge, which crossed the river in the longest span of any on the highway, almost 2,000 feet. She had never spent a night there because for some reason it always seemed to be raining at the times she traveled through, and the wind that often howled down the river was cold and unpleasant in the only tree-less campground.

After trading places with Loomis she belted herself into the passenger seat, but it felt very strange, for almost never did someone else drive her house on wheels. Trying not to be obvious about it, she watched him carefully for a few miles until she was comfortable with his ability to handle the Jayco. Then she settled back and, closing her eyes, found she was more tired than she had imagined. *The stress of the last couple of days has taken the starch right out of me,* she thought.

"Do I pass?" Loomis asked with a grin, keeping his attention on the road ahead.

Caught out when she thought she was being subtle, Maxie tossed her head back and let out her usual hearty whoop of unrestrained laughter.

"And I thought I was being so cleverly indirect—so tolerant. Yes, you pass."

He waited while the headlights of an oncoming vehicle grew brighter and sped by them.

"How long have you had this thing?"

"Well—it'll be three years in August," she mused, remembering that first fall trip down the highway alone. "When my husband died, I decided to see some of the country. So I bought it and took off."

"But you still live in Alaska part of the year?"

"A month to three months in the summer. I'm a snowbird, like so many—head south before winter sets in, usually. Twice I've flown back for the holidays. Doesn't seem quite like Christmas without snow."

"So where have you been in your travels?"

"This last winter I spent in Arizona. Not in Phoenix—it's too hot for me. My blood has thickened living in the north. I like

Flagstaff, though, so I spent some time there—and roaming around in the northern desert and canyon country when the weather was good.

"The winter before that I drove all the way across the country, from California to the Carolinas, stopping wherever I felt like it. Spent a month in southern Virginia, digging up old bones."

"Archaeology?"

"No, genealogy—one branch of my family settled near Abingdon back before the Revolutionary War. One was a drummer boy, and several others fought at Kings Mountain."

"Interesting stuff to a guy who hasn't a clue where his family came from."

"Didn't you ever sit around and listen to family stories? I was always under the table when my relatives talked, whether they knew it or not. Sometimes heard some spicy stuff that way." She grinned, remembering one particular flapper aunt who seemed to have taken full advantage of the Roaring Twenties.

Loomis smiled, hesitated, then shook his head. "My parents died in a fire when I was almost seven. I was raised in an orphanage—never got adopted."

Things were quiet for a time after that statement as Maxie thought of how different their lives had been—hers so full of family and people constantly moving through her life, his so empty of all blood ties. What a curious mixture Loomis was, confident, competent, and insightful, but under it seemed to run an unexpected shy streak and a hunger for acceptance that betrayed itself in his humor—understandable, given his background.

"Did you have any brothers or sisters?"

"One brother, but he was killed in Vietnam."

A loner, then. "Married?"

"Nope—never found anyone to put up with me, or my job."

Was there a hint of defensiveness in his voice and grin?

Remembering that Patrick was also very much by himself, Maxie's attention turned to his recent and similar lack of family ties. His mother dying so terribly must have been especially hard on him. Where had he gone? With Jessie? With that stepfather he feared so much? Both? It worried her.

"You've worked with—what's his name—Patrick's stepfather? What's he like?"

"Yeah, I worked with him, but not much. McMurdock's his name. He's big—kind of a good ole boy that doesn't fool around—takes pretty much what's tossed at him and makes it work—doesn't waste time putting up with nonsense. It took some time and effort to get used to him when I first came up from Denver almost two years ago. We started out working on . . ."

Maxie nodded encouragingly and tried to look as if she was following what he was talking about, but she had stopped hearing what he was saying, as she wondered if there were things he wasn't saying. He sounded as if he knew this McMurdock quite well, but then he would, wouldn't he? The Cody police force couldn't be that large. Was her imagination running away with her common sense?

". . . then they transferred me to homicide, where I've been for the last few months."

"What do you know about his relationship with Patrick?"

"Oh—well." Loomis seemed relieved to get onto something besides his knowledge of McMurdock's capabilities and person-ality. He sat up straighter and glanced in her direction, "Not much, really. The kid's been in and out of trouble, and they didn't get along. But most kids don't like stepfathers, do they? I think Mac's just trying to find Patrick and get this thing with his mother straightened out somehow." *Mac?* "It's hard to imagine him killing his wife—but then it's hard to figure out why the boy would do it either. We've just got to find them—especially McMurdock, before—well, before anything else happens to either one of them."

"Why would he try to drown that boy in the pool?"

"Ah, well, Maxie, we don't really know that he did, do we? Patrick was there too, remember."

She remembered Stringer's comparable suggestion that Patrick might have run from Wyoming because he killed his mother, and it still seemed unacceptable to her way of thinking. But even Jessie had had trouble trusting the boy to begin with. Was there something she was completely missing in the equation?

But she knew she had not been wrong about the expression of tension and fear on Jessie's face as she drove the Winnebago out of the Liard Hot Springs park. And she believed that Patrick was truly terrified when he showed up to hide in her motor home there. The question was *why* was he afraid—and of *what*? She was not quite so sure anymore, but Loomis was right, they needed to find both Patrick and McMurdock—and Jessie and the Winnebago—to answer any of her questions.

"Do you have any idea how far Jessie might drive tonight?" Loomis asked.

She told him about the Dawson Peaks Resort where they had agreed to meet. "I think she would go there if possible. It's the only connection we made. I'd like to stop there anyway, to see."

"Makes sense. Probably should let Webster know about it too."

They had gone almost halfway. It was dark and there was little to see aside from the occasional vehicle that passed them on the road. Maxie was sleepily wishing she were parked somewhere and could crawl into her comfortable bed, when lights ahead on the south side of the road announced the Rancheria Motel coming up, with fuel for sale.

"We'd better stop for gas," she reminded Loomis, who pulled into the parking lot and up to the pumps as a teenage girl came out to fill the tank.

"Good idea," he commented, opening the driver's door to get out. "I'd better see if I can use the phone to reach the inspector. Tell him where we're headed and see if he's left any messages for us."

"Would you see if they've got any coffee?" Maxie asked as he slid out and was about to close the door. "I don't like to drink it this late, but I'm going to be a zombie if I don't."

He trotted off toward the lights in the small store that was part of the service station. Through the window she could see him talking to a woman inside, displaying his identification.

Unbuckling her seat belt, she got up and went for her credit card to pay for the gas. It felt so good to stand up that she decided to walk around to wake up a little. Handing the card to the girl, who took it into the station, she walked back and forth near the Jayco while she waited for the receipt.

The air was cool, and a light, pleasant breeze blew the scent of evergreen into her face. Looking up she could just make out the pointed tops of the trees across the road against the slightly lighter night sky with its sprinkling of stars. She wished it were daylight, for the Rancheria Falls were only a few miles up the road, a place she had stopped before. Those who have driven the Alaska Highway more than once often tend to follow roughly the schedule they have maintained in the past, recognizing and stopping at familiar places, renewing their acquaintance and appreciation of favorite scenery and discoveries. The falls usually meant lunch to

Maxie on drives between Watson Lake and Teslin. But the events on this trip had redefined her timing completely.

Rounding one corner of the motor home, she looked toward the station in search of the girl, who seemed to be taking a long time. Inside she saw that Loomis was now talking on the telephone. A cup of coffee, probably hers, sat steaming on the counter. The girl came out, and at the sound of the door closing Loomis turned his head as if to see if Maxie had decided to come in. He glanced at the window, and she lifted a hand to wave, but he seemed to be focused on the conversation he was having.

It's Mothers Day, the telephone suddenly reminded her.

The girl brought the receipt. Maxie signed it and grinned to herself, knowing how much she did not intend to call her daughter, Carol.

"Cell phones don't work out here, do they?" she asked, curious.

"No, they don't," she was told. "There's a NorthwesTel microwave tower just south of us, but it's only normal phones or radios until you reach Whitehorse."

Carol can't call me again either, Maxie thought.

Thanking the girl, she watched her walk back toward the lighted station, where Loomis was now paying the woman for the coffee. Maxie climbed back into the Jayco, locked the coach door, and got into the passenger seat, ready to take the paper cup Loomis handed in.

"She said it was fresh-made," he said. "Black okay?"

"Only way I take it. Anything from Inspector Webster?"

"Yes. He's sent word to the dispatcher that he's already in Teslin and will meet us there. Hasn't seen any sign of Jessie's rig."

"But he wouldn't if she stopped at the resort this side of it," Maxie said.

"I gave the dispatcher that location and name. She'll pass it on and he'll probably check it out," he said as he took the Jayco back onto the highway.

In less than ten miles they passed Rancheria Falls and continued into the night toward Teslin.

Wondering where Jessie was—and how—all Maxie could do was sit, jittery, wide awake, and worried, beginning to wish she had not had that cup of coffee after all.

"Look," said Loomis, when he and Maxie reached the campground where she and Jessie had arranged to meet and found it dark and seemingly deserted. "Let's go on into Teslin—it's just a few miles. We'll find Webster. Then we can come back to see if Jessie's here, if he hasn't already checked. She might have gone on when she got here and found the access road blocked."

It seemed a reasonable assumption. Maxie agreed, tired and yearning for her bed but too concerned about Jessie and Patrick to consider finding it yet. The effect of the coffee was beginning to wear off, leaving her slightly thickheaded, and she was glad Loomis was behind the wheel.

They drove on a few miles, crossed the Nisutlin Bay Bridge, longest span of any on the highway, and found Webster sitting in his patrol car on the other side where he could watch traffic on the highway. When they pulled in beside him, he immediately climbed into the coach.

"Was beginning to wonder if you'd gone back to Watson Lake," he said, leaning between them with a hand on the back of each seat.

"Have you seen Jessie?" Maxie asked directly, too weary to make small talk.

"No. I didn't see her on the way, and she hasn't been through here."

"Did you check at Dawson Peaks yet?"

"Dawson . . . ? Oh, that RV park outside of town? Why would I check there?"

"Didn't you get the message I left with the dispatcher in Dawson Creek?" Loomis broke in. "Maxie and Jessie had agreed to meet there."

"No—first I heard of it," Webster said shaking his head. "But I've been watching here for almost two hours and was just considering a call to the Dawson Creek dispatcher."

Maxie was beginning to feel as though she were in a stage play with someone else's script in her hand and lines that made no sense at all. Where was Jessie? People and motor homes didn't just disappear into thin air, did they? She thought of Patrick's stepfather and wondered where he was and if he had anything to do with the fact that none of them had seen her. Could she have slipped past without Webster knowing? He seemed too competent to miss the Winnebago, and this was the only road that crossed the bridge and went on through Teslin. Could they have switched vehicles?

Longing for her bed, she sighed as she slumped a little in her seat.

"You okay?"

"Yes, I'm fine—just tired. We'd better do something about checking Dawson Peaks, hadn't we? It was closed, but she seemed very certain about it."

Webster looked at her thoughtfully. "I think we should go and check—meaning Loomis and I," he said. "You look beat. Why don't you find a spot in the RV park here and wait while we drive out and take a look? No need for all three of us to be stumbling around in the dark out there."

Maxie frowned, considering the suggestion. She had promised to meet Jessie, not send someone else. But what he said made sense. What could she do anyway that they couldn't do without her—and probably more efficiently? "You're right—I'm bushed. But you'll come back and let me know—and tell her where I am if she's there?"

"Of course."

In five minutes the two law enforcement officers had gone off in the patrol car. In fifteen, Maxie had registered and parked the Jayco in a space on the highway side of the RV park, plugged in her electricity and water, and was considering the restoring properties of a cup of tea.

I'll just lie down for a few minutes first, she thought, leaving the galley and dinette lights on, as well as the one outside the coach door, and heading for her bed in the back of the motor home. Then I'll get up and wait till they come back.

CHAPTER

In the last, darkest hour before dawn, Jessie suddenly woke and listened intently for the sound she had heard to repeat itself. There had been something outside—an unnatural sound that was not a part of the faint sigh of Patrick's breathing, the soft susurration of the breeze in the leaves of a birch, or the faraway murmur of trucks infrequently passing on the highway above the lodge. She could hear passenger cars if she listened very closely when the light wind took a breath, but the trucks made a purring sort of roar that faded slowly as it filtered down through the trees and drifted in through the window beside her bed, which she had opened a scant inch before going to sleep.

The sound came again, a slight unidentifiable rustle from somewhere up the hill—the sound of something, or someone, in motion. Somewhere near the lodge something had moved. The possibilities were varied and endless. It could be something the wind was tossing against something else. A deer or a moose could be wandering through the dark—even a bear, though she thought that a bear would probably make more noise. Or it could be a person—friend or foe. But if it was, from the lack of normal sounds it was someone carefully trying not to be heard. A soft, dull thump, like the toe of a boot accidentally kicking a root in a trail, a little closer this time, and Jessie was on her stockinged feet, moving swiftly and silently through the dark to lay one strong hand on Patrick's shoulder, the other over his mouth.

He woke, groggy and frightened, and tried to twist away from her firm grip, which held him like a vise.

"Sh-h-h," she whispered. "It's Jessie. There's someone outside—or something. Get up and put on your boots and that raincoat I gave you." She released his face and shoulder, turning back to don her own shoes and jacket, left ready for just such an emergency.

"No," he whispered out of the dark, louder than she liked, and sat up in the bed. "Let's stay in here—where it's safe."

"I'm not going to be trapped in here like a bug in a tin can," she told him fiercely. "Get up and get your shoes on—hurry."

"Okay," he said reluctantly and began to follow her instructions.

Though she had thought it unlikely they could be found, she had slept in her clothes and had Patrick do the same. In one jacket pocket she had put a flashlight and the pepper spray—in the other, a bottle of water and four Power Bars. The keys to the Winnebago were in her jeans pocket.

"Come on," she whispered softly next to his ear. "We'll get out of here until I can find out what's making that noise."

Creeping forward she passed the coach door, which she knew from Dutch Creek experience would scrape against the frame, causing a small squeal of metal against metal. She had parked the motor home headed in the direction that would take them out, so she wouldn't have to turn around if leaving was necessary. It put the coach door on the uphill side, toward the sound she had heard, so she climbed into the driver's seat and carefully worked the handle on that door, which opened with only a small click. One after the other, she and Patrick slid cautiously out onto the ground. Then she closed the door and locked it quietly with the key, gripping the two others on the ring tight in her hand to keep them from falling against each other.

As quietly as possible they became shadows in the dark, slipping away past the cabins, walking on the grass at the edge of a branch of the dirt road that led toward the lake shore, where between them and the water there were trees that would keep them from becoming silhouettes against its pale, breeze-rippled reflection. When they had gone far enough to see around the end of the motor home and up the hill beyond it, Jessie moved them deliberately, one step at a time, into the brush beside the road, timing the rustles of their passage to those the breeze made in the leaves. There they knelt, listening raptly, and waited to see what would happen next.

They huddled in the brush for a quarter of an hour, listening carefully. There were no more suspicious sounds and nothing visible to indicate that anyone had been moving down the hillside toward them. Still, Jessie was not willing to relax her guard. She badly wished Tank were with her, knowing he would have been able to sense the presence of another person in the dark. Again she longed to know that Maxie had found and collected him—that he was with her and Stretch.

Patrick shivered next to her and shifted slightly.

She laid a hand on his shoulder and leaned close to whisper, "Cold?"

"A little," came the soft reply.

Scared, she thought, and hoped she was not frightening him unnecessarily with this quick trip out into the night because she thought she had heard something. It had been quite a long time since she heard anything and she considered going back to the motor home. Crouching here in the dark might be an overreaction and nothing but paranoia, but something kept her from moving, told her that being overly cautious was better than being caught. There was a tense feeling in her chest and a prickle on the back of her neck that made her unwilling to venture out just yet, kept her motionless and alert.

She knew what it was to be hunted, from a terrifying experience on an island not so long ago that had produced a kind of terror and claustrophobia she hadn't easily forgotten. She was not willing to give away the advantage of invisibility easily or negligently.

If the wind had increased, or if it had been raining, they could have disappeared into the forest that surrounded the resort and made themselves safer. Any attempt in that direction now, however, would result in sounds that could be heard, pinpointing their location if there was someone up there listening. It was not worth the risk.

"Can't we go back inside now?" Patrick whispered.

"Let's wait just a little longer."

He shivered again. Odd how he seemed to feel safer in the motor home, Jessie thought, while she felt imprisoned in it and threatened by the inability to escape. Was the comfort of small confining spaces something you outgrew as you aged? She remembered liking to crawl into cardboard boxes as a child, to fold up her arms and legs inside a container just large enough to hold her curled-up body, and lie there feeling secure and safe.

All she could hear was the small sound of the lake lapping gently on the shore, and she was almost ready to stand up and take Patrick back to the motor home when a breath of wind rustled the leaves of the bushes and the trees overhead like a million bits of tissue paper. Suddenly, in the midst of it, there was another sound—the metallic click of someone trying the door handle of the coach of the Winnebago.

A tiny whimper of fear escaped Patrick and he jerked as if he had been unexpectedly touched, then froze into stillness.

Jessie also froze, staring into the darker shadows of the motor home, trying to see as well as hear, but whoever it was stayed on the far side of the rig, out of sight. She knew the coach door was locked, so this person would probably try the cab doors next. She had locked the one on the driver's side, but had the passenger door been locked or not? She couldn't remember and silently cursed herself for not checking it before they slid out. With a sinking feeling she remembered that Patrick had climbed out on that side when they stopped and come to the coach door to get back in. Had he locked it? Most likely he had not. There was no point in asking, with what was almost certainly his stepfather so close.

Was it his stepfather? Could it possibly be Webster or Loomis? Even Maxie? Could whoever had been using the tools to build the unfinished cabin have come in the middle of the night? She thought not. Any one of them, looking for her, would have made obvious sounds as they approached, would have called out to let her know they were there. This person, whoever it was, had moved stealthily and was taking his time.

The sound of the passenger door handle reached her, and as she had feared, the door opened. She could hear him climb in and vaguely saw the Winnebago rock slightly with his movement.

There was a long pause, then the galley light came on and remained on. He was searching. But now there were walls between him and the two of them. It was time to go, and quickly.

"Come on," she breathed in Patrick's ear. "We're getting out of here."

He shrank back. "He'll hear us."

"Get up, Patrick. He'll do more than that if we don't go. He'll be out here and find us in a minute or two."

Hauling the boy to his feet, she half-dragged him out of the brush and onto the grassy verge of road that curved gently down toward the lake. Thinking he would stay close behind her, she let go of his arm and started to lead him away from the motor home as quietly as she could. But Patrick was clumsy in his panic and almost ran to catch up with her, stepping off the grass and onto the road itself, where the sound of his feet made an unmistakable crunching on the gravel.

Behind them Jessie heard a muffled shout from inside the motor home and the screech of the coach door as it opened, then the thud of it flying back to hit the outside wall. There was the sound of running from the side to the front of the rig, and without warning a bright beam pierced the dark in their direction—a flashlight.

"Hey. Stop right there. I've still got a gun," the man yelled.

But Jessie knew that his night vision had been compromised by turning on the galley light. If they could stay out of the beam of light he was waving around, they might make it far enough to put a tree or two between them. Grabbing Patrick's arm again she tried to yank him into a run, but he had taken only three or four steps when he stepped on a rock that rolled from under his foot and pitched forward, falling to his hands and knees in the road.

The sound of boots closing in behind them kept Jessie in motion. She knew instantly that stopping to rescue the fallen boy would only put them both within range; that their one chance might be for her to remain on the loose and free to find help. She dashed on into the dark, paying no attention to how much noise she was making now—knowing he would stop to make sure of Patrick before he turned his attention in her direction.

Reaching the lakeshore, she angled west and continued to run along it, finding it not covered with rocks as she had imagined it would be, but quite flat and covered with grass that muffled the sound of her pounding feet, though she couldn't tell if she was leaving a track he could follow. She ran until she was gasping for breath, then paused to listen for pursuit—leaning forward, hands braced on knees as she panted, held her breath, and panted again. Hearing nothing behind her, she all but staggered into the shelter of the brush and trees that lined the shore. Throwing herself down, she lay completely still on her belly, trying to control her ragged breathing enough to listen—and to not be found.

By the time she was finally breathing normally and had taken the bottle of water from her pocket to quench the thirst produced by her run, she knew that Patrick's stepfather had not followed her along the edge of the lake. But morning was coming, when he might.

What could she do now, without transportation or communication? It was nearly seven miles to Teslin. Should she climb up to follow the highway into town and try to find help there? It would take precious time. Or should she stay where she could perhaps watch for Patrick? Would he keep the boy in the motor home where it was or drive it out and away on the road above? The keys were in her pocket, but she guessed that a policeman would be able to start the vehicle without them.

Leaning back against a fallen birch log, she rested and considered the situation. She mustn't do anything that might get Patrick or herself hurt—or killed. She mustn't put herself back into the hands of this frightening man. But under all her deliberations, she knew she would go back—that there really wasn't a choice to be made—for she remembered Patrick's panic and the terror his stepfather inspired in him. She couldn't leave them alone together.

What she really wanted to know was why all this was happening. What could be so important that this man would make such an effort to locate and capture his stepson? He had evidently killed the boy on the bridge at Kiskatinaw. Would he kill Patrick before she could find a way to rescue him?

Slowly, Jessie stood up and began to move cautiously up the hill from where she had rested in the trees. As she crept through the darkness among the trees that grew more thickly away from the water, every shadow seemed a threat and the slightest rustle of leaves a menace. Feeling extremely vulnerable, as a stone slid from under her foot and hit another with a sharp report, she knew that there was no way to disguise the small sounds of her passage through the forest. There were too many things she couldn't see in the gloom—and one of them might be the very person she least wanted to meet.

C H A P T E R

When Maxie woke early the next morning, it was just growing bright enough to see inside the Jayco without turning on a light. Swinging her feet toward the floor, she came close to stepping on Stretch and Tank, who were curled up together beside the bed.

"Good morning, galahs. Time for a walk before breakfast. Yes?"

Stretch, more than familiar with the word *walk,* went pattering off into the front of the coach, but Tank only sat up and watched attentively while she washed her face, brushed her teeth, and dressed for the day.

"You're really missing Jessie, aren't you?" she asked him and reached to give him a few consoling pats. "So am I. We'll go and find her then, shall we?"

At the sound of the familiar name, he turned his head toward the door, as if expecting Jessie to open it and walk in. When it remained closed, he moved back to sit beside it as he had the day before, silently, patiently begging to be let out.

Maxie took the time to put a pot of coffee on to brew, then attached leashes to the collars of both dogs, put on a jacket, and stepped out into the coolness of the early dawn air.

Across the parking lot she could see Webster, still sitting in the patrol car watching the highway, as a truck that reminded her of Stringer rumbled past, heading for Whitehorse and probably Alaska beyond it. She walked across to the car window, which he rolled down to greet her. In the passenger seat, Loomis was asleep, head back, mouth open, snoring in a soft buzz.

The two law enforcement officers had stopped and knocked on the door of the Jayco when they returned from the Dawson Peaks Resort the night before. Startled awake, Maxie had realized she had gone to sleep in her clothes and that the lights were still on, as she went to the door to let them in.

They had found no evidence of Jessie, Patrick, or the Winnebago.

"It's still closed for the season," Webster had told her. "The lodge is locked up tight and there's no one in the RV spaces. She isn't there, Maxie."

"What shall we do?"

"Wait till morning. Loomis and I will take shifts watching the road in case we missed her somehow between here and Liard Hot Springs. If she goes past, we'll see her. When it gets light we'll go back and search the place again—when we can see to do it right."

There had been little else to suggest. Still, Maxie worried. Now it was light enough and she wanted to see Dawson Peaks for herself. Jessie might have arrived there after Webster and Loomis returned to Teslin.

"I just put on a pot of coffee," she told Webster through the car window. "Shall I bring you a cuppa, or will you come in?"

He would come in, leaving Loomis, who was yawning his way to consciousness, to keep watch, then to take his turn.

While the inspector made a quick trip to the restroom in the Yukon Lakeshore Resort, she walked the dogs. They arrived at the Jayco at the same time and climbed in, Tank, as usual, resisting, then sitting watch at the door, though this morning he ate the food that Maxie set down beside him.

"You know," Webster said thoughtfully, sipping at a steaming mug of coffee as he looked at the dog that so clearly wanted to be elsewhere, "I think that husky of Jessie's might be some help this morning. If she's out there, or has been out there, he just might figure it out faster than we would. Should have taken him last night maybe."

Maxie, who in lieu of cooking breakfast had put out bread and fruit, agreed. "Can we go soon? I'm really worried."

"I'll send Loomis to ride with you while he has his coffee and we'll go now."

Readying the Jayco, Maxie was ready to roll in ten minutes, at the wheel herself this time.

* * *

A caribou moved like a shadow in the unreliable first hint of dawn light, slipping so steadily and silently through the edge of the trees that it was difficult for Jessie to tell if it was actually there or only the product of imagination and fear, for she had watched the area around the Winnebago with anxiety for over an hour from a spot high on the hill above it. Wisps of ground fog drifted almost imperceptibly around the animal, partially obscuring its background. Without sunlight to brighten nature's colors they were all similar neutral shades of gray, and she found that the caribou was almost undetectable when she looked at it directly—only a hint of motion in her peripheral vision. Slowly it moved away and without a sound disappeared among the trees.

The pale sky was scattered with clouds beginning to show the

first of the light that would soon be caught in the glow of the rising sun, reflecting it onto the dark waters below. The breeze had
died and everything was very still, even the lake. Nothing moved
but the mist that flowed slowly from the water across the shore,
just above the long grass through which Jessie had run in her
flight the night before.

She had made her way from the forested edge of the lake back
to a sheltered place near the lodge, where she could see but not be
seen. She had half expected the Winnebago to be gone, that
Patrick's stepfather would have driven it up the hill and escaped
on the highway. But when she arrived at a point where she could
look down, she could make it out still sitting where she had parked
it. She knew it was still occupied for she had heard shouting from
it less than fifteen minutes earlier, though it was now quiet.

Why had he elected to stay there? He must have realized that
she was a threat, that it would be possible for her to reach Teslin
in little more than an hour and come back with help. What had he
waited for?

She couldn't go in after him or go too near the motor home;
he might use the gun on her or Patrick. Her greatest fear was that
he might use the gun on the boy before she could make her way
back, but his shouting had told her otherwise. In the dark she had
crept once down the hill, trying to hear what was being said
inside the rig, but made out very little, only the loudest of his
angry threats and demands. "Where *is it,* dammit. What have you
done with it?"

She wished she had not been so tired the night before that she
had neglected to make Patrick tell her everything, as he had
promised. Now she wanted desperately to know what *it* was. The
boy was evidently stubborn and stronger than he appeared, even
if he was terrified of the man, for as long as the demands continued it was clear he had not told what he knew. She hoped he real-

ized that whatever his stepfather wanted might be all that was keeping him alive. Whatever it was, it must be very important to the Wyoming cop to make him so irate and keep him from making the boy disappear, which would be so incredibly easy in this kind of country. All he would have to do was drive off the highway on some lonely road and either take Patrick into the millions of miles of trees, where nothing of him would ever be found, or dump him into one of the swift-flowing rivers that wound their way away from the few manmade paths into the endless wilderness where man had never, and might never, set foot.

Jessie had gone carefully back up the hill to the space she had found, sat down on a log to keep herself from the cold damp ground, and continued her watch, determined to know if the rig was moved or if they left it, waiting impatiently for daylight.

Not more than half an hour later it was light enough to see quite well through the trees when the door of the Winnebago suddenly opened and the man pushed the boy out onto the ground, from which he picked himself up slowly. He had secured Patrick's hands together behind him with duct tape and applied a strip of it across his mouth, ensuring his silence. Jessie could see that he carried the roll of tape with him in one hand. She remained unmoving in the shadows of the trees and watched between the leaves of a bush as the man looked cautiously around, making sure there was no one to see, then turned back to the boy.

From the way Patrick stood, shoulders slumped, head hanging, Jessie knew he had not only been hurt but had finally given in to his stepfather's demands and told him what he wanted to know, for every line of him had been sketched with the gray mourning color of defeat. He exhibited no resistance and seemed to have only enough endurance to keep himself upright as the man growled something and shoved him forward.

At first Jessie thought he meant to walk the boy up the hill, and began to glance around for some other hiding place, for she would be visible the minute they were halfway up and came around the curve in the road. But instead Patrick was directed onto the path that led to the lakeshore, stumbling slightly, moving on legs that looked as if they might collapse under him.

As the man and boy moved behind a small stand of trees, she got up and quickly slipped farther down the hill. Crouching behind the narrow trunks of a pair of birch trees, she could see that they were heading for two small boats that lay at the edge of the water, each covered with a blue plastic tarp to keep out the rain. She had not noticed them at all, half in, half out of the water, either in her run past them in the dark or in the half-light of this new morning.

It became clear what McMurdock meant to do when he paused to pick up a large rock and carry it along to the nearest boat: drown the boy and be sure his body never surfaced from the deep lake as evidence of the murder. Pulling off the tarp, he pushed the boat out until it floated, then made the boy clamber in and climbed in after him. There he taped the boy's legs together and used the rest of the tape to attach the heavy stone to his feet. Swiftly, competently, he fitted oars into the oarlocks and began to row the boat away from the shore with strong, deft strokes.

Jessie could hardly believe what she was seeing but understood its significance immediately and, ceasing to care if she was seen or not, wanting him to know he had a witness, stood up and shouted.

"*No-o!*"

Then she was running down the hill toward the water, leaping over brush, stumbling, falling once to her knees, crashing through branches that caught and tore at her as she passed, dashing across the lower part of the gravel road and finally out onto the open ground of the lakeshore.

McMurdock's head came up as he heard her yell, but he continued to row. By the time she reached the water, he was twenty yards out and too far away for her to catch.

She screamed at him in frustration and anger. "I'm here, you bastard, and I see what you're doing."

He didn't pause as he looked back in her direction, just kept on rowing steadily, and grinned at her, powerless on the shore.

"You're next, girlie," he called, every word carrying across the still water, over the rhythmic sound of the oars. "I almost got you at Summit Lake and I'll get you now. You're next."

Jessie knew she couldn't stop him, but, beyond fear, she thought she might be able to distract him enough to keep him from drowning Patrick, as he obviously intended. If he threw the boy overboard, maybe she could keep him from sinking irretrievably into the dark depths of the lake. The boy in the back of the boat sat silent and frozen in dread, wide, horror-filled eyes looking back at her over one shoulder as he was carried away over the ominous water.

She went quickly to yank the blue cover from the second boat, shoved the boat into the water, and was turning it around when she noticed a detail he had missed. Canted up so its propeller was out of the water, an outboard motor was clamped tightly to the transom at the back of the boat, invisible until its covering was removed. One single piece of luck, for the man in the other boat would surely have taken this one had he seen it.

Wading into the shallows, Jessie climbed into the boat. It rocked, almost unbalancing her, as she moved quickly to examine the motor.

A can of fuel sat next to it, half under the rear seat, a hose attached to the motor. Someone had taken this boat out recently and planned to use it again soon or the motor and its fuel would not have been left. Another piece of luck.

She tipped the motor on its hinged clamp, easing the propeller into the water.

Now—if it would only start.

A glance in the direction of the other boat told her that its rower had hesitated and was leaning forward against the handles of his oars, had seen the motor, and was watching her efforts closely. As she met his interested gaze, he grinned at her again, then took the handgun from a jacket pocket and held it high for her to see, warning her without words that he would use it if she tried to come out after him.

Very near the boat there was a sudden splash and a low-pitched hornlike call—*ko-hoh*—that startled her into a motion that set the boat rocking wildly again. A large white shape paddled quickly away—a trumpeter swan, returned to the north, that had blundered too close as she looked at the engine and was now vocalizing its displeasure as it fled. *Ko-hoh!* Nothing to worry about.

Jessie squeezed the bulb on the hose to prime the engine, took firm hold of the starter rope, gathered her strength, and pulled. A burp and a gurgle, nothing more. The rope rewound itself. She adjusted the choke and tried again. This time it almost gargled.

Another look toward the other boat told her that McMurdock was rowing again.

Once again she cautiously squeezed the primer bulb, smelling fuel, worried about flooding the engine, then pulled with all her strength and speed. With a sputter the motor came to life, ran roughly for a few seconds, then died. Encouraged, she opened the throttle on the steering handle slightly, gave the starter rope a mighty fourth effort, and was rewarded with a steady roar from the engine. A wisp of smoke hung over it in the still early morning air.

Turning to look toward the bow, Jessie took firm hold of the

steering handle, twisted the throttle, and felt the boat surge forward in response. As it moved away from the shore and out into
the lake, she gradually turned it in the direction of the other boat,
which was moving west toward Teslin, several miles away, on a
long course that was slowly bringing it closer to the shore.

Cutting the distance between the two crafts in half, she slowed
her speed until it matched that of the rower. All she could do now
was follow and watch, being careful to stay out of range of the
gun but close enough to make an attempt to rescue Patrick if the
opportunity arose.

CHAPTER

Webster arrived first at the driveway that led down to the Dawson Peaks Resort and moved the barrels and poles that blocked the entrance, laying them to one side and leaving it open for the time being. They drove both vehicles down to the lodge and got out. Maxie left Stretch inside the Jayco but took Tank with her on his leash. A pickup was parked toward the rear of the building, but no one was in sight.

She and Webster were inspecting the locked front doors of the lodge when Loomis suddenly leaned forward and cupped his hands around his eyes to peer into the shadows beyond the window glass.

"There's somebody in there," he said, startled. "He's coming to the door."

When it opened, a tall, pleasant-looking man in well-worn jeans, and a red plaid shirt with sleeves rolled to the elbow

greeted them with a smile so infectious that they all found themselves smiling back in spite of the situation.

"I was just about to go up and move the barrels. It's our first
day open this season. Can I help you with something?"

His eyes widened and his smile faded and turned to a curious
frown when he saw Webster's RCMP patrol car. "Something
wrong?" He hesitated, then opened the door wide and motioned
them in. "Please, come in." He held out a welcoming hand. "I'm
Dave Hett."

The front of the lodge was one large room divided lengthwise
by heavy posts that supported a gently peaked ceiling. Broad
windows separated the left half from a deck outside that overlooked the lake, but a canvas tent had been erected to fill the
other half, reminiscent of those used by gold miners in the early
days of the territory. Both halves contained small tables with
chairs slid neatly under them. Around the walls, paneled in
rough-hewn boards, stood and hung an interesting collection of
antiques—a wood stove, a sideboard, a huge gold pan, an air-
plane propeller, skis, snowshoes, tools—along with several pho-
tographs, posters, and paintings.

Beyond the tables and chairs Maxie noticed two doors, one
leading to restrooms, the other open to a kitchen, where she
could hear the rattle of pans on a stove and water running.

"We're looking for someone who was supposed to stop here,"
Webster told Hett, but before he could go on, a woman appeared
in the door to the kitchen and walked toward them with a questioning look.

"I thought I heard voices."

"This is Carolyn Allen," Hett said, placing an arm around her
shoulders to draw her into the circle. "We run Dawson Peaks
together."

Shorter than he, she was also dressed in jeans, with an apron over her green T-shirt. She smiled and shook hands as Webster introduced himself, Maxie, and Loomis.

"Did a woman in a Winnebago motor home stop here last night?" he asked. "It would probably have been fairly late."

Both Hett and Allen shook their heads.

"We weren't here at all yesterday," Hett told him, explaining that they had made a trip to Whitehorse for supplies two days before and had not returned until late last night themselves. "We have a separate house a half mile west, so we don't stay here at night anyway."

"You mind if we look around?"

"Not at all. Help yourself, but there's nobody here but us."

He led the way onto the deck to point out the road that would take them down to the cabins and tents as well as the lake.

Looking down at the pale canvas walls of the tents, Maxie frowned as she noticed an odd shape to the side of one of them, something a little lighter cream color than the canvas. As she examined it with more attention, it slowly resolved itself into something that wasn't a tent at all but a shape she thought she recognized.

"Do you have a motor home down there?" she asked Hett suddenly, interrupting his description of the property.

"No, just the tents and cabins."

As she turned to show Webster what she had seen, a whisper of an early breeze from the west rustled through the leaves of the nearest birches. Tank was immediately straining at his leash, all but tugging Maxie off balance as he pulled her toward a flight of stairs that led to a trail down the hill.

"I think that's the Winnebago," she called back. "Down there behind that tent. Tank seems to think so too."

Before they could answer or follow her from the deck, the sudden crack of a gunshot reached them from somewhere out of sight to the west.

"Hey," Hett said, noticing for the first time. "My boats are gone."

As Maxie struggled to keep Tank from pulling her over, the three men ran past headed for the lakeshore. She trotted along after them, soon reaching the lower section of the road, and was able to see that Jessie's motor home was indeed parked beside one of the tents, the door hanging open.

"Jessie?" A quick look inside told her the rig was empty, so she didn't go in but went on toward the lake. When they reached the open grassy shore, Tank stopped abruptly and barked, twice, toward the water. Maxie almost ran over him, but he was off again immediately, this time yanking the leash from her startled fingers and breaking into a lope, dragging the leash behind him as he ran.

"Bloody hell!" she swore and started after him, but soon stopped, knowing she hadn't a chance.

Far out on the lake she could see a small boat and hear the sound of a motor. Between it and the shore was another boat, and from it came another crack of gunfire. There were two people in the second boat, one sitting in the back, one at the oars. But there was only one in the boat with the motor, and that one was Jessie.

Maxie was hardly aware of company when Carolyn Allen, who had followed them all down the hill, came up and stood beside her to see what was going on.

Hett and the two policemen were still running, and Webster was now shouting, though she couldn't make out what he was saying. Loomis stumbled and fell to his hands and knees. As he regained his footing, Tank caught up and passed him. When the dog reached a point on the shore directly opposite the nearest boat, where Maxie thought he must stop, he threw himself into the water and began to swim out toward the boats.

Frightened and worried, Maxie knew she had let Jessie down by letting her dog escape. But there was nothing to be done about it. All she could do was watch him swimming strongly away from the shore and think that the water was icy cold, even for a husky, and it was a long way to where Jessie was running the motorboat back and forth, keeping it in motion in an attempt to evade the shots that were being aimed at her.

The man with the gun had not yet seen the animal in the water. But he, the boy—and his handgun—were all in the rowboat, directly between the dog and where he was determined to go.

What Maxie also knew was that the second figure in the rowboat *had* to be Patrick Cutler. So the man with him was, without a doubt, his stepfather.

Webster was assessing the situation without much optimism.

"You wouldn't just happen to have a third boat, would you?" he asked Dave Hett, without turning his attention from the drama taking place on the lake.

"No—sorry."

"Didn't really think so."

Loomis caught up and they all three stood helplessly watching.

"I've got a rifle at the house. Would that help?"

"Better get mine, I think," Webster said grimly. "If anyone has to be shot, it'd better be with an official weapon. Here's my trunk key. Will you get it for me?" he asked Loomis.

"I can go faster," Hett told him. "I'm used to the hill and can bring it back down in the pickup."

"Go—as fast as you can."

* * *

From her vantage point in the lake, Jessie had seen Tank run along the shore, then leap into the water and start to swim, and she was even more worried than Maxie, but there was no stopping him. Now she had two problems—Patrick and her lead dog—to say nothing of the chance of being shot herself. But at least she was no longer alone. There were people on the lakeshore who could see what was happening, though they had no way to reach or help her.

She was watching closely, however, and saw the tall man with Webster and Loomis begin a long-legged, ground-covering run back toward the lodge. Forgetting for a moment to keep an eye on the other boat, she was startled into a quick turn when a bullet thumped into the stern. Another quickly followed. He was shooting not at her, she realized, but at the motor, trying to disable it and leave her dead in the water—perhaps literally. And he was a pretty good shot.

She wished for a moment for her reliable old Winchester, a bolt-action rifle her father had given her, which had survived the fire that had burned her cabin. Even in a rocking boat she knew she would have a better chance of hitting this madman with it than he had of hitting her with the handgun. But it would have been very tricky to avoid hitting Patrick as well.

Above the whine of the motor on her boat, she faintly heard the sound of another engine and saw a pickup come bouncing from the road that ran between the lodge and the lake. Moving fast, it rocked its way onto the grassy shore and headed west toward the two policemen but was soon stopped by several large rocks.

She could see that Loomis had walked a little way back toward where Maxie and another woman were standing and was waving the pickup to a stop. The man in the truck handed out a rifle, which Loomis took. He headed back toward Webster and was still perhaps twenty feet from the inspector when Jessie's attention was distracted.

The man in the other boat suddenly stood up and, balancing himself, feet spread wide, reached for the boy. A struggle ensued, Patrick cowering and trying desperately to evade his grasp but losing. He was hauled onto the center seat and his knees were lifted over the side, feet dangling in the water, with the heavy rock still attached.

"You see this?" McMurdock shouted to the men on the shore. "Back off, or I'll dump him in. Loomis, you son of a bitch, so help me, I'll . . ."

Loomis and Webster had dropped flat on the lakeshore, and Jessie could now see that the Wyoming detective, who still had the rifle, was aiming it at the man who was standing in the boat. Swinging the motorboat away from his line of fire, she waited to see what would happen next, ready to drive in toward the rowboat if he started to shove Patrick over the side, knowing that she was the only person who had any chance at all of reaching him.

"Give it up, McMurdock," Loomis yelled back.

So, the man had a name.

"Give it up and bring the boy back in." Webster joined the conversation. "We'll work it out."

There was silence for a moment from McMurdock, then he leaned forward and reached as if to take hold of the boy, who was trying, and failing, to pull his feet back into the boat against the weight of the stone.

"We couldn't. Not with—" He started to say something that was abruptly cut off by the crack of the rifle. He staggered as the bullet caught him in the chest. One arm windmilled vaguely and he fell backward, almost in slow motion, it seemed to Jessie from where she had stopped her boat and shut off the motor in order to hear. If he had not been standing, he would have fallen into the boat. As it was, the gunnel caught him at the knees, flipping him over into the water with a splash. For a few seconds he appeared to float face down, then vanished beneath the surface with only a ripple that quickly spread, leaving the surface once again smooth where he had been.

There wasn't a sound from any of those watching. Shocked into immobility, no one moved for a long moment. All was totally silent. Then, from somewhere farther down the shore, the low, lonely *ko-hoh* of the swan came echoing across the water.

As if it broke some kind of spell, other sounds rushed in immediately. A truck grumbled from up on the highway. Webster stood up and shouted something at Jessie. There was a splashing in the water, and Tank came swimming up beside the boat, panting hard from his exertion.

Reaching over the side, she lifted him into the boat and clung to him, soaking her clothes with the water that ran from his coat, and not caring in the least. He wriggled and joyously licked her face and hands, though he was shivering violently with cold, energy all but expended. She took off her jacket and wrapped him up in it.

"Oh, you wonderful dog. You are the best dog in the whole world and I love you more than anything. Good boy, Tank. Good old mutt."

Laying him down in the bottom of the boat, she started the motor and went to rescue Patrick.

CHAPTER

Jessie helped Patrick swing his legs out of the water, stripped the duct tape from them and let the stone fall into the bottom of the boat as she continued to strip the tape from his mouth and wrists. She then headed for shore, where willing hands helped them back onto dry land. Webster and Hett took the motorboat back out to see if they could retrieve McMurdock's body, though it seemed there was little chance.

"You've got a bullet or two in that one," Jessie told Dave Hett as he climbed into the boat. "I'm sorry."

"Not your fault," he told her, "and no great damage done."

"You all right?" Loomis asked her, noticing that she was shivering with delayed shock in the cool morning air, as they watched the two men in the boat drawing a wide circling wake on the lake water as they searched.

"Yes, I'm fine. But I need to get Tank dry and warm."

"Brave dog, but you're cold, too. Here, take this." He took off his jacket and wrapped it around her shoulders with a smile.

"But—"

"Hey, it's okay. I've got another one in the car. Keep it—you might need it before you reach home."

"Mine will be okay as soon as I wash it, but—thanks." Jessie gave him a grateful smile, then turned and took Tank on his leash back to the motor home, where she used a towel to dry his damp coat, rubbing briskly until he stopped shivering and was happily eating a second breakfast, while she sat beside him on the floor, affectionately rubbing his ears.

"Cold and dry is okay for you, isn't it, guy? Cold and wet is not."

She had been very glad to see Patrick, pale but recovering from his ordeal, given a huge hug by Maxie, and had watched them walk away from the shore and climb toward the lodge with Carolyn Allen. Now a knock at the door of the Winnebago announced him, dressed in his own clothes and followed closely by Maxie and Stretch. He handed her the jeans, sweatshirt, and socks she had loaned him.

"I had to leave my backpack at the hot springs when I ran. That cop had it in his trunk."

Wet to the knees and grubby from a night in the brush, Jessie wanted nothing more than a bath and change of clothes herself.

"There's a shower in the lodge," Maxie suggested. "You won't have to wait for water to heat."

Taking what she needed for a good scrub and shampoo, with clean clothes over her arm, Jessie climbed the hill with them and was soon closing the door of the small shower room, ready for the luxury of someone else's hot water.

Tank, not willing to leave her side, followed her in and lay down on the floor of the cubical. Before taking off the jacket Loomis had given her, she plunged a hand into the pocket for the shampoo she had stashed there. Her fingers closed on the plastic bottle and a scrap of paper, which she withdrew to see that it was a piece torn from something, a notebook perhaps, and wadded up as if to be thrown away. Uncrumpling it she found nothing but a phone number, 867-390-2575, evidently one he had decided he didn't need anymore.

She dropped it back into the pocket, quickly disrobed, and was almost immediately lathered with soap and singing happily to herself. "Oh what a beautiful morning . . ."

Outside in the restaurant section of the lodge, where the others had collected around a large round table and were drinking coffee, Hett, who was playing waiter for the group, turned an ear to listen to the muffled gladness that was echoing down the hall from the shower and grinned.

"Gutsy lady," he commented, filling Webster's cup from the pot in his hand and nodding in the direction of the music. "You wouldn't catch me out in an open boat chasing a guy with a gun."

"She's all wool and a yard wide," Maxie agreed, using an Aussie expression that made Loomis grin. "But I think she could do with a rest before we head on up the highway. Would you have a couple of spaces for us for tonight, Dave?"

"Sure. Pick any you want."

Carolyn had volunteered to make everyone breakfast, and by the time Jessie and Tank had rejoined them, she was helping Dave lay platters of bacon, eggs, fried potatoes, and toast on the table, accompanied by slices of her famous rhubarb pie, which Webster attacked with gusto. "My mother used to make rhubarb pie," he said around a forkful. "Haven't had any in years."

"Glad you like it," Carolyn said, pulling up a chair beside Dave to join them.

"She wins ribbons at the fair with this pie," he bragged, cutting into a slice of his own.

When they had finished eating, everyone helped clear the table and carry dishes back to the kitchen. Webster donned an apron and insisted on turning chief bottle-washer, while Maxie and Loomis dried and Carolyn returned clean items to their proper places.

Jessie, taking the two dogs outside for a walk, found Patrick alone on the deck staring out at the lake, which was now bright with sunshine and watery colors. He glanced back at the sound of the door she closed behind her, then quickly turned his face south again. But she had seen the tears on his face.

"Patrick?" she questioned softly, stepping up to the place where he leaned on the rail. "You sorry about him?"

"God, no!" The words exploded from him. "I'm *glad* he's dead."

She waited.

"He killed my mother," he told her through stiff lips. "All of a sudden I just really missed her again. That's all."

"That's a lot." There was little she could say and nothing she could do to ease the pain of that loss. It made her feel ineffectual, but all anyone could do was be there for him and share when they could. "It hurts to miss somebody. I know."

He wiped at his face with his fists and turned to her with a worried look.

"Will they make me go back, Jessie? I don't want to go back— I want to go on to Fairbanks. But he said he told them that I killed her."

"Oh, Patrick—*no-o*. The inspector said that Loomis came looking for you because they didn't believe him."

He was silent for a minute. "I thought Loomis was a pal of my stepfather's."

"No. He was sent after you because he knew there was something wrong with the story your stepfather was telling and they wanted to hear your side. They knew he was the one who'd been hurting your mother—not you. The idea of your killing her didn't make any sense—ever."

He nodded, relieved.

"You may have to go back, but maybe not right now. Would you like me to ask him if you can go later?"

"Would you?"

"Of course."

When they both turned back to look down on the lake, she saw that the swan had been joined by a half-dozen ducks, all paddling along the shore between the two boats, now beached in their usual places.

Jessie thought about McMurdock's body slowly falling and coming to rest somewhere on the deep bottom of Teslin Lake.

Everyone who dies joins everyone else who ever died, through water, she mused, watching a breeze make small waves dance on the lake. Somehow, wherever they fall or are buried, water connects them; rain falls on their quiet resting places and runs off to join other water. It's the melding agent of wars, for the blood of soldiers from all the battles of history has been washed away by the rain and eventually found its way down rivers and streams to some ocean, becoming one with its salt and the blood of others. It was fitting, she thought, that human blood had the same salt content as sea water.

In a few minutes she left Patrick and went to ask Webster what she had promised, only to find that Maxie had already plowed that particular ground. She had arranged with Webster and Loomis for Patrick to ride with her to Fairbanks, where the police would contact him for any information they needed. He might even be able to give a deposition to the local police there, since his stepfather would no longer be making accusations.

Loomis had wandered off to the lake, where he could be seen skipping rocks across the water, to the displeasure of the swan and ducks, but Jessie told Webster all that had happened since the last time they had spoken, at Summit Lake. He listened attentively, asked a few clarifying questions, and took notes of it all.

"How is Patrick's friend doing?" she asked, when they had finished. "Kim, the one I found in the pool at the hot springs."

"He's doing fine. Kids that age recuperate pretty fast, but he was very lucky you got him out when you did."

*   *   *

Well before noon, Inspector Webster and Detective Loomis had gone, heading back to Dawson Creek, where Loomis would pick up the car he had left and continue on back to Wyoming. It would take weeks and a lot of paperwork to complete what had turned into an international and interprovincial situation, but at least it seemed that, given McMurdock's death, there would be no complicating murder charges leveled at anyone alive.

Jessie moved the Winnebago up the hill and into a space next to the Jayco, which Maxie had parked close to the back door of the lodge. Tank was still hanging close, so she took him with her when she settled for a nap that stretched into midafternoon. Patrick, too, chose a snooze, but in the Jayco. Maxie, after a tour of the resort with Dave, cheerfully assisted Carolyn with dinner preparations in the spacious kitchen, where they shared recipes and anecdotes of the highway and its travelers that they had met over the years.

Jessie woke to long shafts of afternoon sunlight pouring between the trees and into the windows of the Winnebago, rested and ready for company again. She could hear Patrick stirring next door and, through the open window, invited him over. There was one question still on her mind, and when he was seated with a can of apple juice at the table, she asked it.

"Last night I went down the hill and was listening outside when your stepfather was shouting at you in here. He asked you what you had done with something. What was he talking about, Patrick?"

He looked up at her without a word for a long minute, then turned his head to watch a bright-blue whiskey jack hop along a picnic table outside the window.

"It isn't important now," he said quietly, frowning.

"Are you sure?"

"Yes." His frown vanished, replaced with acceptance and relief. "It was something he doesn't need anymore—so it doesn't matter. I just want to forget it."

"Will it cause problems later?"

"No."

"Will it ever hurt anyone?"

"No."

"You?"

He shook his head.

They looked at each other in silence, and finally Jessie nodded. "Okay."

He had a right to keep his own counsel, she decided. As long as it would do no further damage to him or to anyone else, let it go.

"Well, hey, let's go find Maxie."

* * *

They spent a pleasant and quiet evening, first over drinks on the deck, then over an extended dinner for five. No one else had pulled off the highway and wandered in to make use of the RV parking, cabins, or tents, which gave Jessie and Maxie a peaceful opportunity to nourish their growing friendship with Dave and Carolyn. The two were working hard to make their resort a growing concern, and it was already one of the best Jessie had found along the long highway north.

Asking them what they did during the winter months, when everything froze into snowy silence and there were few travelers to stop at their door, Jessie was interested to find that they spent part of each winter season in South America. There they collected handmade sweaters to bring back for sale in the small gift and book shop that occupied the front part of the tented half of the lodge. She had noticed the bright colors and patterns, which did not look local, and was pleased to pick one out as a souvenir of her visit. Maxie helped her choose a blue and green one with a bit of yellow in the design that she was assured suited her blond coloring.

By ten o'clock they were all ready for a good night's rest. The kitchen was clean and ready for morning, and they were getting up from their chairs when Dave poured the last of the bottle of wine into their glasses and proposed a toast.

"To new friendships," he said, smiling. "May they grow into old ones."

C H A P T E R 27

It was another glorious day when Jessie, Maxie, and Patrick left Dawson Peaks Resort the next morning, leaving Dave and Carolyn waving from the lodge. The sun was shining and there wasn't a cloud in the sky.

At the top of the hill, Jessie, who was in the lead, turned left toward Teslin and was surprised and delighted to see two bicyclists peddling along the side of highway ahead of her—Craig Severson and his friend Leo Taylor from Fort Nelson. She honked as she passed them and pulled over at a turnoff that came up handily in about a half mile.

"Hey, Jessie," Severson called with a grin, braking to a stop where she stood by the Winnebago, then raising a hand to greet Maxie in the Jayco. "Thought you'd be long gone by now."

She explained their delays briefly, knowing he would be glad to hear that the person who had thrown the boy off the Kiskatinaw Bridge would no longer be a threat to anyone.

"You're moving right along, aren't you? Good weather makes a difference."

"Yeah, a lot. We've been making over a hundred miles a day. It's a great trip now that the rain's gone."

They soon glided back onto the highway and Jessie headed the motor home to Teslin, where she and Maxie had agreed to pull in for gas. Filling both tanks, they went into the Lakeshore Motel to pay for it, leaving Patrick and Stretch in the Jayco and Tank content to watch from the window of the Winnebago to be sure Jessie did not disappear again without him.

Waiting for the clerk to finish with a customer, Jessie looked around curiously at the people having their breakfast and noticed a couple she recognized.

The elderly couple she had seen at Fort Steele, then again at Liard Hot Springs, were sitting together at a small table near the middle of the room, their matching blue windbreakers hung over the backs of their chairs. The woman had a cup of coffee in one hand, almost as if she had forgotten she held it, and was staring blankly out the window at the RV park behind the motel, a slightly bored and forlorn expression on her face. The white-haired man forked pieces of a cinnamon roll into his mouth and did not look up or speak between bites.

How sad, Jessie thought to herself. There were times she regretted her single state and thought about the possibilities of growing old alone. But there were others when, noticing a couple like this one, she knew exactly what she did not want in a relationship.

Maxie signed her credit card receipt and went back outside, leaving Jessie at the counter. Handing her card to the clerk, Jessie waited for her to ring up the price of the fuel, but before she could, a waitress came bustling across the room with a question. "What's the phone number for the restaurant, Jean? It's not the same as the motel, is it?"

"Nope. Different: 390-2575."

She turned to the cash register.

Jessie stared at her, confused by what she had just heard.

"What's your area code?" she asked.

"What?"

"Your area code. What is it?"

"Oh. It's eight-six-seven."

Reaching into the pocket of Loomis's jacket, Jessie retrieved the scrap of paper she had found earlier: *867-390-2575.* The numbers matched.

Dropping it back in the pocket, she automatically signed the receipt and handed it back with the pen.

"Do you ever get phone calls for people in the restaurant?" she asked.

"Yes, sometimes. There's a pay phone, but it's only for outgoing calls—doesn't ring here."

"So anyone trying to reach a customer would have to call this number?"

"Right."

Her mind in a whirl of speculation, Jessie went back outside and directly to the Jayco, where Maxie and Patrick were waiting, ready to take off.

"Maxie," she asked through the driver's window, "did Loomis make any phone calls between here and Watson Lake, when he was riding with you?"

The older woman thought back to the long, sleepy evening ride two nights before, remembering the image of Dan Loomis standing in the small store that was part of the service station at the Rancheria Motel. "Yes," she said. "He called Inspector Webster. Why?"

"Did you hear him make the call?"

"No, I was outside having the gas tank filled."

"So you're not really sure who he called—just who he said he called?"

"I guess not, but he came back and said he'd talked to Webster." Then she recalled the information about Dawson Peaks that Webster claimed not to have received when they met him here in Teslin. "What's wrong, Jessie?"

"Let's pull these rigs away from the gas pumps and talk about it."

Maxie came to the Winnebago, leaving Patrick with Stretch in the Jayco. "I thought maybe this would be something he didn't need to be involved in," she said, climbing in and settling at the table. "What's going on?"

Jessie explained about the phone number and what it indicated to her.

"I keep wondering just how McMurdock found us so easily at Dawson Peaks. He couldn't possibly have seen the motor home from the highway, or known we were there, unless . . . Did you tell Loomis where we were supposed to meet, before you got to Rancheria?"

"Yes," Maxie said, slowly nodding. "I'm sure I did. We'd been talking about Patrick's relationship with his stepfather. Then he asked me where you might go for the night. So I told him. When we stopped for gas, he said he should call Webster."

They looked at each other in hesitation and perplexity.

"But Loomis *shot* McMurdock," Maxie pointed out.

Jessie agreed. "And I'd like to know if there was another reason for that killing, wouldn't you?"

"How would we ever find out? Webster wouldn't know. McMurdock was about to drown Patrick. It seemed so . . . so . . ."

"Yes. It did. And if he had other motives, what a perfect opportunity it offered to stay in the clear. If McMurdock was about to go down for his wife's murder, couldn't Loomis have thought it was possible that he might be implicated, too?"

"The good ole boys club would only go so far, you mean?"

"Yeah, sort of. I think that maybe we should make a call to Webster. Let him work it out."

* * *

The rest of the drive home to Knik was not only uneventful, it was the most pleasant part of the trip for Jessie. The weather held, and the country she passed through seemed to be showing off its fresh spring green like a woman with a new dress, proudly and with the grace of knowing she looks well.

There seemed to be wildlife everywhere. A black bear sat in a field of early sunflowers, hungrily munching on them and ignoring the traffic that passed practically at its back. Moose waded in ponds for the rushes that reach up through the water. Flocks of birds were completing their long migrations to the north, and there were more swans and ducks floating on the lakes and rivers, geese winging their way across the sky with noisy honks.

Outside Whitehorse Jessie spent a last night with Maxie in the Wolf Creek government campground. They parked their motor homes next to the stream that murmured its way through the tall trees and walked their dogs around the circular road.

A red fox dashed through an empty campsite near to them and disappeared into the brush on quick, silent feet. Squirrels chattered from the branches and descended, hoping for crumbs, driving Stretch wild with the desire to be after them. Tank watched him with tolerant dignity from his place by Jessie's feet, knowing from experience that it was foolish to try.

The two women relaxed in Maxie's comfortable chairs with the bottle of Jameson's on the table between them, quietly appreciating good whiskey, the setting, and each other's company. Patrick had gone off on a walk of his own but would soon be back for dinner.

"I'm going to miss you, Maxie," Jessie told her friend.

"We'll have to get together this summer. You should come down to Homer for a few days. I'd like that."

"And you could stop with me on your way to the Lower Forty-Eight this fall."

"I will definitely plan on it."

"What do you think Webster will do about Loomis?" Jessie asked, thinking back to the phone call they had made before leaving Teslin. It had been a long, all-night drive back to Dawson Creek, but they found him in his office, about to go home and to bed for the sleep he had missed.

"Nothing without more substantial proof. Everything we feel we know is circumstantial. But I think he won't forget it. Sometimes things like that take time."

"Who do you think broke into the Jayco in Prince George? Could that have been Loomis?"

"It might have been, but it could also have been completely unrelated—just a chance kind of city thing. It doesn't actually relate in any way that I can see."

"You're probably right and we'll never know."

Patrick came walking back toward them, an open, friendly grin spreading over his face at the sight of them taking their ease.

"Hey," Jessie said, taking a closer look. "Your brown hair is turning red again at the roots."

It was. He was turning gradually back into the mischievous boy who had stolen her lunch at Fort Steele—but not quite.

There was now an older, more experienced expression that never quite left his eyes, and a confidence he had not had before.

·   ·   ·

The next morning, after taking a look at Miles Canyon, where stampeders had run the rapids on their way to the Klondike a hundred years earlier, they parted company. Maxie had decided to make a quick two-day swing from Whitehorse to Skagway on the Alaskan coast before going on to Fairbanks by way of Dawson City and the Top of the World Highway. Jessie, eager now to get home, was headed for the border by the fastest route.

With much waving, they split up at the junction and Jessie went on alone into town for enough groceries to take her the rest of the way. The highway ran along the top of a bluff south of Whitehorse, which lay on the banks of the Yukon River below. A loop route took her through the city. It was familiar, but she knew it best as the start for the Yukon Quest, the distance race she had run in February. Now the streets were bare of snow and ice, and it was bustling with people without heavy boots and down clothing. It was pleasant to drive through, but she only stopped for a few minutes at the market and went on out the other end of town where the loop route rejoined the Alaska Highway.

She drove ninety-eight miles to Haines Junction on the shoulder of a broad valley that spread east and west. For the next sixty-seven miles the world she passed through was framed with the almost unbroken chain of the Kluane Range, which ran into the Saint Elias Mountains, highest in Canada with Mount Logan's 19,850 feet, Mount Saint Elias's 18,008, and others that commanded the western horizon. Though she couldn't identify, or even see them all, she knew that Mount Lucania, King Peak, Mounts Wood, Vancouver, and Hubbard, even Mount Steele (named for the same Superintendent Samuel Steele of the North

West Mounted Police that she remembered from Fort Steele), were all there in their regal snow-covered splendor.

It was still early when she reached Kluane Lake, but she stopped for the night at Congdon Creek government campground and found a space for the Winnebago near the shore. In the shadow of tall mountains the sun set early, so she built a small blaze in the fire pit and sat outside with Tank to watch the rosy alpine glow fade slowly on the Ruby Range to the east and the moon rise to cast a shining path across the wide water.

The breeze died and it was very quiet. Jessie toasted a few of the marshmallows she had found in the Whitehorse grocery and began to review everything that had happened in the last week. As she remembered how pleasantly the trip had started out so many days ago, she suddenly decided to let it all go. From here to Knik was time to take peacefully for herself and reset her internal sense of balance. So she simply enjoyed her surroundings and went to sleep with an appreciation of her own solitude and the moonlight that fell through the window onto her bed in a pale square.

She was on the road at seven o'clock the next morning and crossing the border between Canada and the United States, with its flutter of flags, at ten. For the second time on the trip she crossed a time zone and moved her watch back an hour. Thanking the woman who had welcomed her with a smile, she drove away from the border and was back in Alaska at nine.

Stopping briefly in Tok for lunch and fuel, she turned off the Alaska Highway and headed directly south on the long straight first section of the Tok Cutoff that would take her to the Glenn Highway and the last leg of the trip. The cutoff ran between the Alaska Range and the Mentasta Mountains, eventually opening up above the wide valley of the Copper River, with Mount Sanford rising alone at the northwest forefront of the Wrangells to dominate the skyline. Seldom so gloriously displayed, often cloud-covered at 16,237 feet, pure white with snow and glacier ice and with deep blue shadows, it drew her attention like a magnet as she drove a long southwest curve around it and finally reached the Glenn Highway intersection just before Glennallen.

A last stop for gas, and she knew she was only 150 miles from home. *Home!* It struck a cord that continued to reverberate in her mind in eager anticipation. *Home!* The rest of the drive was all so familiar that it seemed to belong to her—the Chugach Mountains to the south with their collection of glaciers flowing from deep valleys, the Matanuska River from high on the hill above. Then she was driving through Palmer, turning off at Wasilla onto Knik Road, passing Iditarod Headquarters on the right, and finally—Tank sitting up attentively, catching her impatient expectation—turning into the driveway of her own place.

Her mutts in the kennel set up a welcoming racket and her handler, Billy Steward, stepped out of the storage shed, saw her coming, and trotted toward the Winnebago with a huge grin. Parking the rig beside the tent she had been temporarily living in, she shut off the engine and climbed out with Tank, who went immediately to investigate his box.

Hank Peterson's backhoe was parked in the middle of the space where her new cabin would soon rise, ready to dig the hole for the basement so Vic Prentice could start raising logs.

Jessie stood surveying the one place in the world that belonged to her, with pure and simple pleasure.

Home!

CHAPTER 28

The old man woke in the gray early morning light, rolled over in his bed, and swung his legs over the edge. Joints aching, he trudged to the bathroom and shoved up the window to see what kind of a day it was going to be. The sky was almost clear, and the single fluffy cloud he could see through the narrow opening was faintly touched with coral from the sun that was about to slide above the horizon.

Somewhere a meadowlark sent out its distinctive call. A robin hopped into sight and tilted its head, listening for worms in the dewy grass of his lawn. The lawn needed mowing again, and he wondered how he could go about finding some young person to hire for the regular mowing of it. The boy next door had not returned, and it didn't seem to the old man that he was going to—that he would want to live in a place with so many ugly memories. It made him sad, for he missed the boy and their talks at the kitchen table. It seemed no one wanted to waste time in conversation with old people these days. Everyone was so busy and in such a hurry, they never seemed to stop long enough to take a leisurely look at the world around them. Or perhaps they were just afraid to look at what they would become someday themselves.

He supposed that sooner or later a For Sale sign would go up in front of the house next door, now that McMurdock was dead—drowned in a lake somewhere in Canada, according to the article in the newspaper. The boy, it had said, was staying with friends in Fairbanks, Alaska, for the time being. So that was where he had gone, and he *had* made it. It was nice to know he was safe—and that he had been cleared of all suspicion in the death of his mother.

If they sold the house next door, he guessed that the money would probably go to Patrick. Maybe a family would buy it—and maybe they would have a boy of an age and inclination to mow lawns. He could always hope.

Closing the window to its usual crack, he washed his face and brushed what few teeth he had left, then went back to the bedroom to put on his clothes, propping his left heel on a stool so he could reach down far enough to pull on his socks and shoes.

In the kitchen he spooned coffee into a filter in the coffee maker, poured water in the tank, and turned it on. While he waited for it to brew, he ate a bowl of raisin bran with milk and a little honey. If he didn't eat something first, the coffee he loved didn't always agree with him these days—even decaf. Pouring himself a cup of the fresh coffee, he stirred in sugar and low-fat milk and sat back down at the table to enjoy it in small sips and watch the sky brighten into blue through the window that opened onto the backyard.

Though he needed to take his cart and go to the grocery store three blocks away, he decided to wait until tomorrow. Today was a day to work in his garden. It was divided up into sections, which he cared for on a rotating basis. He couldn't do all the work on his knees in one day, only a part of it, or he would pay for it in aches and pains later. So though he would do the weeding around the beds of spinach and lettuce today, the carrots and radishes would have to wait till Wednesday, the zucchini and cucumbers would claim most of Friday morning, and the tomatoes and green onions would have to be fitted in over the weekend, one at a time, when he felt like it. If he worked at it consistently, he could just keep ahead of the weeds. The beans he had planted by the shed also needed weeding, but he could do it standing, with a long-handled tool, loosening the soil around them as he liked to do before adding plant food.

Every year his garden seemed to be growing smaller to accommodate his diminishing ability to care for it. Once it had fed a family of four. Now, alone, he periodically bought vegetables at the store to augment his homegrown supply. He was philosophical about it, but it saddened him nonetheless.

Draining the last swallow of coffee from the cup, he got up and rinsed his dishes in the sink, then put on a floppy-brimmed hat and made for the back door. Before he started on the weeding chores he would water everything in the garden and set a sprinkler going on the front lawn. It was best to water while it was still cool outdoors, before the heat of the sun evaporated half of it and raised his water bill beyond what he could afford on his limited income.

He went from the kitchen to the porch and paused for a moment on the steps that went down into the backyard, looking at the house next door. The yellow tape and other evidence of the police investigation was gone now, and the house had taken on an empty, abandoned air. The blinds had been drawn over the windows, as if the place had closed its eyes in shame. One of the blinds was crookedly caught on something and pulled to one side, making it seem to peer from under an eyelid.

Keeping an eye out, the old man thought, not for the first time. Someone should have kept an eye out for the people who had lived in it, as well. But that was all over now.

He went on down the steps and into the yard, where he unrolled the hose that hung over the faucet on the side of his house and set about watering the garden.

.   .   .

An hour later, he looked up from his position halfway down the lettuce bed to see a familiar figure coming along the side of his house, carefully avoiding the sprinkler that was soaking half the front lawn. Sitting back on his heels, knees on the piece of old carpet he had tossed down to keep his pants clean, he waited, watching his visitor approach.

"Ah," he said finally, "the salesman again."

Daniel Loomis stopped at the edge of the lettuce bed, nodded, and grinned. "Yup, the salesman."

"Watcha want this time?"

Loomis pulled off his baseball cap and scratched his head. "Got any more coffee?"

"Might."

"Well, Mr. Dalton—I've got a question and some information for you if you do," he said in his slow way of speaking, and waited for a response.

When the old man began to make getting-up signs, the detective stepped forward and reached out. "Give you a hand?"

"I'm not quite crippled yet."

Reaching for the hoe he kept handy, the old man used it as a prop to heave himself to his feet, knowing there would be hell to pay in getting back down again but determined that he would, to finish today's job when this man had gone. Without a word, holding himself carefully so as not to limp, he led the way to the kitchen, where they settled, as they had before, with coffee, Loomis's cap on the edge of the table.

"Information first," Dalton demanded. "How's the boy?"

"Fine. He's fine," Loomis told him. "He's in Fairbanks and seems to want to stay there. He asked me to tell you hello—to say that he's sorry he won't be here to mow your lawn."

"Can mow my own lawn if I have to. What about the house?"

"It'll be sold."

"Can you tell me now just what went on over there?"

Loomis pursed his lips thoughtfully and nodded.

"It was pretty simple really. McMurdock hit his wife and she fell against the corner of a bedside table—hit her head. Patrick had come up from his room in the basement and saw what happened. He smacked his stepfather from behind with the baseball bat, dropped it, and took off. McMurdock came to after he left and, finding his wife was dead, evidently put on some gloves so he wouldn't leave prints and used the bat to beat her head in, hoping he could blame it on the boy, especially since the kid had disappeared. He went after Patrick to make sure he didn't talk his way out of it—couldn't if he was never found, which was what McMurdock intended."

He stopped and there was a silence, as the old man considered what he had heard.

"Well—he won't be around to hurt anybody again, will he?"

"No," Loomis agreed slowly, finishing his coffee. "He went down in the lake where he was going to drown the boy. They may never recover the body."

"Harumph." The old man scornfully cleared his throat, then

curled his lip in a sneer. "Good riddance to bad rubbish," he said, rocking his whole upper body in an emphatic nod. His face was a study in satisfaction.

Loomis waited until he stopped rocking and looked up.

"Mr. Dalton, you probably can't help, but I thought I'd just ask. We've searched the whole house for McMurdock's notebooks—you know, the records of his cases that every policeman keeps—but haven't found them. You wouldn't have any clue where they might be, would you?"

A frown of puzzlement creased the old man's forehead. Why was this supposedly smart detective asking him? He shook his head. "Nope. He wouldn't have given me the time of day. So why would he have given me anything else?"

"Well, I didn't really think so, but—ah—you know. I thought I'd better ask."

He pushed back his chair and got to his feet, holding out a hand. "Good-bye, Mr. Dalton, and—thanks."

The old man hesitated, something in him not wanting to shake this man's hand. Reluctantly, he got up and shook it anyway. No reason to insult the fellow, who had been his one thin link to the boy.

"If you should speak again to Patrick, tell him that I miss—aw-w—well—just tell him my lawn'll be okay, and I hope he is, too."

"I'll do that, sir."

From the porch, the old man watched the detective disappear around the corner of the house. When he was sure he was alone, he allowed himself to limp back to his piece of carpet and finish weeding the lettuce, his back aching by the time it was done.

Taking the hoe, he walked around the house and moved the sprinkler to the other side of the front yard, left it splashing a few inches of the front walk as well as the lawn, and returned to the garden. Going into the shed, he retrieved the plant food and traded the hoe for a long-handled claw with three spikes. It would be easier to use in loosening the soil and breaking up any clumps of dirt.

Leaning close, he examined the beans that were climbing the strings he had tied up on nails. They were doing well, would soon bloom and begin to make baby beans. He loved fresh beans of all kinds, even raw and straight off the vine, sun-warmed and crunchy. He could almost taste them already.

Cautiously, he began using the claw to turn over the topsoil around the bean plants, careful not to catch one of the vines in its spikes. He had done half the narrow patch and was getting tired from the up-and-down motion of his arms, his back aching again, when he dug in the claw a little deeper than he intended and it hung up on something. Jerking at it impatiently, he tried to pull it loose, but one spike was caught on something that refused to let go.

Using the handle again as a prop, he lowered himself to his protesting knees and dug his fingers into the dirt, feeling for the obstruction, expecting a root of some kind. What he felt was soft and pliable. Digging with both hands, he removed a small pile of soil, exposing what appeared to be a piece of plastic, wrapped firmly around the spike. Removing more, he clutched the thing in his fingers and hauled at it. How had some plastic bag gotten into his bean patch?

The plastic came loose suddenly and flew through the air into his lap, liberally sprinkling his pants with dirt. It *was* a plastic bag, from some grocery produce department, with a knot holding it closed over something inside. The spike had pierced it and made a rather large hole. He tore it open all the way across and was astonished when five fat bunches of bills held together with rubber bands tumbled out, along with a small black notebook.

Dalton sat staring at what lay on the ground in front of him until he realized how painful his position was becoming. Then he pulled himself up again, leaned the tool against the shed, gathered the plastic bag and its contents, and took it all into his kitchen, where he spread it out on the table.

Picking up one of the bundles of bills, he licked his thumb to wet it and flipped them over one by one—fifties and twenties mostly, with a few fives and tens scattered between—hundreds of dollars worth. When he had finished a rough count of all five bundles, he figured there was ten thousand to each one—*fifty thousand dollars!* We-ew!

He got up and poured himself the last half-cup of coffee, added sugar and milk, and sat back down at the table to stare at the money and think about it. There was only one place it could have come from—the house next door. And he didn't imagine that McMurdock had buried it in the bean patch. His wife would have been terrified to touch what didn't belong to her, and the cop had kept her on a tight leash—no possibility that she could have collected this much cash. The only alternative was—Patrick.

The old man thought back to how he had prepared the bean patch just before the night of the murder—loosened the soil, ready to stick seeds in the ground. The boy could have brought this across and buried it the night he ran away, when he knew he wouldn't be around for his stepfather to punish when he discovered it missing—for it must have belonged to McMurdock.

Or . . . ? Maybe it wasn't really his. This was not the kind of money an honest cop would keep lying around in cash. But if it was dirty money, he wouldn't have wanted to put it in a bank, now, would he?

Dalton picked up the notebook and thumbed through it as well. The pages were filled with initials, dates that stretched back four or five years, and amounts that seemed to be divided in half, each with a letter after it, *M* and *L*. McMurdock . . . and . . . *L?*

The old man was no dummy. His mind immediately drew the only possible conclusion. He sat staring at the initials on the page, then slowly closed the notebook and set it down with the bundles of money and the remains of the plastic bag.

What to do? There was no one connected with the police department that he would trust to bring him a glass of water, let alone do what was right—what ought to be done with what he had found.

This much would keep his lawn mowed for the rest of his life and then some. Or it would buy all the vegetables he could ever eat, wouldn't it?

The word *theft* crossed his mind uncomfortably, upping his blood pressure slightly—and again, *Patrick*. Rightfully—whoever it had originally belonged to—this should now belong to the boy. But he had no idea how that could be accomplished, and there was no one he was willing to ask.

Perhaps the boy *would* come back sometime. It might be prudent to go on being dumb and blind for the time being, to wait and see.

The coffee had been in the pot too long and tasted scorched. He rose from his chair, dumped the last couple of swallows out into the sink, and rinsed the cup. Opening a drawer, he fished inside for the plastic bags he saved from the grocery, found two with no holes in them, and put one inside the other to make a double thickness.

Going back to the table, he put the notebook in the bottom of the doubled bag, then, one by one, tossed the bundles of money in on top of it. Carefully tying a knot in the top, he carried the package to the porch and back through the garden to his bean patch, where he stuck it back in the hole from which he had taken it. Smoothing the dirt back over this secret, he took his long-handled tool from the side of the shed, pulled himself back to his feet, and continued to till the soil around his beans until the job was finished to his satisfaction.

He slept very well that night, waking only once to visit the bathroom, but he did not bother to open the window to peer across at the empty house next door.

ACKNOWLEDGMENTS

With sincere thanks to:

Barbara Hedges, Kate Grilley, Alice Abbott, and cousin Jack Ellis, for company and assistance in researching the Alaska Highway from Anchorage to the Lower Forty-Eight and back, twice.

The many people of the United States and Canada met along the way or contacted afterward, who provided insight into the character of the communities, residents, and travelers on the long road north.

Claire McNab, my favorite Aussie, for assistance with "down under" slanguage.

David Hett and Carolyn Allen at Dawson Peaks Northern Resort (Mile 769.6/1282.5 km) east of Teslin, Yukon Territory, for remarkable hospitality and generosity in sharing their wonderful resort home, experiences, and rhubarb pie.

Aayric Hooten, RV Consultant of A&M RV Center, Anchorage, for assistance in understanding many different makes and models of motor homes, their operating systems and options.

Wade Cobb of The Bicycle Shop in Anchorage for information on bicycles and equipment for long-distance trips, and for putting me in contact with:

Skip Thomason, who bicycles year-round in Anchorage, often travels the wilderness on two wheels, and who referred me to:

Dave and Barbara Taylor, former Alaskans, who pedaled part of the Alaska Highway on a bicycle-built-for-two on their honeymoon trip and generously shared their memories and photos of that trip.

Chuck Foger, Crown West, Inc., authorized dealer for Precision Craft Log Structures and Lodge Logs, for information on materials and the building of log structures.

Mike Davis, Operations Manager for Lynden Transport, for detailed information on the big rigs that haul heavy commercial loads from Canada and the Lower Forty-Eight to Alaska on the Alaska Highway—what they carry, who drives them, fascinating tales of past trips.

Marilyn Howard of the Dawson Creek Visitor Information Centre.

Larry B. Ballard, Area Manager, Bridges, British Columbia Ministry of Highways and Transportation, for information on the height and history of the Kiskatinaw Bridge.

And to my son Eric, for his research assistance, for putting up with my sometimes backward and excessive methods of collecting information, and for patiently keeping a sense of humor—but particularly for designing the map in this book.